HANDICAP

HANDICAP

A NOVEL BY

JOHN PACE

Editor: Whitney Evans
Cover Design: Robin Vuchnich
Interior Design: SGR-P Formatting Services

Indigo River Publishing
3 West Garden Street Ste. 352
Pensacola, FL 32502
www.indigoriverpublishing.com

Ordering Information:

Quantity sales: Special discounts are available on quantity purchases by corporations, associations, and others. For details, contact the publisher at the address above.

Orders by U.S. trade bookstores and wholesalers: Please contact the publisher at the address above.

Printed in the United States of America

Library of Congress Control Number: 2017964033
ISBN: 978-1-948080-06-4

First Edition

With Indigo River Publishing, you can always expect great books, strong voices, and meaningful messages. Most importantly, you'll always find...words worth reading.

For Molly,
with whom, after reading long into so many nights, the idea of
writing stories first took seed.

Contents

Chapter 1

So this salesman, lawyer and midget walk into a bar . . .

Moe Norman, a talented if peculiar Canadian golfer, once proclaimed, "The golf course was the only place I felt comfortable. Away from the course, I wasn't in my world." Golf was Thom Loudon's world too. It lifted him above the tedium of the prior three years and obscured memories of his foul existence before that. Thom—just Thom—and all that green—green grass, green leaves, green swamp, green bugs and snakes, even the air smelled green— this was his heaven. Golf, however, could not transcend all the world's evils. Some evils, say corpses, guilt and love, the sixteen-year-old would have to resolve for himself—or die trying.

Thom knelt to plant a tee in the sandy Florida soil between the blue markers on number one. He crowned it with a spotless white ball and looked skyward. "Hey, God," he called to the boundless expanse above, "Unless you have other plans, just leave my dead carcass down here, engulfed in verdancy. By the way, God, just how tall are you? Six-foot, one-eighty-five, Caucasian, brown hair with blond highlights, like your kid? I've seen the paintings. Then again, maybe Jesus took after his mom, and you really do resemble that painting on a ceiling in Italy that looks to have you going some six-three, two-forty."

Thom addressed the ball, already savoring that *tink* of a metal driver launching it skyward and two hundred yards down the fairway. He drove to within fifty yards of the typical lay-up spot in front of a fingerling swamp, beyond which stretched the putting green. He'd known from the clean sound and feel of contact where the ball would come to rest. Most players reached the lay-up spot with no more than a simple three-wood. From there, they'd loft their approach to the green so high it was a wonder that none hit any of those jets flying north out of Orlando packed with brats wearing mouse ears. Thom required a hybrid six—a club that resembled a metal driver but played more like an iron. He did not possess the long game of most players.

That, ladies and gents, is where the others' advantage ended and Thom's began. With but three years of experience, he had the best short game this side of the Golden Bear himself. It often took Thom three shots to reach a green everyone else hit in two. Wielding his custom-made putter, however, Thom only needed one putt to finish, whereas they'd take at least two or three. Just as a heart beats without intent, Thom simply felt how the ball would break depending upon how firmly he hit it, how it might slow just before reaching the cup. He knew without stepping off the distance, consciously inspecting the length of grass and lay of the grain, or calculating up-, down- and cross-slopes. Perhaps it was his proximity to the ground.

That Saturday morning on number one, as a sticky sliver of orange sun rose from the swamps of North Central Florida, Thom's second shot blasted off the hybrid club head with a low trajectory. Owing to backspin, the ball suddenly gained altitude, reached its peak, and simply collapsed straight down, three feet past the cup. On the green, he repaired the blunt force trauma inflicted by the ball upon its landing, and drilled the putt for a birdie. One under after one—he'd take that. On to the second hole, an even shorter par four.

Some drove the second green with a single swing and two-putted for a birdie three. Thom required a driver and a mid-iron to carry the deep, steep-sided sand trap that guarded the left front of the putting surface. His second shot landed hole high, four feet to the right. His blue cart cleared a small slope twenty-five yards in front of the green. Thom, who piloted his craft like a captain at the tiller, squinted into the sun at something lying in that front bunker. An alligator? Could be—one of the fetid canals that fed the course's ponds and swamps moseyed nearby.

In Thom's three years laboring as the club pro's chief assistant (read: *only* assistant for a worn-out booze hound who accomplished very little without considerable assistance), he'd occasionally stumbled upon a gator. Truth be told, he couldn't tell if it was one or several because they all looked the same to him: a thousand razor-sharp fangs framed by indomitable jaws. Thom calculated how fast this one might scramble up the steep edge of the sand trap were he to sneak onto the green's backside to play out the hole. He knew he could sink that putt for another bird, leaving him two under after two.

A raven so black that the sun's rays glared off its back hopped along the big trap's lip as if deciding whether to jump in. Thom drove another ten yards and stopped. An unkindness arose from within the bunker just as Thom realized the figure lying in the sand wasn't a gator at all. He kneeled on the seat, which did not improve his sightline. In frustration, he climbed to a standing position, which was also a mistake because when he saw a girl lying there it might have been a lot further to fall from the shock.

He drove nearer, stopped at the edge of the sand trap, and eased out. The girl lay so still, that's why he slid over the side and bent down. That's when he saw the gaping wound in her chest and how she was lying on her back, a foot trapped under her bottom like an extreme hurdler stretch. That's when he reached for the golf ball in his pants pocket. He saw the sand on which she rested, sand usually whiter than Wonder Bread, now rust stained where blood from the hole in her heart had been more than her yellow blouse could absorb, and the blood, dried brown like dirt, caked at the corner of her mouth and down her chin. That's when he saw his mother lying there and scanned the trees for his murderous son of a bitch old man. That's why, instead of staring at this dead girl, a total stranger after all, he should've holed out and headed straight to number three. But he didn't, and that's why a foursome found him later, Thom couldn't say how much later, lying next to Savannah May Paulson's corpse and sobbing like a newborn babe craving the shelter of his mother's womb.

Chapter 2

Moisture infusing the midmorning air intensified the sun's radiation like a magnifying glass. Thom craved an escape—away from the sun's glare, away from the inquisitive, intrusive people, away from the dead body still lying in the sand. To where, given his meager savings and no car, Thom hadn't a clue. Besides, State Highway Patrol Corporal Tony Laboda and his rotund colleague, Putnam County Deputy Sheriff Howland Ricketts, kept jabbing him with questions. Other officers in various uniforms blue and tan stretched yellow tape, planted stakes around the girl and took pictures. A few more just mulled about trying to look busy.

"What's your name?"

"What were you doing when you found her?"

"The golf course? Where do you *really* work?"

"Where were you last night?"

"This morning?"

"Can anyone confirm that? Witnesses?"

Thom might have answered these questions with ease, but, just then, he could scarcely breathe. So he nodded, struggled to produce one-syllable responses and, in so doing, only made the cops more impatient. Especially Ricketts. As their inquisition grew more intense, so did Thom's breathless panic.

A uniformed man near the dead girl said something. Thom's interrogators turned. Thom stumbled toward the blue golf cart. The cops turned back and ordered him to *stop* or they'd *shoot*. He didn't stop, but before they shot, Laboda realized he could simply jog alongside as Thom rolled back toward the clubhouse in his obsolete electric cart on its three small wheels, steered by a handle attached to the one in front. It was the slow-motion O.J. Simpson chase all over again, except that, instead of a white Bronco, the officers followed an even slower powder-blue golf cart, rusted along its edges, on foot, with chubby Ricketts bringing up the rear.

The cart hummed to a stop in the shadow of what was once a western-themed motel and whorehouse, which now functioned as a western-themed golf pro shop and Nineteenth Hole—with "guestrooms" still located upstairs. The two officers hobbled to Thom's side. The dry spots of Ricketts's uniform shirt stood out as islands amid the sea of sweat-saturated blue polyester. "What the hell you doin,' boy?"

"I couldn't breathe," Thom managed between pants.

"What say we all take a deep breath," Laboda said, still looking crisp and cool in his tan shirt and slacks. In fact, he appeared the only one capable of a deep breath. "We need to know what happened back there, Thomas. From the beginning."

"I was dying," Thom said.

"Goddamn it, you pint-sized prick." Drops of sweat running off Ricketts's crooked nose aerosolized as they passed his sputtering mouth. "You done it, didn't you?"

"It'll go lots easier on you if you just level with us," Laboda said. "We're here to help."

Thom understood buffoons. He'd grown up with one. He worked for one. Therefore, he understood Ricketts. Laboda, on the other hand, seemed competent, sincere. Categorizing him would take more effort. First, however, Thom looked past the cops for any sign of his father. "I told you," Thom said, "I found her, and then . . . I don't know."

Ricketts stomped. "You don't know? How the hell don't you know—unless you're just lyin' out that midget pucker hole of yours."

"Don't call me that," Thom said.

"What the hell you think you is—a center for the Miami goddamn Heat?"

"A little person."

"That's what I said, a midget."

Before Thom could decide whether to explain which words showed disrespect or simply call Ricketts an asswipe, Ricketts produced a plastic baggie from his tan trousers. "Do you recognize this?"

Thom's eyes grew large. Inside the bag was a golf ball bearing the initials *MN* in black ink on white enamel. It was the closest thing Thom had to a friend. He vaguely recalled reaching for it when he saw the bloody body lying in the sand.

"*It's mine*," Thom shouted, tumbling from the cart as he grabbed at the treasure. How could he have missed its absence?

"Moe Norman, *the* Moe Norman, signed it himself."

"Well now," Ricketts said, dangling the bag just beyond Thom's reach. "Looks like we finally gettin' somewhere. We found it sort of half shoved under the dead body. Had to a been left by the murderer, right?"

"What do you have to say for yourself, son?" Laboda said.

"For starters, your sidekick is an asswipe. And that ball, it's mine." The cops waited. "It was a gift. I *need* it."

Ricketts reached in one pocket, then another, finally found his wallet in the third, and extracted a small laminated card. "You have the right to remain silent," he began.

"I didn't kill anyone. I found her there. Gimme back my ball!"

"Anything you say can and will be used against you in a court of—"

"Ricketts," Laboda said.

"—law. Huh—what?"

Laboda stepped away and Ricketts followed. Thom couldn't hear their conversation, outside of a few vulgar protestations from Ricketts. Laboda returned, hands on hips; Ricketts followed, hands deep within pockets.

Laboda's expression hadn't changed, yet Thom felt an increased intensity of gaze. "Look, young man, like it or not, you're tied up in this young lady's murder somehow. You may be telling the truth. Then again, some folk are lots better liars than others. So you tell me—if it wasn't you, who was it?"

"My old man. Had to be." Thom again peered around and through the officers for any sign of his father.

Apparently sensing Thom's certainty that the real murderer was near, Ricketts jumped and looked around. Seeing nothing that posed an immediate threat, he returned his focus to Thom. "Your old man? Your goddamn old man? He live in Hollister too?"

"Not as far as I know—not even close."

"So'd he just parachute his ass down here in Putnam County, murder that girl out there, and get airlifted back out? Just what the hell do you take us for, you, you—"

Thom felt on the verge of melting under the sun's relentless intensity, combined with that of the officers. The more sinister the scenario involving his old man, and the further from Pointe-Saint-Charles it occurred, the more plausible it seemed.

The Pointe, wedged between an abandoned shipping canal and the St. Lawrence River, lay just south of Montreal. It was the "working class" neighborhood where Thom was born and raised for thirteen years yet never called home. The Loudon family was poor, but so was everyone in the Pointe. Mr. Loudon drank too much and beat the crap out of Mrs. Loudon and Thom, but drunks and domestic brutality weren't all that uncommon either.

The Loudons lived in stacked housing—three floors, a flat on each—and theirs was number two. Thom slept in the den. They called it the den because the sink, mini-fridge and two-burner hot plate lay at the other end of the common room, so that part became the kitchen. Thom's parents slept in the second, smaller room. The chunks of missing plaster, higher than any of them could reach without a chair, meant the previous tenants had hammered nails into the mustard yellow walls to hang pictures.

Thom's father found odd jobs wherever he could, if not to feed the family, then at least to buy more drink. He typically worked off the books a couple of nights each week on a loading dock where produce from trains and large trucks was transferred to smaller trucks to be shipped in and around Montreal. The old man was as strong as most. He could maneuver pallet jacks and hoist crates with the best of them. Yet he was relegated to cleaning out the maggot-infested spillage from the backs of those trucks before the rats started feeling a little bit too much at home.

One night, the old man returned late with two friends. They'd most likely left work and, after a few hours of good cheer, gotten thrown out of the kind of dive that hardly ever tosses anyone. Spurred on by buddies and booze, the elder Loudon's cocksure "big man" act may have entertained ironically at first, but would quickly run thin with laughs turning to shoves and shoves to the old man throwing a punch. Upon their noisy arrival at the Loudon flat with a fifth of hundred-proof rotgut, one of the tall guys noticed Thom getting off the couch to go into the other room. The man was so plastered Thom couldn't tell if he was muttering between guffaws in French or English.

Thom's mother was awake. She lifted the sheets as Thom climbed onto the bed. She hummed a few familiar tunes and rubbed Thom's back in gentle circles, apparently thinking he needed reassurance. She'd always been like that. When she was hungry, she fixed Thom a plate; if she was cold, she made him put on a sweater; when she was scared, she offered comfort.

They were still awake an hour later when the old man threw

open the bedroom door and shouted at Thom: "Get out of here you little shit."

Thom slipped out from under the covers and into the big room. The tall men managed to resist laughing at Thom for a good two, three seconds. The old man slammed the door behind him, but Thom still heard the arguing. One man tendered Thom the near empty bottle. Thom looked away. The other man said it would only stunt Thom's growth. The men laughed even harder.

Thom's mother emerged a few minutes later, followed by his father. She wore an orange robe that felt like a worn washcloth. She surveyed the room, the men, the bottle, and clenched her fists. "No," she said.

"What?" the old man said.

"No."

He pushed her; she fell back. He pushed her again, this time towards the kitchen. They were dancing just like Thom had seen so many times. The men laughed, slapped their knees. "Midget fight! Bloody midget fight!"

His mother steadied herself, and before the old man understood what was happening, she pushed him so hard he fell on his ass. That's when Thom knew this was different. All he could do was watch. Well, no—all he *did* do was watch. He watched the old man get up and start swinging. He watched his mother raise her arms for protection. She even tried hitting back, which just pissed off the old man that much more. Thom watched his father grab a steak knife from the counter, one that had never seen steak, turn it sideways, and slip it between his mother's ribs right where her heart was. Thom watched a red spot blossom amid the orange terrycloth.

The men didn't shut their pie holes until she went down to one knee. She glared at her murderer with something worse than hate. Blood, having saturated her robe, dripped on the bare wood. When it started coming from her mouth, she looked at Thom with hope and no hope. That's what Thom saw all right: hope *and* no hope.

Maybe it sounds impossible, like white and black at the same time, but it's not. Hope means a person wants things to be different, maybe to be somewhere that's not a shithole. No hope is where the chance of finding that somewhere else is nil without luck, good luck, and good luck's GPS didn't even register the Pointe. If a guy had hope and a plan instead of no hope, he had a ticket out, and a ticket out was one hell of lot better than banking on luck.

Thom's mother? She was hopeless and without a plan. She had no path, no ticket. So, of course, she hoped that *Thom* might find something better and pitied *him* because the only luck they'd ever known was bad.

More blood spilled from her mouth. She made a gurgle, then a convulsion like an electric shock. She fell back, the knife clattered to the floor and the blood from her heart continued to ooze. The leg on which she'd been kneeling ended up trapped under her bottom like an extreme hurdler stretch.

The old man just looked. Thom couldn't place his expression, except to note there was no hope there. As for Thom, he was thirteen at the time—and hopeless. But if getting away from his old man, away from the goddamn Pointe, was a plan, then at least he had one of those.

Thom stole across the border at the Thousand Islands Bridge north of Syracuse in the back of a sixteen-wheeler driven by a man Thom had gotten to know at the warehouse where the old man occasionally worked. The driver took a risk to help Thom. Then again, the driver knew Thom's old man, and he realized it was a risk worth taking when Thom told him about the murder. Before the driver hid Thom under shipping pads among crates of tomatoes destined for the States, he loaned Thom his cell phone to call the police.

Some three years and 2,200 kilometers removed, Thom turned in the direction of Savannah May's body, her muscles tightening into the full rigor of death. The stiffness in his own neck and shoulders caused pain.

"That's exactly what my mom looked like," Thom explained to the officers. "The way she's laying there, all the blood—exactly. And that bastard's the one who murdered her. I mean, who else. . ." He turned away from the corpse.

"But he's in jail, right?" Laboda said.

"Gotta be," Thom said.

"Ah, for Christ's sake," Ricketts said. "Tony—what are we waitin' for?"

Laboda raised a hand and Ricketts backed off. "We're not arresting you, Thomas. Not yet anyway," Laboda said. "But we need you to stick around. You're not planning on going anywhere, are you?"

Thom shook his head. He didn't bother to ask where else he

had to go or how the hell he was supposed to get there.

"What kind a car you drivin,' boy?" Ricketts said.

Thom nodded toward the rusty blue cart.

"Smart ass," Ricketts muttered.

Laboda offered a business card. "Here's all my phone numbers and emails. If you remember anything, anything at all, let me know." Laboda pulled back the card just as Thom reached for it and wrote a number on the back. "Just use that one, okay? It's my wife's cell, and she's the only one who never forgets to have the darn thing with her. She'll know where I am better than me."

"What about the ball?" Thom said with a trace of desperation. "It's mine."

"Tell us how you done it first," Ricketts said.

Laboda said, "It's evidence, Thomas. We'll be keeping it until we figure out what happened."

The officers ambled off in the direction of the second green, with Ricketts leveling a parting sneer over his shoulder. Only then did Thom notice the others gathered around the clubhouse entrance, staring, listening. The crowd included Jimmy Simms, the chair of the BRGC's board of governors, his son, Brett, and his son's oversized shadow, L.T.

Thom wanted nothing more than to escape into the cinderblock storage garage where his mattress lay in a back corner among shovels, rakes, irrigation equipment, and stacks of members' clubs. Both the hinged garage door, whose rusted rollers and sections remained seized shut absent a fresh bath of WD-40, and the steel entryway door were equipped with heavy brass padlocks that could be secured from the inside. Thom's father couldn't get past those. News of a local girl's murder, however, had brought out even the pretend golfer crowd—the ones who paid the fifty-dollar annual fee to store their clubs in Thom's bedroom so that the clubs might gather dust somewhere other than the corner of the pretend golfers' own mudrooms and garages. The storage garage had to remain open.

A formidable woman strode forth through the gawkers. Her tight blue skirt barely concealed ample thighs and hips that might, for some, bring to mind certain lascivious pursuits. Just then, however, said thighs and hips were embarked upon a mission of mercy. She took Thom's arm.

"Jade," Thom said.

"You think?" Jade said.

"Have you seen him? My old man?"

"Now just how am I supposed to know that? He don't look like you, does he?"

"Well, yeah."

"Why didn't you say so? I ain't seen him, but Lord only knows how many places a little bitty person like you might hide. Follow me."

Jade ran the Nineteenth Hole of the Breeders' Roost Golf Club in Hollister, Florida. For twenty years, the BRGC had occupied the same space and buildings as had the Breeders' Roost Hotel for decades previously. She also kept the club's books and served as its unofficial historian. Shortly after Thom began working there, Jade allowed as how she wasn't sure whether the Breeders part of the golf club's title referred to the ranchers who, at one time, made Florida home to more cattle per capita than any other US state or the activities that occurred in the eight rooms upstairs. That the so-called hotel was built a mile and a half off the nearest paved road leant credence to the latter theory. She'd explained that the nightly booze sales in the Nineteenth Hole and hourly rentals on the upstairs beds put water in the pool, kept gasoline in the lawn mowers, and thus ensured their continued employment. Knowing just how little Thom was paid (albeit under the table and free of taxation), Jade had suggested a business opportunity: "Midget sex. You team up with some of them girls what drive over from Gainesville, and you'd earn yourself a pretty penny. Midget sex—yessiree—now that's something you don't see every day."

"I don't need any pretty pennies," Thom said. "And I am not a fucking midget."

"In case you ain't noticed, you're pretty damn short."

"If I'm a midget, you're a nigger."

As soon as the word left his mouth, Thom fully expected to have the crap beaten right out of him by a person nearly two feet taller and perhaps a hundred pounds heavier. He could not outrun Jade—even in high heels, one of her strides would cover three of his.

Nonetheless, it had to be said. He was who he was: a little person, a short guy, altitude challenged, but not a goddamn midget. That word carried too much baggage and none of it good. It had become a hate word. It was used to degrade. It was the kind of label normal people attached so they wouldn't have to see a freak like him as a real person, to meet him on equal terms. A label that lived on precisely because it caused separation. Hate words were an excuse for abuse. *He ain't normal like us, so we don't have to treat him normal.* Maybe someday little people would claim the word, take back the word's power for themselves, in the same way black people had with nigga. Nigga: Migga. Thom liked that—migga. Meanwhile, he was waiting for Jade to decide whether she would start the ass-whooping with her feet or her hands.

She'd said, "What should I call you?"

Thom thought for a moment. "Thom. With an *h*."

Thom followed Jade through the crowd that had watched his interrogation and near arrest, up the five plank stairs splintered by golf-shoe spikes during daylight hours and spiked heels at night. They passed through the glass-door clubhouse entrance. The pro shop lay to the left where a hotel lobby might once have stood, the Nineteenth Hole to the right where one might have imagined a cathouse bar and restaurant. More stairs rose in front of the main entrance.

Jade left Thom's side long enough to grab a tallboy of Colt 45 malt liquor from the bar. "For purposes of sedation," she explained, "cause you look plum out of sedate."

He was indeed but he wouldn't imbibe. Thom was prone to overdo anything he enjoyed. His was an addictive personality. He'd read about addictive personalities, and lots of other personalities, precisely because reading constituted one of his addictions. Golfing by himself also qualified, which worked out well since solitude was yet another. However, harboring no desire to further resemble his old man, he'd never been tempted to drink. He'd smelled enough cheap booze and beer to have some idea how they might taste. He'd seen more than enough regurgitated in and outside their flat in the Pointe to know it was poison. Knowing also that Jade was not easily dissuaded, Thom accepted the cold, perspiring can and followed her up the stairs.

At the top lay a dimly lit hallway flanked by four doors on either side. Another descending stairway marked the hallway's far end. Faded pink and yellow roses decorated the peeling wallpaper. Jade retrieved a key from a pocket of her white, white lace-trimmed blouse that, along with the tight skirt, constituted her uniform. She stopped at the third door on the left.

"Number seven. We don't use number seven except when it gets real busy, so you can have it for a while."

Inside the room, cigarette burns blemished the bedside table, just as carved initials scarred the twin bed's slat headboard, whose connection with the bed frame seemed tenuous at best. The mirror above the headboard was cracked and Thom didn't want to know why. He engaged the deadbolt immediately upon Jade's departure. While the door itself wasn't particularly substantial, the lock worked. Were his old man to break in, Thom would at least enjoy sufficient time to—what—hide under the bed? He likely wouldn't have been the first to seek such refuge.

Thom had read every glossy golf magazine left lying around the pro shop and so understood plenty about relaxation techniques guaranteed to steady any golfer's nerves and cure the yips. Thom had never personally experienced such maladies. The key, as any

Moe Norman devotee understood, was focusing upon opportunity. Most players envisioned threats in the wind, trees, water, long grass, and bunkers, threats that dominated their thoughts and so their minds and muscles. The wise golfer experienced each swing as a gift—a new beginning. Thom saw the ball where it lay and the potential of launching it within feet, if not inches, of where he wanted it to lie. On the golf course, distinct from any other setting, Thom felt gratitude, not fear, a thankfulness that occupied Thom's psyche prior to every swing. This is why the course was Moe's world, Thom's world.

Even so, Thom had read the advice. There was little else to satisfy the reading addiction. Perhaps it would come in handy when he was playing in the final Sunday pairing at the Masters. Who knew what it was like playing before a crowd—Thom certainly didn't. Within a year and a half of escaping the Pointe, playing golf every spare moment, he was shooting scratch—and better. No small accomplishment, all things considered. No one would have believed how good Thom had become. In fact, no one did, because during those three years at the BRGC, he never golfed with anyone. Never once a twosome, threesome, foursome. When Thom golfed all by his lonesome, he wasn't anything in anyone else's eyes. He was not a dwarf, a little person, a midget, a freak. He was Thom Loudon, hitting a ball, unconstrained by the expectations of others that governed all other aspects of his life, watching the ball soar through the air and, anymore, landing pretty much where he intended.

He practiced the abdominal breathing extolled in a magazine's advice column by one teaching pro who'd probably never played on the Pro Golfers' Association Tour, let alone the Masters: in through the nose and out through the mouth—smell the cake and blow out the candles. Envision the cleansing breath washing over sweaty hands, wobbly knees, sour gut, the very soul itself, ridding mind and body of all tension, all anxiety. Breath, gentle and pure like sun-glistening water, rinsing away the shadowy sludge. In fact, all Thom wanted just then was to get in enough breath so that he no longer felt like he was suffocating inside one of those plastic bags parents are supposed to keep away from toddlers.

The painful spasms in Thom's neck and shoulders subsided first, then the trembling in his hands. Whether his breath came easier as he quit thinking about it or vice versa was of no moment. He closed his eyes and played a game in which he designed golf holes in every imaginable terrain: holes traversing rivers and lakes; fairways lined by white sand bordering opal-blue tropical coves; hazards such as sheer cliffs, deep bunkers, and live oaks lurking in the most inopportune locations—a world where risk was reward and opportunity promised life. Then Thom would typically play all those holes, calmly overcoming every hazard, for birdies and eagles. But he couldn't that morning, nor would he over the weeks that followed, because fear rather than opportunity engulfed him at the first imaginary tee.

He managed a series of naps instead, the shallowness of which blurred any border between sleep and consciousness. By the sixth or seventh time he came to, night outside was falling and the noise downstairs was rising.

Thom left via the back stairway. It was marked *Fire Escape*, but *Wife Escape* was more like it. The back door opened onto a less frequently used pathway around the rear of the clubhouse, which provided an alternative route to the pool. Walking slowly and straining to detect movement behind each building and tree, Thom left the path, squeezed past a dumpster, and cut through the space between the clubhouse and storage garage.

He was panting before reaching the entryway to the garage, otherwise known as his bedroom, even though it was barely thirty yards from door to door. He had even stopped twice to make sure he wasn't being followed. Why were there more shadows after sunset than before? The very shadows in which a man—say, a little man—might hide. Even after curling up behind the locked door on his familiar mattress, under the covers and blanketed by a square floor fan's wind and white noise, Thom felt as if someone else were present, someone sucking up all the oxygen.

Chapter 3

Thom awoke hungry. While he had snarfed a milk chocolate bar from a vending machine before teeing off Saturday morning, he had not consumed real food since Friday evening, not even a sip of malt liquor. He headed straight for the BRGC snack shack, which was strategically nestled between the modest swimming pool and the tenth tee, where golfers could grab a beer and a burger from the take-out window before starting the back nine. It also took an occasional food order from the Nineteenth Hole, because what was left of the Breeders' Roost original kitchen now served as storage space for an ever-growing inventory of broken but theoretically fixable furniture, alongside bags of dirty linen and stacks of clean. And roaches. Except in Florida, these roaches, fat, ripe six-legged date fruit large enough to trip the unwary, particularly the species *Paraplaneta americana* (a.k.a. the American cockroach), were known as palmetto bugs.

Like the storage garage, the snack shack and neighboring swimming pool locker rooms were cinderblock affairs painted white and trimmed in blue. Among this poolside suite of dressing and cooking facilities, the shack, true to its name, was the smallest structure. Its door and window were around the corner from the pool, overlooking the tenth tee. Hungry golfers and swimmers ordered and received their burgers and fries, candy and shakes, via the window. Customers were not allowed inside. There wasn't room.

Aisha had run the snack shack since before Thom's arrival. She wore a headscarf. Thom had seen more women wearing headscarves and also the veils that obscured all but the wearer's eyes around the Pointe and Montreal. Maybe there were fewer Muslims in Putnam County. Or Muslims in Putman County simply eschewed additional layers of clothing amidst the stifling heat and humidity. Or, as Thom suspected, perhaps they, like him, just hated standing out around all the pickups, gun racks, and confederate flags.

Thom was authorized one free meal a day at the snack shack. Aisha and her occasional stand-in let him eat twice—typically around 10 a.m. when the snack shack opened and just before 6 p.m. when it closed.

Aisha knew without asking what Thom would order at every meal. Double cheeseburger, fries, full-sized salted nut roll, large Sprite. Extra lettuce, tomato, and pickle on the burger to ward off scurvy and because Thom liked pickles. That's why, despite his affinity for anyone else who didn't fit in, Thom didn't like Aisha. Aisha was rude to presume to know what he wanted, never mind that she was always correct. It was as bad as a drugstore cashier assuming that every old geezer in line was there for XXL diapers and denture cream—no matter how badly one of them might have been dying to demand the ribbed condoms. Her presumption, despite its accuracy, was bad enough. Her twice-daily inquiry of, "The usual?" only made it worse. Who wanted to be reminded that he craves the security of predictability? Thom wasn't about to mount a Harley and ride whichever way the wind blew, even if he were able to reach the foot controls, but he sure as hell did not need to be reminded of that fact nor have it regularly broadcast to all within earshot.

Some might confuse golf with the banality of routine, especially golf played by someone as proficient as Thom. After all, on the same course, under consistent weather conditions, Thom would play the same shots to the same spots using the same clubs nine times out of ten. Those people, however, did not understand the difference between routine and ritual. The former, while safe, is drudgery, mindless. The latter is self-affirming. Those eighteen individual journeys, so pleasant and peaceful, so predictable when Thom's game was on, were where Thom escaped the fear and expectations that others projected. Fear and expectations, of course, being redundant, as expectations reflect nothing if not fear of the different and unknown. Golf was where Thom engaged the world on his terms, where his ruler set the standard. Where his routine was his and his alone. Where three to get on and a single putt constituted a regulation par-four just the same as two to reach plus a two-putt. Where six feet tall was not necessarily the norm. A place that had been Moe's world and now was Thom's.

He reached the snack shack window at ten sharp, hungry as hell and already bitter that Aisha knew exactly what he was about to order. She'd say, "The usual?" He'd grunt, "Why not?"

That's when a woman asked, "What, sir, may I do for you?"

"What did you do with Aisha?" Thom said. "She never asks."

"I am Dyleane. I do not know this, this Aisha." Her accent was French—or at least a fair approximation. She was tall like Jade, rounder face, same dark skin, a fraction of the makeup, half the poundage. Her braids were so tightly twisted that straight scalloped lines of scalp stretched in between.

"Okay, then, why the hell are you talking like that?" Thom said.

"Because I am from Montreal, and I do not appreciate your tone of voice."

"Aisha runs the snack shack."

"You are not only impertinent, you are most sorely mistaken. Starting with this day, it is I who runs the snack shack."

"And you're not from Montreal. The accent isn't bad. But it's not so great either."

Dyleane looked down upon Thom in exasperation. "Who are you, and how do you presume to know anything about me or my upbringing?"

"Then prove it."

"I have nothing to prove, *merci beaucoup*."

"Fine. Tell me which night is Hockey Night in Canada?" Nothing. "Who's the greatest center in NHL history?" More nothing. "Hint: the Pocket Rocket." Still nothing. "What's the toughest neighborhood in Montreal? Hell, what province is Montreal in?"

"Quebec? Quebec!" She'd lost the accent.

"One out of four, eh? That's one better than most Yanks."

Rather than escalate their disagreement into a full-blown argument, which Thom assumed to be the normal course of most conversations, Dyleane smiled. The smile was, what, friendly? Cute? Thom had precious little practice at interpreting such nuance, let alone appreciating it. Most of his experience around girls his age involved turning away and not noticing. Even though a friendly face might occasionally punctuate the routine looks of scorn, why fantasize about Gay Paree when you lived in a bloody backwater and always would?

At the same time, her imaginary Canadian self was more plausible than, say, a homeless half-pint from the land of perpetual winter trying to master a big man's game for rich people who live where flip-flops constitute appropriate year-round attire.

"I'm just trying to get away," Dyleane sighed.

The smile remained despite this foreboding admission. Inviting? Maybe it was the big brown eyes, a shade darker than the skin around them, or the rosy fields beneath her high cheekbones. No one else was waiting in line, and Thom experienced an odd sensation. It was almost as though he felt like talking or at least looking. How, he had pondered on more than one occasion, do people talk simply for the sake of talking? And why? It was almost as though some actually enjoyed discussing topics that bore no tangible relation to matters immediately at hand. What did they say that was neither too blunt nor too personal nor laughably trite?

"What," Dyleane said as Thom stared. "I got something stuck between my teeth?"

"Get away? You just started here."

"Actually I started yesterday."

"Where are you really from?"

"Marianna, Florida, if you must know," she said. Her vowels began deep down and rolled out like a slow dance.

"Never heard of it." This small talk wasn't so tough.

"In the panhandle. And you wouldn't, unless you had some interest in the upbringing of Florida's most racist governor ever, which is saying something in these parts. And what white person would be interested in such a minor thing as that? Dude committed suicide—on his plantation run by slaves—actually committed suicide when he heard the South surrendered the Civil War.

"Or the Dozier Reform School where more black boys were murdered than they could keep buried deep enough that the coons and polecats wouldn't dig them back up. It's also where my stepfather still lives and where that drunk son of a bitch is going to stay if I have anything to say about it."

"So you're not white—er, I'm not black—" Damn overconfidence!

Dyleane laughed before Thom could dig any deeper. She opened her mouth, appeared to reconsider, and finally explained that she and her mother had just escaped to Interlachen, and the French-Canadian affectation was her way of fitting in with the mostly white kids at the high school there. The name Interlachen might conjure images of towering snowcapped alpine mountains and crystal-clear glacial lakes. Several lakes did surround this North

Central Florida town, but the water was more a cloudy green, and cowboy hats and boots greatly outnumbered lederhosen, just as boiled peanuts were more widely available than actual Swiss chocolate. Interlachen, however, did constitute the largest nearby settlement, thus relegating the tiny hamlet of Hollister to the status of Interlachen's trailer park exurb.

A background involving Dyleane being kidnapped by a circus troupe and forced to walk tightropes in scanty glimmering outfits would have grabbed Thom's rapt attention. Her actual story, however, one of abuse and escape, was one with which Thom was already too familiar. Just then he was occupied enough with finding a happy ending to his own tale to worry much about someone else's.

"That's me. Who might you be?"

"I might be Thom Loudon—with an *h*."

"LaHoudon?"

"*Thom* with an *h*."

"All right, all right. That *h* must be pretty important."

Thom hesitated. "I really hate getting called Tom—with*out* an *h*—Thumb, okay?"

"But you're way bigger than him. I mean he was only as big as a—"

"Right, a thumb. Got it. So, I'll have a double cheeseburger with—"

"You're the one who found Savannah May yesterday, aren't you?"

"—extra lettuce and tomato. And—" he paused. "How'd you

know her name?"

"She goes—went—to high school with me. Even though she was a cheerleader and really popular, she was actually nice to me. *Me.* I mean, who could hurt such a sweet young thing? There are so many mean girls at that school. And I mean, *mean.* One of them pushed me on the steps between the library and gym on my very first day." Dyleane pointed to a chipped upper tooth. "That one didn't even lie about it being an accident. Just laughed and walked off with all her friends."

Thom's expression darkened. "Someone did that—to you?"

"But Savannah May, she wasn't that way. She wouldn't hurt anyone like that. And I'm sorry for you."

"Me? Why me?"

"I heard you were, well—they say you murdered her. Did you?"

"Did I what?"

She shook her head. "I didn't think so. I was eavesdropping on two policemen who ate here yesterday—"

"Let me guess: a skinny one and a fat one."

"Yeah," Dyleane said. "You ever wonder what it is about cops and chilidogs? The skinny one, he did most of the talking, going on about how the rain had washed away Savannah May's footprints and soaked her blood into the sand. But your footprints came after all that. I guess it rained like heck out here that night."

Thom recalled that his clothes had been wet when he finally climbed from the sand trap that Saturday morning.

"Extra pickles, fries—"

"Oh, I'm sorry. You're still upset, bless your heart." Folks around there were always blessing someone's heart. Sometimes they may even have meant it. It was better than when they patted Thom's head like a kitten. "You want to talk about it?"

"Talk? Like, what, just for the sake of talking?"

"If you haven't noticed, some people like talking with other people, especially when something's bothering them."

In fact, all this talk had reached the point of enough bother to put Thom right off food—as well as any further human interaction in the foreseeable future. "No one I know." Just then, he craved sustenance from the single pursuit most capable of providing it, even more than food or the books he had once consumed like ketchup chips (a junk-food delicacy Thom had yet to find south of the border).

That Sunday morning promised to be slow, what with so many people showing up to play the day before, or at least to gawk, when news broke about the dead cheerleader stabbed through the heart, fueled by rumors that the perp may have been that Canuck midget with the perpetual sneer. Thom figured to squeeze in a quick nine before the regular after-church men's foursomes began teeing off. On his way back to the storage garage, he saw a cop taking down the yellow tape that had blocked off the front nine. No one else was heading for the first tee. Thom tapped on the window next to Reinhold "Dill" Pickle's table in the back corner of the Nineteenth Hole and pointed at the blue cart parked nearby. This constituted notice that Thom would be out for the next seventy minutes or so. And were Dill so inclined, he could actually get off his drunk, lazy head-club-professional butt and help out in Thom's absence.

Upon reaching number one, Thom was sweating more than called for on a relatively bearable September morning, trembling too—probably just low blood sugar. Or someone was watching. Thom had stashed sour candy balls in his golf bag for just such an occasion—hypoglycemia, not being stalked. He crunched a purple ball and chose a red one to suck on. Problem solved—almost. His hand still quivered as he set a ball on top of the tee. It obviously took a minute or two for a body to get the sugar where it needed to be. Thom, per usual routine, would stand behind the ball and visualize its flight, address the ball, take one last look at the target, swing easy and let the club do the job it was precisely crafted to perform. Done, done, done, and *swing*. The driver barely caught enough of the ball's dimpled white cover to send it rolling merrily across the well-manicured tee box and about ten yards into the long grass that preceded the fairway.

He was alone (he hoped). No one was watching (he hoped). He could take a mulligan. Anyone else would. Thom used to, when he was a total newbie, especially on the first tee. Whether taking a do-over on the first tee was cheating depended upon whether a recreational round really began with that very first swing or with the very first swing that was actually counted. Thom knew the answer: a mulligan was cheating. But assuming he was alone, who would know? Thom would. And he wasn't in the mood for metaphysical musings, ambiguity, or areas shaded gray. He would play by the book, duck decisions that needn't be made, just hit the damn ball, and watch its graceful flight through the calm morning air. He chose a hybrid with extra loft to lift the ball free of the rough and carry it somewhere close to the layup spot. "Lift," of course, being a term of art, because, as every golfer understood, you hit down on a ball to make it fly. The divot should come after ball contact. From there, he'd get up and down in two and save par, which, just then, struck Thom as an acceptable outcome.

Golf was perfect that way. The last shot was irrelevant to the next shot. Make a mistake? Take the ball where it lies and decide which shot will best move it towards where it ought to be. A game with so much history and yet best played in the here and now. Moe said most golfers played from fear, trying to avoid danger. Moe's advantage was that he focused only on what he wanted that next shot to accomplish. If he wanted the ball to fly three hundred yards straight down the fairway, that was his only thought. It didn't matter if the fairway was lined with water, cliffs, forest, or dragons. Every shot promised an opportunity to leave the past behind and craft a present more to his liking. For what more could a misfit loner like Moe ask? Absolutely nothing, a truism that Thom Loudon understood all too well.

Head down. Relaxed grip. Aggressive forward move. Follow through with the club head low. In other words, smooth and strong through the long grass. Thom knew without looking where he wanted the ball to land and how many bounces it would take before coming to rest. After a deep, cleansing breath, he initiated a swing patterned upon the image ingrained in his mind—and promptly plowed a pond-sized divot four inches before the ball, a divot so deep that it stopped the metal head cold, jerked the grip from his hands, and left him following through as though he were playing air golf. The ball traveled an inch, propelled not by the club but from the earth the club had excavated in front of it. He finished the first hole with an eight—a quadruple bogey—rather than the customary birdie three.

After a start like that, no wonder Thom was anxious and short of breath. That many strokes meant getting in and out of the cart and swinging more than twice as many times as usual, and from parts of the course that, anymore, Thom only saw from a green John Deere tractor. It also dashed any hope for a low final score. Thom's focus upon nothing but the next shot, however, almost erased such negativity from his mind. Even so, with three candy balls down and another locked and loaded, why still the trembling hands, tight chest, and queasy belly?

Here was where the capable golfer must summon a positive outlook. Smile through the frustration to tell mind and body alike to relax, to announce that things were fine, just fine. This was gospel from the more spiritual pages of those glossy golf magazines left lying about the pro shop. Not one, however, contained a photograph of Jack or Tiger grinning in the middle of a bad round. Of course, Moe permitted himself a smirk every now and then, but mostly after shutting up some heckler in the gallery with a shot no one thought possible. Outside of golf, Thom had always expected the worst, and if the worst didn't happen, it was a pleasant surprise. Inside of golf, it wasn't so much an expectation as a simple understanding of cause and effect: Do your job, and the ball will do its. Just then, after firing a quad and feeling like a man about to have his legs cut off without anesthesia, he no longer understood what to expect, which was best because what happened next was worse than he could have imagined.

Still sweating, panting, shaking, he wobbled onto the second tee. His extremities may as well have been overcooked noodles. Attempting to borrow a page from those glossy golf mags, he forced up the corners of his mouth. This produced not even the whiff of a smile. An attempted laugh emerged a cackle. A force greater than Thom could comprehend tightened across his chest. No air moved in or out. None. This was what a drowning man felt upon realizing God himself was holding his head under the water. That, indeed, the man was surrendering his very soul to the black unknown. Barely one gasp short of final surrender, Thom jumped back in the cart, not bothering to pick up the ball, and retreated toward the first green. The constriction loosened a bit. A little further from the second tee, it loosened even more. Still shaking, still sweating, he waited, tried to breathe, grateful that no one had teed off number one. He was alone. He had time. No hurry. Watch the flag on number one wave this way and that in the gentle morning breeze. Breathe.

In a few moments, he didn't feel much worse than when he'd first teed off. He turned the cart and re-approached the second tee. This was stupid. This was his refuge, his church: *Thom's World*. But no sooner did he step from the cart than the metal jaws of death re-gripped his chest. The breath rushed out as though he'd ventured into the ultimate vacuum of outer space. Then there were bodies scattered just beyond the rise in the second fairway—at least a dozen, another few lying partially in and out of the sand trap, some tall, some short. He knew without looking that more lay inside. Each girl with a foot grotesquely trapped behind her. Each with a massive bloodstain growing on her yellow blouse or orange robe where a blade had been expertly slipped between the ribs into her heart, the bloody daggers randomly strewn among the corpses. Of course, this was impossible. Thom knew that. But there they were! Present also was the certainty that Thom's old man lurked nearby, waiting, watching.

He'd been over every blade of BRGC grass dozens of times—playing it, mowing it, watering it—yet as everything turned upside down and spun backwards, Thom wasn't sure of the path back to the pro shop. He couldn't get too lost—a three-strand barbed-wire fence marked the property's perimeter. So long as he avoided the damn fence—and the swamps—he was bound to get back sooner or later. Unless he ran into his old man first.

He reached for the Moe Norman ball. Its absence was another slug in the gut. The fence and swamps be damned, he maxed out the rusty blue cart's speed, which wasn't much, turning only to avoid trees. There, finally, was the cowboy clubhouse. Jade nodded through a window of the Nineteenth Hole. Thom nodded back—he needed a hiding place where he could lock the door. Jade appeared and said something about Thom looking paler than a ghost and how he'd better not be one of those. At the foot of the stairs, Thom requested a Sprite instead of a beer.

"With a straw?" she asked. He nodded again.

Thom accepted the can. He took two steps for each stair. Alone and with number seven's deadbolt fully engaged, Thom sipped the soda, smelled the cake, blew out the candles, envisioned a course wending through a mountainous rainforest crisscrossed by whitewater streams. It did not help. So Thom cried. He hadn't cried with such abandon since—since the first time he was conscious of his daddy beating his mommy? The first time he was conscious that the old man beating him wasn't normal? Or understanding that it was? No, it was just the day before when he'd collapsed next to Savanna May Paulson's bloody corpse. Then he fell into a restless sleep.

By late afternoon, Thom was roused by the noise downstairs from half-pissed golfers recounting their Sabbath exploits on the links. This racket would not morph into the more raucous exclamations and deep pounding stereo bass that characterized the rutting ritual for another couple of hours. (Admittedly, any line separating the two often ranged from blurred to nonexistent.)

A queasiness grabbed Thom's gut and announced an immediate need for sustenance, the food kind, and sour candy balls wouldn't do. Thom, in fact, was turned right off sour candy balls—the mere thought turned his stomach. He left via the mislabeled *Fire Escape*. After checking for corpses outside the backdoor, he headed up the more heavily traveled pathway leading from the members' parking lot, around the front of the clubhouse, past the pool, and to the snack shop. A couple of kids in the shallow end skipped a tennis ball back and forth off the pool's surface. They were Thom's size, which put them around ten years old. They would likely end up about six-foot by the time they graduated high school. If finishing high school would similarly affect Thom's stature, he'd re-enroll in a second. It wouldn't, of course, and he'd be looking up at those same goddamn boys in another year.

Thom wondered, often while lying awake late at night, whether finishing high school might at least lead to employment more rewarding than temp jobs alongside rats in the back of produce trucks. Only it wasn't his old man's lack of education or his drinking that held him back, at least not at first. It was the ignorance of others—many of whom had themselves never finished high school. Thom didn't need more formal education to understand this. He'd been educated by stares and giggles on the streets of the Pointe. He'd gone to college on jokes and trash talk from the golf club caddies, mostly black kids, who didn't fit in a whole lot better than he did. His invisibility around golf club members constituted his Ph.D. He was a doctor in suffering the disdain of others.

Golf, Thom had convinced himself, would be his elevator shoes. In just three years, he scored lower and more consistently so than even the best club regulars. Thom played like the proverbial well-oiled machine. He was nowhere near his ceiling—all height-related wiseass remarks aside. He certainly played the wheels off head pro Dill Pickle, although at this advanced stage of Dill's career —end-stage was more like it—that wasn't saying much. Yet excelling in what, fundamentally, was a public pursuit would eventually force Thom out into that same public. At least it would if Thom desired some return from his excellence. And he did. Thom appreciated this drawback. As is often the case with long-term plans formulated in the mind of a sixteen-year-old, however,

Thom chose not to dwell upon his plan's potential downside. Perhaps it reflected his approach to each golf shot—focusing where he wanted the ball to travel, not upon the hazards that might lie in its path. Still, as even Thom had to concede, this sudden inability to breathe thing constituted a significant concern.

The air around the snack shack always smelled like grease, even at night, as though fries perpetually boiled in that vat of liquefied lard. Thom reached the shack just as Dyleane was closing the order window for the night. Much to his surprise and more than a little bit of consternation, Dyleane welcomed Thom inside because, so she said, she might need his guidance to ensure everything was properly prepared. She locked the window and shooed Thom toward the lone chair. He climbed up and watched. She moved confidently within the cramped kitchen as if everything were second nature. Dyleane didn't need Thom's help, and the food tasted fine without it. Then again, Thom was hungry enough to enjoy skink sushi. Dyleane scraped down the grill with a black pumice brick and loaded the dishwasher. After cleaning the table she called a prep station, she sat on a cylindrical tank of Coke syrup waiting its turn to be tethered to the soft drink dispenser whose rattletrap refrigerator motor cycled on and off. She not only invited Thom to describe that morning's golfing nightmare, she even appeared to listen.

"You always carry around a golf ball in your pocket but not to play golf with?" she asked when Thom finished. He resisted the urge to check his pocket for what he knew wasn't there. Instead, he bit off a chunk of nut roll just as she said, "That's creepy."

All he could do was nod and chew before saying, "Used to," and explaining the ball from Moe Norman was in police custody.

"You're shitting me," she said. "Moe?"

"You know about him? Really?"

"I *love* The Three Stooges. I never knew they golfed though."

Thom crammed in the other half of candy bar. This talking thing had its ups and downs.

Dyleane, however, had not finished asking questions. She asked why Thom wasn't in school. He offered his pat explanation: as long as he never had to add threes, fours, and fives to any total in excess of seventy-two, which was par on most golf courses, he'd be just fine. "Anyway, no one around here has ever mentioned it. And I don't suspect they will as long as I keep doing my job for what little they pay me."

Dyleane asked about the corpses. Merely the thought made it harder for Thom to chew and swallow. She waited. He finally washed down the last fry with a swig of soda, buried a hand in the empty pocket and wondered why he was sweating in this air-conditioned cubby. He told her about the Pointe and his mom—how that's who he'd seen in the sand trap. About how his old man murdered that girl just as surely as her blood stained the white sand red, even though it couldn't possibly have been him. About hope and no hope. About how, since watching his mom bleed out on that bare wooden floor, golf was the only thing that had ever made him hopeful.

"That's it," Dyleane said.

"What's it?" Thom said.

"Why you couldn't do your golf thing."

Thom's mouth opened, but nothing came out.

"You ran away when you saw your dad—you know—that night, back home."

"Not *home*. The Pointe." Although this conversation was fast losing steam, that was an important distinction. Plus it might've been rude to take off before letting Dyleane finish whatever the hell she was talking about.

"You never dealt with your anger, your sense of loss," she said. "Your guilt."

"What's to deal with, eh? My mom was dead. My dad was heading off to jail—he's a damn murderer isn't he? I was going to foster care as a ward of the province, which is dangerous enough for a normal kid. One like me, well . . . "

"You're suppressing your anger. You've never grieved the loss."

"You're a shrink when you're not flipping burgers?"

Dyleane rested hands on hips. With an air befitting a French Canadian, she explained, "I *am* starting a third class in psychology. Well, one was sociology, but they are very similar. Besides, I'm right and you know it."

"Thanks for the diagnosis, Doc. Just post the invoice."

Later, back at the garage, Thom placed the big square floor fan at the foot of his mattress and turned it on high, both to drown out the noise from the bar and to create a reason to pull the covers over his head.

What the hell did grieving loss and suppressing anger even mean? He'd run across that tripe about the stages of grief in his reading. Maybe all that held true for Yanks. Canadians, however, were a task-oriented people who valued the time they were given. Americans went out of their way to create occasions for "sharing feelings." Look at their television programming chock full of talk shows and so-called reality TV, where would-be celebrities prattled on, playing the martyred narcissists. Hell, look at football. The delay following any occurrence of note provided sufficient time for choreographed one-act plays. In hockey, by contrast, there hardly existed time after a goal for the obligatory scuffle and a line change before the puck was dropped back into play. The cold nourished nothing if not pragmatism.

Sure, Thom had feelings. He missed his mother every single day he woke up on a mattress resting on dusty concrete in the corner of a storage shed and even more each time a so-called palmetto bug scampered across his face in the dark. Meanwhile, this emptiness waged daily battle against anger for possession of Thom's soul. Anger, though, enjoyed all the advantages in that war. Anger stimulates, motivates. Moroseness sedates. As often as not, Thom was mad about something or at someone and couldn't really be bothered about who knew. Outside of golf and the occasional book, what wasn't there to be mad about? What emotion besides anger was better suited to meet head on the endless frustrations of everyday life? Given Thom's current, if *temporary*, hiatus from golf, he was more pissed off than ever.

Besides, what did it take to *un*-suppress anger? Just for the sake of argument. Something ridiculous like beating up a pillow?

He slammed his pillow with a fist and slammed it again. And

again. He beat the holy crap out of that damn pillow. Then the boy whose eyes had remained dry even as he watched his mother bleed out on a bare wooden floor bawled for the third time in two days.

Chapter 4

Monday morning, with two days "off" and a good dinner under his belt, Thom hit the course before dawn, first atop the green John Deere tractor to pull banks of whirring reel mowers over the fairways and then, after increasing the clearance of the blades, over the rough. During the warmest months, March through October, this meant fairway grass less than four-tenths of an inch and the rough well under an inch. Dill's goal: keep the Bermuda grass as short as possible without killing it. The shorter it was, the easier the swing, the further the roll. The further the roll, the lower the members' scores—assuming they hit the ball in the general direction of the correct green and not so hard as to go right past it. The lower the scores, the greater the members' love of the course and, presumably, for Dill. Dill needed all the love he could get or, failing that, sex. He actually preferred sex. While Dill may long ago have lost his passion for the game of golf, the embers of abject lust remained aglow. Considering the primary economic driver of the golf club had less to do with firm putting than stiff putters, one might say he had found his niche.

Stopping long enough to exchange pleasantries with Dyleane,

which still constituted a significant interaction, Thom ate his standard meal while dragging industrial-sized sprinkler heads and thick black hose behind the tractor from one buried water outlet to the next. Two caddies, Alfonso and Jade's son, Corey, helped out by cutting new holes on the greens and using each newly extracted plug of dirt and short grass to fill the old hole. They finally trimmed, rolled and sprayed down each green. In exchange, Thom offered preferential caddying assignments and permission to play the club course on occasion, such as hot, steamy afternoons when the pool and cold drinks won over most locals with time to relax. For Corey, caddying was an occupation, while needling Thom was sport. He would likely have helped out Mondays simply for the additional opportunity to irritate the little white guy. That morning, Corey asked more than once whether Thom might be able to escape prison by squeezing between the bars once convicted for Savannah May's murder. Corey even pantomimed such efforts to the great amusement of the other caddies, if not Thom.

Mondays were also the one day each week when women and, while school was out, kids enjoyed first swing at tee times. Most men wouldn't be caught dead playing while dodging sprinklers or making way for mowers. Besides, they already had the course mostly to themselves all of Tuesday through Sunday. On Monday, they rested.

In the midst of ground keeping, Thom also cleaned off the clubs and stored the mountain of golf bags that Dill had been piling just inside the garage entryway since Saturday morning. The bags of members' clubs were stored alphabetically on two levels of racks crudely constructed from plywood and two-by-four along two aisles dimly lit by overhead fluorescent tubes. Taking down and then replacing bags on the upper shelf, which sat even with the top of Thom's head, was no mean trick. Thom attributed his surprising strength to all the lifting.

The grind, for once, provided some sense of accomplishment, almost satisfaction, beyond the simple and humiliating security of routine. It must have shown: Thom received a couple of five-buck tips from ladies pleased with how promptly he retrieved their clubs and loaded up the carts. Perhaps he would make pillow assault a nightly ritual.

Around four, darkening skies, accompanied by distant, slow-tumbling thunder, promised a storm. Thom quite happily sounded the air horn that closed the course for members due to lightning but opened it up for him. This time, Thom felt things would be different—knew things would be different. All that green would once again become Thomas Loudon's world—the place he shared with Moe's Canadian spirit and with no other two-legged mammal.

During his three years at the BRGC, Thom had played a thousand rounds of golf. It didn't matter if it was in Florida steam bath heat and stifling humidity, the gathering dark, tropical storms, or a tornado warning. He'd dabbed balls with fluorescent paint for chipping and putting practice in the dark—some rounds he'd retrieve one of those to complete the final holes. In the afternoon flash-bang monsoons like the one then brewing, lightning posed a deathtrap for the unwary sportsman holding a metal object over his head in the middle of a wide-open space. Thom, however, had customized the blue cart, the only remaining electric vehicle from the fleet replaced a few years before by sportier four-wheeled models powered by gas, with a chain to throw out like an anchor. He'd rigged the cart with a lightning rod he could raise at will. The rod was actually nothing more than an old two-iron someone had left on the course and never reclaimed. Thom had stripped the leather grip at the top of the shaft and shoved the exposed steel into an old metal flagpole holder to which he'd wired the chain. Based upon zero evidence whatsoever, Thom theorized that a bolt of lightning would prefer a golf cart grounded by a chain to a short guy standing nearby, never mind that the short guy might also be holding aloft his own lightning rod at the same time. If his theory held true, Thom would still have been blown head over arse when a bolt fried the cart sitting only a couple of yards off. But this wasn't about actual safety. A mere illusion of safety sufficed. A hypothetically decreased risk of death engaging in what every golfer recognized as sheer folly helped him rationalize golfing during thunder and lightning storms. The hypothetically decreased risk was all he needed when the alternative remained waiting out a storm somewhere inside, precisely when he could've had the course all to himself.

The BRGC back nine wasn't Thom's favorite. Its longer holes made it harder on a short hitter. Rather than landing on the green of a par-five in regulation three and two putting for par, Thom often needed four or five just to reach the undulating green carpets. A one-putt might only guarantee a bogey. Still, it meant avoiding number two. If a few rounds on the backside were what it took to settle Thom's nerves, so be it. Focusing on his long game might even prove beneficial.

The cart path to the tenth hole passed the snack shack. Dyleane looked up and smiled through the pickup window. Thom noticed. He could've stopped but the course was calling. He tipped his white, sweat-stained BRGC visor and parked next to the slightly elevated tee. Ten was a 170-yard par-three that Thom could birdie two times out of three. Screw the coming lightning and rain, ladies and gents, it was a new day in Thommy and Moe's world. Teeing off before a gallery of one—just this once—only enhanced the beautiful tension of opportunity.

Thom made a show of deciding which club to use even though, absent hurricane-strength head or tail winds, it was always an easy swing with a metal three-wood on number ten. While the thunderstorm was closing in, the winds weren't yet howling, so he grabbed the regular along with a tee and an impeccably white ball. The sweaty palms made him wonder about wearing a glove on each hand next time, instead of just the left. The shortness of breath, well, he was excited at reclaiming such a vital part of his life, of his very being.

It hit just as he teed up. A lightning bolt grounded out on the flagstick 170 yards off. Its blinding flash silhouetted a short figure dancing on the green, ignited a fuseless bomb of thunder, and sucked every trace of breath from Thom's breast. He began sobbing, except that it's impossible to sob without air. He turned toward the cart, stumbled, and rolled down the embankment.

This was it; he was going to die, if not at the hands of his old man, then from suffocation. He lay against a wheel under the cascading rain. He smelled the grass, the rain, the wet rubber of the old bald tire next to his face. What would death smell like? That's when someone pried the club from Thom's hands and practically lifted him into the cart's passenger seat.

Dyleane drove the thirty yards back to the snack shack through sheets of rain and hydroplaned to a stop in an inch-deep puddle before the snack shack door. Thom stole breath between blubbering sobs.

Dyleane yelled, "You know you'll drown out here before anyone else if we don't get inside."

Under different circumstances, Thom might have seen humor in such a remark. Just then, it was all he could do—even with Dyleane grasping his elbow—to spill out of the cart and splash through the door. She led him to the chair and shut the window. It barely muffled the crashing, bashing thunder.

"Did you see him?" Thom wheezed.

"Who?"

"My dad."

"Thom, the only damn fool out there in that weather was you. And me, of course."

Thom reached into his pocket and came up empty. He made a face that caused Dyleane to exclaim, "Jesus Christ!"

"*The ball.*"

Another detonation shook the cinderblock shelter as Thom raced for the door, prepared to dash back to the tee box no matter what.

"Thom," Dyleane implored, "The police have it—the cops."

Thom stopped with his hand on the round silver knob. The cops, the corpse, the fear, all of it hit him like a ton of bricks. His shoulders fell. He looked at his feet.

"What the heck were you doing out there anyway?"

"I was dying," he wheezed. With chin firmly planted on chest, he shuffled back to the chair, leaving a puddle with each step.

"That's a full-on panic attack right there," Dyleane said.

"If I didn't die on my own, the old man was there to make sure. I know it was him. He murdered my mom, then the girl, now me."

"That's it! You have to—"

"Not now. God, Dyleane, not now."

Dyleane turned a complete circle plainly searching for something that required her attention before it got the better of her. "You have to make sure it's not your dad. You're so screwed up —no disrespect intended—but you are." Thom nodded. "You are so screwed up. You need to find out who it really was." She sat down on one of the cylinders. "You hungry?"

"No."

"I'm turning off the grill then."

"No—I mean no about finding my dad, the murderer, whoever. No bloody way. That's what cops are for."

"Listen. You saw the very worst thing possible: your very own father murdering your very own mother. They were the only people you've known that look like you, think like you, who actually know who *you* are."

"Knew," Thom said.

"The ones who brought you into the world and kept you alive until you could keep yourself alive. The last people you saw falling asleep at night and the first waking up. The ones who taught you to wear a coat when it was cold."

"Got it, Dyleane. Only Disney never filmed a family show in the Pointe."

"They showed you how to laugh, how to cry—helped you understand when one made more sense to do than the other."

Thom glared at Dyleane. "Got it!"

"Thom, you are them and they are you. One half of you, the half you cherished, was murdered by the half you hate. And, if you'll excuse my frankness—"

"Why not—Frank's your damn middle name, eh?"

"Ever since, you've been walking around with the half you hate still inside you, controlling you, making you feel guilty. And you're missing like crazy the half you loved, the half murdered by the other half, the one you hate."

"And you're crazy—no disrespect or anything."

Dyleane's voice lowered. "And you do feel guilty, don't you? You can't forgive the part of you that watched that terrible thing happen and then ran away. How you should have done something. You as much as helped your dad. You let your mama down."

"What the fuck, Dyleane?" Thom stood, grabbed the object nearest his reach, a silver ladle, and whacked his open palm. Their eyes met, and the last thing Thom wanted to do was let on how badly his hand now hurt. He pulled up his sagging rain-saturated

shorts and stormed to the door, slamming it behind him without looking back.

Weathering a steady shower, Thom's fury had barely eased by the time he reached the garage. He dragged in a couple of golf bags abandoned near the door by rain-averse golfers. He made sure the heavy lock was securely joined, toweled off, and set the fan to maximum noise. He considered battering his pillow once again. He hid under the covers instead. Tonight that damn pillow might hit back.

Chapter 5

Before the sun could pull the covers of darkness all the way back, the seniors would jump out of bed and ready themselves for a round of golf—jump being a relative term. Whether on their last unsteady legs or with spry agility, they appeared shortly after dawn every Tuesday through Saturday, and only slightly less frequently Mondays and Sundays. Many were long-time Putnam County residents without the means to retire gulf-side in condos set a mile or more off the beach. A few actually moved into Interlachen or surrounding environs following retirement—usually to be nearer grandkids. This crowd knew their tee times and where in the garage their clubs were stored. They did not invite distraction, particularly the ones already struggling to remain on task. They were driven by habitude, a trait with which Thom identified and, if he stopped to ponder, resented. They wasted little time, as if they had somewhere important to be later in the day other than the Loblolly Inn's three-to-five-thirty seniors buffet. This haste was not borne of an apprehension of mortality. That's an anxiety best savored in the dark of night. Rather, it gave their lives purpose. They were not merely focused on golf, but on their focus on golf. Even so, Thom wondered whether he ought to dig out the AED manual just in case restarting someone's heart wasn't as easy as Dill had once assured him.

Tuesday afternoons featured a couples' league for husbands and wives—or members and significant others, still exclusively of the opposite gender in this time and place. The league provided an opportunity to escape the job, the home, the kids, driving those kids here, there and back again—a moment of calm respite in the luxuriant glory of the pastures, swamps and clear-cut forests of North Central Florida. In reality, the likelihood that any couples actually mired in such bondage would set aside some five hours on a weekday afternoon to endure the day's maximum heat and humidity just to struggle through eighteen holes was slight. The few who did participate already had enough spare time that they'd likely spent their allotment of *quality* time together somewhere else. Whatever the cause, arguments on couples days, particularly those arising over the back nine, had become pillars of BRGC legend.

When the couples began returning, Thom would normally have loaded up the rusty three-wheeled cart to play eighteen. Even a half-pissed Dill could handle the pro shop by himself at that point.

Life for Thom, however, had become anything but normal. Now? The thought of golfing made Thom want to padlock himself in the garage and hide not merely under the covers, but under the mattress. The mere prospect of hitting a bucket of balls or playing a game of eight-in-a-row on the practice green left him nauseous and short of breath. So he changed the hole locations on the practice green for the second time in as many days, swept out the garage, dragged the driving range—and still had time enough to play nine, damn it.

Thom was going cold turkey on golf without a twelve-step program. This particular afternoon, he envisioned wrapping a set of gold-plated irons around one of the parking lot's metal light standards, club by club, just to see how far each would bend before snapping. He longed to rip apart a pristine putting surface by spinning donuts on the green tractor—never mind that the green tractor would likely tip over if forced into a tight turn at any rate of speed exceeding two miles an hour (which only enhanced the yearning). He fantasized about spraying the entire course with herbicide from a crop duster—a particularly toxic herbicide that killed every square inch of grass and left anyone touched by the mist sterile and covered in hideous skin lesions.

These desires were not simply a case of "If I can't have you, no one can." Thom had to convince himself that while others might need golf he did not, that he could take golf, leave golf, or, better still, wreck it all to hell without a second thought. By this, he sought to trick addiction into loosening its hold on him. Addiction, however, is an unrivaled trickster. What else besides love and fear is capable of motivating an otherwise rational person to lie, cheat, steal, and even kill to obtain more and more of something that, as often as not, is prodigiously unhealthy. In fact, what is addiction if not love and fear? Thom's strategy, like addiction's strategy, was a lie: Thom still loved golf and pined for the ritual, safety, and satisfaction it had afforded. Yet this lie was all he had to dull the stabbing pain of separation from his one true love, a love that, like his beloved mother, had been stolen by his murderous bastard of a father.

Thom was barred—excommunicated—from the only place he had ever been himself—truly himself. "Only heretics get excommunicated, right God?" he muttered to himself. "And not just for breaking a few rules, only the big ones—*after* being warned. What rules did I break? I counted all my strokes, replaced every divot, and haven't taken a gimme in forever. And the warning? There wasn't one. Not a bloody hint. So everyone gets a second chance but me? When's *my* Easter?"

That's what Florida was supposed to be: Thom's rebirth, his resurrection. Florida meant golf. They went together, if not quite like Canada and hockey, at least like hope and a ticket out. Thom had never so much as held a golf club before arriving in Florida. He'd never seen an actual golf course or driving range. There wasn't even anything green growing on his block in the Pointe outside of scraggly weeds that emerged amid concrete crumbles during the few months winter rested. The sporting goods store a half mile away from the family flat sold darts, fishing rods and hockey gear, but not golf balls or clubs. However, prior to watching his mother die on the bare wooden floor in flat number two, Thom had read a Moe Norman biography at least six times—not counting the first time through when it was still merely a book. Moe Norman, a man inept and clueless at anything involving other people, had become a Zen master at hitting a little white ball anywhere he wanted it to land. With his unconventional stance and unique single-plane swing, he could hit low-trajectory balls with a wedge and soaring rainmakers with a one-iron. He could make the high shots go far and skim others just above the grass, stopping them dead ten yards away. Moe proved a guy, a Canadian guy no less, could be terrible at everything but golf, remain alone, and thrive, mostly.

"I'm not asking for much. You hear that up there? Hold the glory. I don't need to sit at anyone's right hand. Just a second chance. It's not like my first one was all that damn peachy."

Thom entered the Nineteenth Hole and avoided eye contact with the last table full of spouses, not necessarily each other's, swilling liquor from sweaty highball glasses following their couples' outing. He glanced at the TV. The sound was off, but there was Nicklaus wearing the green and white pullover, white slacks, and white shoes. Then Tom Weiskopf and Johnny Miller—Miller pumping his fist. It had to be the '75 Masters, one of golf's greatest closing rounds ever. Miller played the last six pressure-packed holes in three under, but Jack birdied two of the final four to win it in regulation, just a single stroke up on Johnny and Tom. Jack was a machine. Brutal. Cold. White looked good on Jack. That's why, despite greatness, he was never a fan favorite during his prime.

It was the opposite with Tiger. Everyone loved Tiger when, in fiery red and black, he dominated all comers in the closing round of the big tournaments. That changed when Tiger cheated on his beautiful wife. And cheated in the 2013 Masters—the *Masters* of all places. And suffered his fifth straight season without a major title.

Jack finally won over the carpers because, if for no other reason, he was always who he was—not merely a great golfer or simply better than the other great golfers, but a golfer who beat those other greats and left no doubt about it. Steady on the course and off it as well, or so it appeared prior to the proliferation of cell phone cameras. Tiger? Who knew—perhaps he would recapture some of the adulation following a final graceful exit from the game he once dominated, if not like a golden bear, at least as a big cat.

Thom's dad? No question there. He was born to slide a knife between a woman's ribs straight into her heart.

A razor blade commercial interrupted the rebroadcast. Jade was slouched in her chair, head back, mouth open. Thom cleared his throat. Nothing. He forced a cough and slapped one of the bar stools for good measure.

Jade opened an eye. "I ain't asleep if that's what you're thinking."

"Your eyes were closed," Thom said.

"I'm resting."

"You were snoring."

"It got plenty crowded for a Tuesday. I been busier than a dirty old bishop in an orphanage."

"I need a favor," Thom said.

"It's gotta be a little favor." Jade laughed. "Get it? A *little* favor?"

Thom explained he needed help finding an address, as he enjoyed no access to cell phones or computers and Canadian phone books were in short supply down in gator country. Thom provided the basics, and Jade's fingers swished across her phone's screen, playing keys with both thumbs as an ancestor might once have plucked a karimba or thumb piano generations before. She even hummed a tune—one occasionally punctuated by a grunt and a grind.

"I didn't know you wore glasses," Thom said.

"That is because I don't," Jade said, despite the drugstore pair perched at the tip of her nose through which she peered at the phone held with an extended arm. "These are just so I don't never *need* to wear glasses—I'm just resting these baby blues." In response to the glare that shot over those glasses she didn't need from her eyes brown, not blue, Thom merely nodded.

In another minute, still focused on the phone, Jade pulled a sticky note from a drawer under the cash register and wrote down an Ottawa address. "Second thing you need to do is write these folks a letter with the name and birthdate of the person you're looking for."

"What's the first thing?"

"Tell little old Jade who the hell you're looking for in that prison way up there."

Thom's conversational style tended toward the passive-aggressive. He either clammed up or, occasionally, forced whomever was listening to listen until he was done talking.

This night, he told Jade about his mom, his mom's murder, about hope and no hope. How that dead body in the sand trap could have been his mother's, and the little man dancing on number ten between bolts of lightning.

"I just need to find out," Thom said.

"Yeah, me too," Jade said. "Find what?"

"Whether—you know, about my old man."

"Oh, right, your old man. Uh-huh. You know something? You're making about as much sense right now as man nipples."

Thom had to concede that man nipples didn't make much sense. "Whether my old man is still in prison, damn it. Or whether he's down here doing to people what he did to my mother. Maybe getting ready to do it to me!"

"Cops know who did it," Jade said. "He works right here at the Breeders' Roost."

Thom shifted his gaze from Jade to the main entrance, then to the emergency exit. Upon ascertaining that the emergency exit provided the most immediate means of egress, he said, "Well?"

"Troy Cotter."

"*Yes*," Thom said, entirely too enthusiastically.

"Or you," Jade said, entirely too nonchalantly.

Troy, like Dyleane, attended Interlachen High and had been a classmate of Savannah May. He'd managed the BRGC pool for four years. "Manage" meant he unlocked the locker rooms in the morning and made sure the chemicals in the pool were somewhere close to prescribed levels. At night, often late at night, he returned to pick up the used towels, skim the pool surface, hose cigarette butts off the pool deck, and lock everything back up. Sometimes he'd sit and alternately pick, pluck, and strum an electric guitar untethered to any amplifier. He leaned toward blues, the kind that sound easy if they come from the soul. There weren't any lifeguards —just signs at each end of the pool warning, *Swim at Your Own Risk!*

One night soon after Thom's arrival, Troy caught Thom

bathing in the baby pool. By midsummer, the small, shallow pool constituted not merely a bath, but a warm bath. Thom chose to attribute this increase in water temperature to climatological factors rather than the toddlers still in need of potty training. Instead of ripping on Thom or reporting him, Troy showed him where he hid the locker room keys. Thom could then take a proper shower so long as there weren't any adult members around to complain about having to mix with the help. Despite enjoying similar shower access, plus whatever was available at home, Troy's long black hair remained stringy and oily. He was a big kid too, but from Thom's perspective, who wasn't? Occasionally, when it was too hot to sleep, Thom rested against a massive live oak along the back pathway to the storage garage to listen to Troy's twangy blues.

"Seems Troy asked little Savannah May to this Friday's Fall Formal up to the high school," Jade said. "He even offered to play her some mushy song at the dance since he knew a boy in the band well enough to let him sit in. She said no and Troy's been the laughing stock ever since. You know how mean those kids is. I heard it straight from Jimmy Simms."

"How the hell would Jimmy Simms know?"

"He got it from his boy."

"Brett Simms? He's an asswipe."

"Don't I know it. But for so long as Jimmy Simms is president of the BRGC Board of Governors, he is my boss. And I shall treat Mr. Simms's boy all syrupy sweet no matter how bad he deserves little gator babies shoved up his lily-white crapper canyon. That big ugly shadow of his too."

Brett Simms and his high school football buddies, almost always including L.T., the aforementioned shadow, paraded around the Breeders' Roost like banty roosters. They were buff, tan, crew cut, and typically wearing little more than shorts and black sandals with white swooshes. They treated everyone like dirt, including Jade, Dill, and, not surprisingly, tall, pudgy Troy. Of the working stiffs, Thom was the most fortunate insofar as they simply refused to acknowledge his existence. When Thom fetched their clubs or filled a bucket of range balls, Brett and L.T. would retrieve them as if they had simply appeared.

"I'll bet that crowd tormented Troy even *worse* when Savannah turned down Brett," Jade said.

"Wait. She turned down Brett Simms?"

"Don't you know it. *The* Brett Simms. Shut him down cold. That's tough on a boy like him what lives on the attention of others. So he builds his-self back up by taking someone else down even lower. Brett and L.T. done everything they know how to push Troy into a fight. But Troy, bless his heart, he ain't bit. Not yet anyway."

"Troy's a little odd, but who isn't that works around here?" Thom said.

Jade peered over her spectacles. "You gotta point?"

"I just can't see him hurting a girl for not going to a dance, let alone murder her. Who the hell wants to go to a dance anyway?"

"Oh, honey. Don't never underestimate the darkness that lurks inside a man's soul. You're all the same. Only I know it wasn't you because there weren't no torture involved. A person always as pissed off as you is would've carved your initials in her poor little white-girl boobs."

"I'm learning to un-suppress my anger."

"Besides, they didn't find no ladder at the crime scene."

Thom was descending the stairs outside the main clubhouse sideways, one step at a time, when a commanding voice summoned him as "Master Thomas." He turned and accepted the outstretched hand of Father Rodden Crittenden, a.k.a. Father C., a lanky, chain-smoking pasty man, tall by *any* person's standards. He also was bald as an egg, which became evident whenever any disturbance greater than a gentle breeze displaced his toupee. Given the number of BRGC members who chose to spend Sunday mornings worshiping fertilized fairways, Thom had never been free to attend the father's Sunday masses had he been so inclined. Thom was sure, however, that should Father C.'s pathetic rug ever slip during the sermon, his authoritative bass would nip any sniggers in the bud. The father sat next to Thom's feet and offered him a cigarette. Thom declined so he lit it for himself.

"It's been a rough few days, hasn't it, my son?" Father C. said from within a cloud of fresh smoke.

Thom shrugged, watching the toupee inch slightly forward.

"You know my door's always open."

Thom said, "Thanks." The pelt slid a little further. It fell completely free when it reached the perspiration on the man's forehead, and Thom plucked it from thin air. The bristles were stiff, the inside lining damp. Thom immediately tendered its return.

"Goddamn," Father C. said.

"None of my business, sir, but aren't you supposed to use glue or tape or something?"

"You'd think they'd come up with an adhesive that functions in this damnable heat and humidity, wouldn't you."

"Why have one if—"

"If it's always falling off and everyone knows what I look like without it?"

"Well, yeah."

"I've been wearing one piece or another for some thirty years now, since before my first pulpit. Its proclivity to fall off or blow away with little warning has, for me, come to symbolize man's struggles in this temporal realm. Moreover, it has become a metaphor for man's fall from grace—often very much a gradual slide preceding the final plunge—as well as our resurrection. You might say it's become a part of my ministry, a veritable inspiration. It also keeps persons who might otherwise be tweeting, texting, or playing Words With Friends during service a reason to look up, just to keep tabs upon its progress."

The cleric replaced the toupee and unfolded his skeletal frame to stand. The wig fit about as well as a tuft of grass tamped into the wrong divot. Holding his head level to ensure the hairpiece's stability, he looked down upon Thom with just his eyes. He turned at the sound of car doors closing. Two women of uncertain age, one with platinum hair except where it was parted, the other pink, were approaching one long, bare leg at a time, showing as much skin as the lingerie models in the magazines Thom had stashed under his mattress. Syrupy perfume accentuated by the smell of tobacco smoke preceded their approach.

"Remember, my son, the door is always open. You might be surprised at the knowledge I've gleaned during the course of my administrations and how helpful this information sometimes proves. Now then, back to the flock." Before Thom could respond, the priest offered each woman a boney elbow and escorted them up the spike-scarred wooden steps and through the doors. Smiling as though he already knew the answer, Father C. asked his escorts, "And to what do we owe the pleasure of your early arrival?"

Thom checked the wall clock visible through the pro shop window. He had just enough time to get to the snack shack before Dyleane put the griddle and fryer to bed, which meant he'd have to resist the siren call of those lingerie catalogues brought to mind by Father C.'s tartish congregants.

"Am I ever glad to see you," Dyleane said.

"How is it you can stay in school and still work all the time?" Thom asked.

Dyleane explained she went to school early mornings and on her occasional weekday off, still turned in all her assignments, and most of her teachers didn't mind communicating at night on the computer. Her counselor emailed Dyleane college and financial aid applications to complete. Oh, and that she'd given up the French accent at school. "And no one even noticed," she added with a hint of disgust.

Then, without an additional breath, "You're off the hook!" She handed Thom a thin rectangular computer screen. Thom had seen these devices before but had never touched one. He overcame the urge to hand it back. He held it before him and pretended to read, only to become particularly enthralled at moving the display with a finger as he'd seen Jade do on her phone. An animated shoe advert appeared. Dyleane reached over his shoulder. Following a tap accompanied by a two-finger swipe, the news article reappeared. At first grudgingly, then eagerly, Thom read that Troy had become the second "person of interest," which interest appeared to have eclipsed Thom's own. Dyleane placed Thom's typical fare on the prep table and set about spraying this and wiping down plenty of that while Thom read the story a second time just to make sure he really was in the clear.

Relieved, practically giddy, he offered, "It couldn't have been me. There wasn't a ladder at the crime scene."

Dyleane shot him a look that might've melted iron. "If that was supposed to be funny, Mr. Man, your sense of humor needs practice."

In response, Thom meekly pointed at the pad and said something about there still being insufficient evidence to arrest Troy.

"No prints, no witnesses, DNA tests still pending," Dyleane recounted straight from the article. "All they have is a BS motive about a stupid dance, the fact that he's big enough to overpower a woman, and that no one has come forward to swear he didn't sneak out that night. How lame is that? Could anyone besides you swear that *you* didn't leave that storage thingy last night?"

Thom only briefly considered repeating what Jade had said about the darkness lurking in a man's soul. "Excellent point,

Dyleane."

"So how do we figure out who really did it?" Dyleane said.

"We?"

Thom sure as hell didn't know; he was, after all, just a migga. A migga who only wanted to golf. A migga only then comprehending what regaining his world, Thom's World, might entail.

If there existed a trace of fairness in this life, Thom's blissful means of escape and self-affirmation should not depend upon his having to discover the person who murdered a complete stranger, one who just happened to choose Moe and Thom's world for the crime scene. The cops had science, tape-recorders, cars, helicopters, satellites, and the third degree. Thom? He had a rusty old golf cart jerry-rigged with a lightning rod that was of no current utility whatsoever. He'd lost his mom. He'd lost his eighteen-hole lover. His custom-made putter gathered dust. He'd even lost his Moe Norman ball. Now he had a bullshit job and a mattress on bare concrete in the back corner of a dusty, roach-infested storage thingy.

Three years before, the likelihood that he might end up as a has-been pro's assistant at a second-rate golf club in Putnam County, Florida, was improbable. So improbable that the only plausible explanation was fate. Fate is what people credit when, instead of *B* following *A*, as one would rationally expect, *X*, *K* or *37* follows *A*. The more outlandish the outcome, the more credit or blame is palmed off to fate. Just then, however, as day surrendered to dusk and birdsong to crickets, Thom attributed his plight not so much to fate as to yet another ethereal screw up. "Yeah, God, I'm looking at you."

"Say what?" Dyleane said.

"Nothing."

"Don't you nothing me, young man."

That sounded so much like Thom's mother he looked up to make sure it wasn't. "Just thinking how the hell I ended up here."

"Tell me."

"You don't—"

"What did I just say?"

"It's—well, other than getting away from my damn old man, it was about golf."

"Imagine that," Dyleane said, smiling. She pulled up an empty coke cylinder and pinched one of Thom's once-warm fries. "Do tell."

The last trucker of the half dozen that had aided Thom's fateful escape from the Pointe let him off on a busy highway called the A1A, somewhere east of Jacksonville in a posh beachside suburb. Thom still faced a stiff hike to his ultimate goal: the Tournament Players Club at Sawgrass, operated by the PGA itself. Upon his arrival in Florida, strictly on the dime of the last trucker, Thom had eaten grilled biscuits and cream sausage gravy, and shrimp and grits. While not poutine, the grits weren't all that bad. From his seat high in the diesel cab, Thom had seen a shipping port on a mile-wide river, dozens of strip malls, tall palm trees, and cookie-cutter cul-de-sacs. He'd caught glimpses of the boundless ocean beyond which lay sites purportedly more foreign than Florida.

In the midst of all this sat TPC Sawgrass's famous stadium

course where the green on seventeen is surrounded by water. People have criticized the TPC island hole for being too cutesy, especially as the penultimate hole on a championship course that annually hosted what everyone regarded as the unofficial fifth major tournament of the year: The Masters, US Open, The Open, PGA, then The Players. Its fifth-major status was cemented when, following a birdie-birdie finish in 1982, champion Jerry Pate pushed two tour officials into a pond and then dove in right after them. While it's one of the shortest holes on the PGA Tour, stretching a mere one hundred twenty-one yards to the front of the medium-sized green, that tacky little par-three seventeenth had managed to affect outcomes and careers. In 2007, ninety-three drives missed the green and went for a swim—*fifty* in a single round—and these were the best golfers in the world. Tiger won a championship on seventeen; Sergio Garcia lost one. In 1997, Freddy Couples aced it. Two years later, he plopped his first drive in the drink, which added a penalty stroke. He then lofted a dry ball from the tee that dropped straight into the cup. For all that fortune, good and ill, his scorecard read a plain old par three. While the thirteen-year-old Canadian had, at that point, never once teed up a golf ball, he intuited that his fortune would someday turn on that island green.

Within the first three minutes of Thom's walk along the road that wound its way between gated communities, he could've wrung sweat from his shirt and from his pants. His knees were about as stable as popping corn by the time someone in the golf club parking lot pointed towards a castle that would've made

Buckingham Palace blush. Thom followed the signs to the pro shop, walked in the door, felt the cool air, saw the dozens of mannequins wearing shirts and pants of every imaginable pastel shade, and fainted.

He came to with a dozen faces forming a dome above him worthy of a Hieronymus Bosch painting. Each face sat atop a green polo, and they were using up all the air. A large black man shooed them away. The man handed Thom a glass. Propped on one elbow, Thom then experienced his first taste of Gatorade, lemon-lime green, cold like it was fresh from a freezer. That's when it sunk in that he had truly arrived in Florida, USA.

"What are you doing down there?" the man said.

"I need to golf," Thom said.

"You got four hundred dollars?"

Thom had never seen four hundred dollars. "How about the back nine?"

"You play the front nine to get there, so I'd say about—"

"Four hundred bucks."

The man helped Thom stand. Still wobbly, Thom followed him past fitting rooms and locker rooms into an office trimmed in gleaming dark wood. The man, tall and broad, hair short, wearing a green blazer with the TPC logo over a pink pastel golf shirt, settled himself behind a desk nearly as large as Thom's parents' bedroom had been. "I'm Sonny Waldron. I run that golf shop back there. Guys dropping unconscious in women's wear isn't good for business."

"I'm Thom Loudon—Thom, with an *h*." Thom recounted why

he'd left Canada, the murder, hope and no hope, shrimp and grits. Then they looked at each other.

"That's one helluva story, Thom. Now what?" Mr. Waldron said.

"How about a job?"

"How old are you?"

"Sixteen."

"No you're not."

Thom might have been made a fair liar had he practiced. Imagination is the key to good lying, and Thom had that. Alienation from community helps. Thom had that too. At the Pointe, though, he was as likely to get beat for lying as for telling the truth. Given there wasn't much to be gained from lying, Thom had never practiced.

"Even if you were old enough to legally work in this state, every job in the golf shop is taken," Mr. Waldron said. "And we have a box full of applications from lots of others with permanent Florida addresses who also want to work here."

"It's because I'm short, isn't it."

"No, Thom with an *h*. It's because you're too young and I don't have any jobs. You have heard about the recession, haven't you?"

Thom, in fact, hailed from a locale mired in perpetual recession —he'd known nothing but. That day, however, he'd walked down lanes lined with mansions fronted by circular drives and Greek columns and was just then sitting in an opulent office larger than his former flat. Economic hardship was not the first thing that leapt to mind. He decided against accusing every American of being self-absorbed, spoiled and greedy, no matter how true it might be. "What recession?"

Mr. Waldron sighed. "First off, there aren't jobs anywhere in this state. Second off, you're looking at a man who knows a thing or two about not looking the part, so I would not shit you. Besides, you stink something awful. Let's at least do something about that, shall we?" He told Thom to sit tight and left.

A blade putter leaned against a mirrored wardrobe opposite the man's desk. Thom's heart began pounding, and it had nothing to do with needing another liter or two of Gatorade. He picked up the club. The sweat-stained grip smelled of fine leather. He stood facing the full-length mirror as though it were the fourteenth fairway at Pebble Beach—a 580-yard dogleg right, the toughest hole on the Tour. There was plenty of sand on the right to dissuade any but the longest hitters from attempting to cut the corner. Then there was the firm postage-stamp-sized green that curled around a gigantic sand trap on one side. Even a ball well hit to the other side might roll right off and down a five-foot embankment before coming to rest next to a tree. Thom resolved to play it honest and drive for the middle of the fairway.

Mr. Waldron's putter was a little long to serve as Thom's driver, so Thom choked up a few inches and assumed a wide stance. He gripped the club firmly in his palms, eschewing reliance on the squirrelly fingers for guidance. Moe always said, "Fingers are fast, fingers are fast, palms are calm, palms are calm." By this time, Thom's personal putter also stood erect. He started the club back low and straight, his left arm bent slightly as he reached the peak of the backswing. His flexed wrists loaded up for the downswing, just like Moe. It felt exactly as he knew it would. He'd practiced this swing thousands of times—watching PGA closing rounds on TVs in a Pointe second-hand shop, lying awake while his old man drank and fought with his mom, and more than once in the street wielding a stick—but never with an actual golf club. Thom started the downswing, focusing all his weight and energy down and forward, hands leading the club head, not yet releasing the wrists. That's when Mr. Waldron reentered the office and slammed shut the substantial door.

The noise distracted Thom. It would have distracted anyone, eh? If there'd been turf instead of carpet, the club would have dug up a divot the size of a manhole. As it was, the club head scuffed hard against the carpet, which sent a painful shock up Thom's arms, which made the club fly out of his hands, which sent it flying blade first into the mirror. The wardrobe clearly was not as sturdily built as one might reasonably have expected given the elegant surroundings. The club head not only shattered the mirror, but pierced right through the wood behind it. The head had also unwoven a run two feet long in the carpet.

"What in God's name are you doing?" Mr. Waldron demanded. "That's the putter Michelson won the oh-seven Players with."

"Teeing off the fourteenth at Pebble." Only the grip and a little bit of the shaft of Phil's putter were visible outside the wardrobe door and shattered mirror. "The marshals shouldn't have let you in during my swing."

"Well, that is not a driver, this ain't Pebble Beach, I control who comes into my office, you just destroyed the carpet, and that was the goddamn *ugliest* swing I have *ever* seen. *No* one worth a damn swings like that!"

Thom might have conceded each point until, that is, the crack about his swing. "For your information, that is a single-plane swing. Or it was going to be," he said. "Made famous by none other than—"

"Oh, Lord. Don't even say it. You're Canadian so Moe Norman, right?"

"Uh-huh. Merely the greatest ball striker in history."

"He was crazy."

"A little different, maybe. But what you Yanks can't stomach is that he was better than Hogan and Sneed combined. Even Tiger says so. Twelve Canadian national championships, thirty-three course records—"

"Seventeen holes in one, yada, yada, yada. I know all that for Christ's sake. But—"

"How many rounds sixty and under has Tiger shot?"

Thom had few friends in the Pointe and fewer black friends. Until then, therefore, he was unaware that a person with black skin could turn red. Their exchange grew more heated and included allegations related to nationality and snobbery. They just as quickly calmed back down when it became apparent that neither was about to budge on the matter of Moe Norman's character and golfing expertise.

Mr. Waldron handed Thom the white plastic sack he'd been holding since interrupting Thom's maiden swing. He told Thom where the men's guest showers were and said he'd make some calls.

Inside the bag Thom discovered a pastel-lemon-lime-Gatorade-colored polo golf shirt, a pair of cream-colored shorts, pastel Gatorade socks, and an honest-to-God pair of white shoes. To Thom's disappointment, the shoes were canvas loafers, not the ubiquitous spiked saddle shoes worn by golfers the world over. The locker-room sink counter was crowded with stacks of fresh towels and dispensers of shaving cream, body lotion, toothpaste, and aftershave—everything but scissors. Thom used his teeth to cut the tags from the new duds.

"I've got a couple of surprises for you," Mr. Waldron said upon Thom's return. This claim did not set Thom at ease: How far can one trust a person who disrespects Moe Norman?

The first surprise was that Mr. Waldron had lined up a job for Thom working at the Breeders' Roost Golf Club in Hollister, Florida.

"Hollister," Thom said. "That's not on the tour."

"You got a better offer?"

Thom had just added a single change of clothes to his wardrobe. He was too young for most jobs, too short for the rest, homeless, dead broke, and over two thousand kilometers from where anyone other than Mr. Waldron knew his first and last names. "Maybe I do, maybe I don't."

"The Breeders' Roost is a little down on its luck right now," Mr. Waldron said. "And probably Dilly too."

"Dilly?"

It turned out that the head pro's last name, the only pro's last name, was Pickle, so he'd been known as Dill or Dilly for as long as anyone could remember. Mr. Waldron explained that Dill was famous in the region for scoring an albatross on day four of the Jacksonville Open on the eighteenth at the old Selva Marina course. Likely known only to avid golf aficionados and crossword puzzle fans, an albatross is when a golfer holes his second shot on a par-five—the equivalent of a triple birdie. It's rarer than a hole in one.

"That was Nicklaus in 1966," Thom said.

"No it wasn't, Thommy with an *h*. Jack did indeed hit one at the J-Open in '66, but Dilly holed his in '65. He came out of nowhere because of it and took home third-place cash. Just between you and me, likely the only top-twenty finish of his career."

Dill Pickle was looking for an assistant. Thom asked what an assistant did. Mr. Waldron said anything Dilly didn't want to do and probably a bunch more that Dilly didn't even know needed doing. Mr. Waldron pointed out that Dill was a great pro, excellent teacher, and fine human being—"deep down inside." Thom did not yet appreciate that one person's opinion about another person's fundamental character came with fewer guarantees, and often less conviction, than an extended weather forecast. In Thom's defense, aside from the overt disrespect with which he regarded Moe Norman, Thom had no reason to question Mr. Waldron's credibility. No reason, that is, other than suggesting that this great pro and fine human being would be so hard up for help that he would welcome as his assistant a four-foot-seven (and a *half*) thirteen-year-old who had never before set foot on a golf course. One whose one and only golf swing had launched a prized putter through a nice piece of furniture.

"And there's this," Mr. Waldron said, extending a hand. Thom drew back. "Take it for hell's sake."

Thom did, warily. It was a shiny white Titleist golf ball bearing the initials *MN* hand-written with a felt-tip pen.

"No way," Thom said.

"Moe used to spend winters in Florida," Mr. Waldron said. Everyone knew that. "He played an exhibition here way before my time—probably just hit a few hundred balls at the practice range and chirped away at anyone nearby." Mr. Waldron was probably right about that too. Moe loved his long game. Who wouldn't when each and every shot went exactly as high and far as he wanted, no matter what club he used. For most golfers, shots on and near the green required calculation of limitless variables. Calculation led to weighing alternatives, miscalculation, and self-doubt. Off the tee box or in the fairways, by contrast, all it took was a firm grip, a perfectly refined swing, and optimism. Neither Thom nor Mr. Waldron could know that day of Thom's destiny to become one of the few humans ever for whom such benign excellence would extend to the short game. "Anyway, his sponsor left us fifty balls exactly like this."

"Why are you being so nice?" Thom said.

"Take this and we're down to forty-nine. Besides, the putter doesn't look damaged, I always hated that carpet—why's everything around here gotta be green?—and I like people who don't fit in.

"Because you're, uh . . . "

"Yeah. Because I'm 'uh.' And let me tell you right now, son, you are in your very own league of 'uh' round these parts. Good luck, because you're gonna need it."

"Mr. Waldron was right about the league of uh, wasn't he?" Dyleane said, helping herself to another of Thom's cold fries.

"It has been a pretty strange trip, all in all," Thom said. Then, realizing he wasn't the only person in the room embarked upon such a journey, added, "You too, eh?"

"Me too."

"Ever wonder when it ends? When you get somewhere you're supposed to be? Like, when the trip is finally over and plain old regular life begins?"

"I'm not sure there is such a place. As far as I can tell, just when you figure you're settled, that's the start of another trip to somewhere else you never imagined."

"That's kind of depressing."

"Who knows—maybe it's a good trip. Maybe around the next turn there really is some good luck. For *both* of us."

Thom squelched his immediate inclination to prick at Dyleane's balloon full of optimism. Later, alone in the storage garage, Thom turned off the fluorescent overhead tubes and wondered what good luck around the next turn might look like.

Golf, for sure. Maybe even playing all the par fives at least even par or better. An albatross of his own? Then Thom wondered whether Dyleane had a date for the Fall Formal that coming weekend—the dance that someone had made sure Savannah May Paulson would not be attending.

Chapter 6

Relieved at no longer being a prime murder suspect but still bereft of Moe's World—*Thom's* World—Thom spent the next few days watching, listening, and comparing wholly insignificant observations with Dyleane. On Friday afternoon, Corey accused Thom of eavesdropping on the caddies congregated around the Caddie Availability Sheet. The CAS was actually a flimsy letter-sized white board duct-taped near the storage garage entryway, which Thom updated based on each caddie's relative experience—and thus the going rate—and how long each had been waiting for a job. Absent extenuating circumstances, golfers typically chose the name on top. It was an imprecise process over which Thom enjoyed considerable discretion.

The caddies, like Corey, were mostly black kids who'd dropped out of high school or were well on their way to so doing, hoping to earn up to forty bucks under the table for dragging a bag around eighteen holes over the course of five hours until something better turned up.

"I work here," Thom halfheartedly offered in defense, surprised to have been noticed.

"If that was you working, you wouldn't just be standing. And if you is listening, you wouldn't be working. Hear what I'm saying?"

Thom had heard. So, too, had the other caddies who nodded in apparent agreement. For Thom, however, hearing didn't necessarily mean understanding. Thom often wondered whether Corey intended to be understood or simply enjoyed scoring points at Thom's expense. Thom spoke roughly the same language as these young men, so many of whom were raised in cramped one-story houses set along roads leading to nowhere. Thom was about the same age as most. He, like they, lived in one form of poverty or another—financial, emotional, nutritional, spiritual. Those who were not recently acquainted with such deprivations (i.e., most BRGC members) took little notice of these others unless or until any one of them acted so as to cause discomfort or fear. For club members, the bar for discomfort or fear was set low, particularly as compared to the bar for noticing anything positive, which was set improbably high. Of course, everyone saw what they wanted to see. And if the club members saw the others as good, honest, talented, and hardworking young men, they'd have to concern themselves with why these fine young men lived in poverty and were stuck pursuing a dead-end vocation. It caused far less discomfort to look for the negative, see the negative, and conclude that it's no wonder those people live like they do.

Despite shared aspects of poverty, as well as immutable physical characteristics that set them apart, Thom felt no more at home in the caddies' world than in that of the club members. In the caddies' eyes, Thom was a salaried employee of this elite establishment from which he received room and board. Thom controlled the CAS and he was white. He, therefore, was The Man. Thom meanwhile envied the caddies' freedom to work when they wanted, to head home and socialize with friends and family when they were done. They enjoyed community. Thom was unfamiliar with this concept and thus uncomfortable with it. So it was that within the larger tribe of outsiders, the caddies and Thom each viewed the other as another other—a divide unnoticed by club members, but obvious within the tribe.

"Any of you guys heard or seen anything about that murder last week?" Thom said.

The silence grew in volume until Corey volunteered, "My mom says you done it."

"The evil that lurks in my soul, right?"

Corey surveyed Thom as one animal might another, but not so intimately as to countenance an exchange of butt sniffs. Corey may even have smiled before turning back to his own others.

Chapter 7

The typical first-, second-, and third-hand teen tales surrounding the previous night's Fall Formal circulated about the BRGC that Saturday morning like flies around a shithouse. They were the same stories that followed similar events through the years; only the names had changed, primarily to implicate the innocent. As usual, Thom recognized but a few of those names. What stood out were ones he did not hear mentioned—not once—particularly Savannah May and Dyleane. This latter omission provided some relief.

Saturday also marked the official end of summer at the BRGC, commemorated by the annual Fall Blast and BBQ. Thom had no idea why the club celebrated the end of summer on the second Saturday in September rather than, say, Labor Day. Even so, the date annually signaled the change on the club's list of regularly scheduled events, for example, the Summer Wednesday Afternoon Bridge Club to the seasonally adjusted Autumn Wednesday Afternoon Bridge Club.

The "Blast" part of the title owed in part to what was known as a shotgun start among the regular Saturday morning men's foursomes. Each foursome was assigned a different starting hole, and each began teeing off precisely at 8:00 a.m. when Dill fired a shotgun. Dill was already three-fourths blasted when the anointed time rolled around, so Thom kept a safe distance until Dill, coifed for the occasion in a coonskin cap, had discharged the 12-gauge's single shot. Once all the golfers were loaded up and on their way, the simultaneous start guaranteed five quiet hours back at the pro shop. Of course, it also meant that dozens of golfers would simultaneously converge on the clubhouse five hours later to check in their carts and clubs.

A café in Interlachen called The Rib Joint, conveniently owned by a member who served on the club's Board of Governors, would cater a poolside barbecue later that day. Fireworks, the other reason for the "Blast" part of the event's title, would follow at sunset. At the pool, Troy would stage games for the kids beginning at ten.

This would constitute Troy's fourth occasion to oversee the Autumn Blast and BBQ pool festivities. From Thom's perspective, Troy had become more adept at handling this, his single occupational commitment that required some social grace. (Thom was alternately impressed by and disdainful of such an accomplishment.) The kids were fine—their fondness for water and games was fairly unqualified. However, the moms, and there were always plenty of moms because women were barred from the golf course on Saturdays until the men's foursomes were done playing, were not merely interested observers but often fiercely partisan advocates. If a child ended up on the wrong side of the greased watermelon or had been impeded in one of the relays by anyone but a sibling there was hell to pay. Just as Thom sometimes strove to anticipate and roll with certain golfers' eccentricities, Troy learned to foresee these potential Blast Day conflicts and how best to avoid them. The previous year's events had gone off without a hitch.

This time around, Thom wanted to see how all the gossip about Troy might play out. It wasn't every day a suspected murderer was left in charge of kiddy games. Between the pool crowd and steady stream of golfers, Dyleane was too busy to talk, so Thom chose to observe from the safety of the live oak on the back pathway. Whether to amp up the general mood or more as a personal tonic, Troy piped a mix of traditional blues and upbeat zydeco through the pool-area PA. Whose mood wouldn't be elevated by the likes of Buckwheat Zydeco and Clifton Chenier?

That question was answered upon the arrival of Brett, L.T., and their football player posse via the front pathway. They began with cannonballs off the stiff little diving board. They progressed to wrestling and chicken fighting right in among the kids, using language small children should not hear, and splashing all the poolside sunbathers who did not particularly care to be splashed. They ridiculed Troy's music as swamp-nigger tunes. It might not have been so bad had the kids been safely segregated in their separate portion of the pool, but this was not the case. In the final and most anticipated event of the day, Troy had just thrown in hundreds of nickels, some in the shallow end for younger participants, some in the deep end for older ones. A few football players started picking up coins for themselves. Children fought to be the next at the ladders to escape the mayhem.

Speaking loudly enough to be heard over the music and screaming, Troy advised Brett that the pool was closed for the kids' games. "But it'll open back up in another ten minutes. We're almost done."

This apparently was the provocation Brett had been hoping for. Backed up by half the high school football team, the Caucasian half, Brett swaggered up to Troy and pushed him. "What kind of crap kind of music is that?" It was actually Taj Mahal's cover of a 1920s classic blues song, "Corina, Corina," but Brett's agenda just then did not include musical appreciation. He pushed Troy again.

"How's it feel to be a murderer?" Brett said loudly enough for all to hear. "Just because the cops aren't ready to throw your punk ass in jail doesn't mean you're getting off that easy with me."

He pushed Troy again. Troy tumbled backwards over a cheap plastic lounger, landing hard on the concrete. He staggered to his feet and was feeling the back of his head when Brett sucker punched him in the gut.

All Thom could do was watch. Well, no—all he did do was watch.

The moms whose children were witnessing a brutal assault, whose dear offspring constituted the very reason Troy had confronted Brett in the first place, watched impassively. Brett's buddies egged him on. Brett grinned at his audience. Before he could refocus his attention on Troy, however, Dyleane marched around the corner of the snack shack with a black 12-inch cast-iron fry pan raised above her head.

She looked at Brett and said, "Cut that shit out."

L.T. and two other players approached Dyleane. Thom rose from the base of the tree. Before he stepped forward, Dyleane cocked the heavy skillet back behind her ear. With unnerving calm, she announced, "I guarantee that at least one of you boys are going to be really sorry if you come one step closer."

L.T., by far the largest of the three, stopped and smiled. "Calm down, girl. We're cool. We're cool."

Dyleane's glare looked anything but cool.

Pointing back over his shoulder at Troy, who was just straightening up as blood from the back of his head ran down his long, greasy hair, L.T. said to the louts on either side, "That boy there is the problem, not this little lady."

Dyleane, with the pan still locked and loaded, hesitated briefly before saying, "Little lady? I'll show you a little—"

"This ain't over, boy," Brett declared. "Just wait till we catch you when your bitch ain't around to save your sorry *ass*."

Thom had just returned to the clubhouse via the back pathway when Brett and the rest of his crew strutted by. They were laughing, pushing and playfully punching each other. All save Brett and L.T. continued to the parking lot where they departed in an assortment of late-model cars, trucks, and SUVs. Brett and L.T. headed for the storage garage. They betrayed no sign of having committed criminal assault just minutes before. The bravado was routine.

They had grabbed Brett's clubs and his dad's and helped themselves to four large buckets of range balls from a counter when

Thom walked in. Because Brett and L.T. consistently outdrove the range itself, it meant Thom would sooner or later have to crawl through a patch of stumps, palmetto and thistles rife with skeeters, chiggers and snakes to pick up those balls by hand. But not until Dill asked why the large reservoir of range balls in the plywood bins was running so low.

"Brett," Thom said. No response. "Dude."

"Yeah?" Brett said, looking surprised that he and L.T. were not alone and yet not nearly as surprised as Thom felt at drawing attention to himself.

"I like your sandals. You know, the ones you're wearing. Those —on your feet."

"Gay," said L.T.

"I was wondering where you get them. Seems like all you guys have the same kind."

"You were?" Brett said.

"Dude, he's gay," L.T. said.

This was not a conversation for which Thom had prepared. Yet he plunged forward like an armadillo craving the warm pavement of a busy, dark highway. "Yeah. I'm thinking of getting a pair. They look like you could wear them for just about everything." In fact, Thom had already splurged on golf shoes, for whatever purpose they currently served. And he wore sturdy boots for working on the course or near the clubhouse where it was all too easy to drop a bag, box, or bucket on one's toes.

Brett explained that the mother of a teammate, Crazy Jay-Z— probably a black guy because, "You don't know him, he never comes around here"—worked at the Wal-Mart Supercenter in Palatka and could purchase as many as she wanted with her employee discount.

"What size?" Brett asked. He looked on the verge of laughing.

"They don't come in kid sizes," L.T. apparently felt compelled to point out. Brett gave in when L.T. started giggling.

Thom had them there. People with achondroplasia dwarfism may have a higher incidence of clubfoot and of other maladies not just of the feet but also affecting the hands, spine, etc., but many have average-sized hands and feet. Thom also knew, but chose to keep to himself, that the males' other appendages reached sizes that were pretty damn normal too.

"Size seven—*men's*. And extra wide if they come that way."

"Hey L.T., his feet are as big as yours," Brett said, still smiling.

L.T. didn't appear to see the humor. Brett, however, was right. Only then did Thom notice how dainty this apish young man's feet and hands looked compared to the pale, freckled trunks to which they were attached. Thom permitted a small smile and reached for his wallet.

"Nah, wait and see if we can get 'em," Brett said. "We can settle up then."

"Let's go, man," L.T. said.

Already through the door, Brett turned. "It's what—Tommy?"

"Thom. With an *h*."

"Fucking gay, with an *h*," L.T. said, followed again by laughter.

Troy appeared a few minutes later walking alone and uncertainly down the main path from the pool. He pressed a towel marked by red splotches against the back of his head. His eyes didn't look right. "I kind of slipped and fell," Troy volunteered upon Thom's approach.

No, you didn't, Thom thought. "Sit tight," he said.

Averting his gaze from the bloody towel, Thom asked Corey to drive Troy to the Palatka urgent care some fifteen miles away. In response to Corey's scowl, Thom offered, "I'll keep you on top of the CAS for the next week."

"Forever," Corey countered.

"A month," Thom said.

Corey accepted the compromise with a look of acute physical pain. He did not own a car, so they took Troy's.

The BBQ caterer forced the snack shack to close at 4:00 to eliminate any competition—the more meal tickets sold, the greater his haul. Thom reached the snack shack at 3:59.

"It sure as hell wasn't Troy," Dyleane fumed as soon as the top of Thom's head became visible through the window. Thom ventured inside just as Dyleane slammed shut the order window with no apparent concern for the potential of shattering glass. She threw a basket of frozen fries into the fryer.

"Happy Blast Day," Thom said.

Without pause, Dyleane assembled Thom's meal and explained what had occurred between Troy and Brett. Thom admired the objective accuracy of her account of the incident that he himself had witnessed—a fact he chose not to share. Dyleane continued, "Instead of being pissed at that total jerkoff, Troy was embarrassed. *Embarrassed.* That is *not* a boy who murders a girl for not going to a dance."

Thom couldn't disagree and, given Dyleane's disposition, would not have done so even if cause had existed. She appeared still ready to take a frying pan to anyone offering the slightest provocation.

"But you know who damn sure *is* capable of murdering a girl for not going to a dance?" she said.

"My dad?" Thom said. "Me?"

"Brett."

"He's got an alibi."

"Oh, sure. Some besties like L.T. saying they were at some kegger in some field some miles south of town." Thom had heard some of this story as well—there'd been more gossip about the murder than hungry mosquitos at dusk. The party celebrated the high school's first football game of the season—apparently a rousing victory. "And that's okay? Mr. Big Shot Quarterback with an offer from Florida State gets someone to buy a keg—probably his dad. Never mind that he's underage, trespassing, driving home drunk. But it gives him an alibi and that's all that matters when it comes to our precious little Brett Jerkoff Simms."

Of course, Thom thought. *That's* why he had asked about those sandals he didn't need. Befriending a potential suspect was the perfect ploy. This realization relieved a nagging sensation Thom had been trying to shake. Yet, despite this estimable sacrifice on his part, Thom did not let Dyleane in on his plans. Perhaps it was best not to risk exacerbating her displeasure. She had taken the griddle brick to the steel grill top vigorously enough to wear a furrow right down its middle. This ritual seemed to have a calming effect.

When she'd finished her chores, turned out the lights, and was locking the door behind them, Dyleane said, "I was thinking about coming back for the fireworks later tonight. Now I'm not so sure I want to be around these people. I might just park a little ways up the road and watch. You want me to pick you up? We could hit a drive-in afterwards for a fresh strawberry shake."

Thom's breath caught. He mumbled something about being tired from working all day and having to get up early, only it came out that he was getting up early from being tired all day. While Thom preferred chocolate shakes, he did enjoy fireworks. But just sitting there? Dyleane, him and no one else, in the front seat of her car? Others driving by, watching, judging? And what was supposed to happen at the end when she dropped him off and he was getting out of the car, as they were saying goodnight? These were not issues Thom felt at all equipped to address.

"Thanks anyway, Dyleane," he said, then added with some urgency, "Maybe some other time? Oh, and, uh, how was the dance last night?"

"Dance?"

"You know, that Fall Formal thing?"

"You think I went to that?"

"You didn't?" Thom said hopefully.

"God, no. I knew you wouldn't come, even if I asked."

Thom watched the fireworks from between the clubhouse and storage garage, a space just then that he shared with the club's dumpster and no one else. The rockets and displays were staged from the opposite side of the eighteenth fairway, which ran alongside of the main path to the pool. A hundred people watched from seats and blankets spread out next to the pool. Rousing Sousa marches blared from a crudely amplified boom box. Adults sat, ate, mostly drank, occasionally oohed. The kids, hyped by the pyrotechnics, ran and chased each other through, behind, and in front of their inebriated parents, thus missing most of the actual fireworks. In a display that became more elaborate each year, accompanied by a rousing men's glee club rendition of "I Wish I Were in Dixie" that issued from the boom box, the final barrage of aerial bombs and rockets exploded into flowers and stars. Thom was thinking that a shake might taste pretty good just then, even a strawberry one. As he pondered what parting after an evening with Dyleane might entail, Dill and Brett's father strolled past, deep in conversation, on their way to the Nineteenth Hole. They did not notice Thom in the shadows. Thom could not make out much of what they were saying. Mostly it was Jimmy Simms telling Dill to remember: "They were near her car in the parking lot."

That night, even the fan jacked to extra high and a pillow over his head couldn't drown out the party next door. Didn't anyone else have to work Sunday morning? Ah hell—none other than Father Crittenden was likely leading the revelry.

Thom had suffered nightmares and insomnia ever since escaping the Pointe. He'd attributed them to the interminable Florida heat and humidity suffered in his windowless bunker of a bedroom devoid of air conditioning. The climate, however, explained neither the nightmares and insomnia that persisted during cooler months nor why they had worsened since finding Savannah May Paulson's body. That night, the one-week anniversary of finding her bloody corpse, Savannah May, along with Troy and Brett, played through every dream. As did the image of Dyleane with a strawberry shake, Dyleane going after a gang of sandal-sporting thugs with a fry pan, Dyleane driving herself and Thom around together. Thom did not actually dream about the taste of her lips wet with strawberry milkshake, but he woke up wondering.

Chapter 8

Sunday mornings were steady. Out of respect for churchgoers and/or the hungover, the regularly scheduled men's foursomes didn't start teeing off until eleven. Until then it was first come, first served. At ten, Thom knocked on the Nineteenth Hole window next to Dill's corner table and pointed at his mouth to signal he was taking a break. Through the glass, Thom could not tell how loudly Dill spoke, but reading his lips was easy: "She-it."

Thom considered telling Dyleane about his brief interaction with Brett and L.T. After all, she was as committed to finding Savannah May's murderer as he was, perhaps even more so. He did mention the letter he'd finally gotten around to posting to the prison authorities in Quebec. "Just making sure he's still behind bars," he explained.

"Whatever with your father," Dyleane said. "It's still gotta be Brett. If you'd seen that raw malice in his eyes. . ."

"Maybe he was really in love with Savannah May and he's, like, heartbroken or something."

"That doesn't explain his look and how he made it such a show for everyone watching. There's something seriously sinister about that boy."

Thom thanked Dyleane for the food and retired to eat with the caddies. He had regularly warned them to be on the lookout for an older guy who was short like him. Corey had twice claimed to have seen just such a man hiding in the trees off the second hole. Thom would say, "Yeah?" Corey would say, "Or not." Then he would laugh at Thom, at which point the other caddies would also laugh at Thom.

Thom, pursuant to the agreement struck the day before when Corey agreed to serve as Troy's ambulance driver, secured Corey an eighteen-hole gig within minutes of his arrival. Corey was fortunate. Caddying was fast going the way of golf clubs called brassies, mashies, and niblicks. Apart from the several geezers who teed off daily around sunrise, not many still walked the course. Thom had tried walking during his first year in Florida. After all, that's what the pros did—except for one guy, Casey Martin. Casey was born with a bad leg. He had to go all the way to the U.S. Supreme Court to force the PGA to let him use a cart. Thom, meanwhile, had worn completely out by the fifth hole. Before then, the smell that walked with him, feet getting damp in the morning dew, staying warm and loose between shots instead of jumping out of a cart, hitting the ball, and climbing back in, made golf even more special. Thom knew Casey would walk if he could. Call it youthful optimism, or myopic avoidance, but just as Thom did not worry about playing before massive crowds when he became a professional golfer, neither did he concern himself with potential Supreme Court proceedings required to secure the use of a cart.

Except, of course, at night. Thom fretted over everything at night.

Some who walked the BRGC course did so for their love of the game. Others persisted upon doctors' orders—many Floridians desperately needed more exercise and fewer fried Twinkies à la mode. Whatever the reason, most who regularly used a caddie appreciated how much a good one could improve their game. A competent bag tender determined yardage to the hole without reference to a GPS phone app. By the second hole, a caddie would know what club a specific player needed to reach a green out of the rough at 165 yards. The caddie could accurately predict whether the ball would slice, hook, or even fly straight from how the player stood and started his or her backswing. Thom understood, and thus was grudgingly forced to acknowledge, that Corey had long ago mastered the technical aspects of the job. He could also be personable when it suited his mood. Precious few at the BRGC, however, would ever avail themselves of these benefits. Doing so would require them not only to walk the course but also to regard these others with black skin as full-fledged members of the human race who deserved full portions of respect and dignity—not to mention a share of the credit and an appropriate gratuity.

Thom was getting clubs, selling tees, balls, the occasional glove or set of head covers, and arranging the singles and couples into foursomes—and missing golf. So he didn't notice the black county sheriff's SUV pull up and park in the handicap stall closest to the clubhouse entrance until the asswipe who a week before had wanted to book Thom for first-degree murder climbed out and slammed the door.

"Oh, it's you," Deputy Howland Ricketts said.

Just as no one can resist messing with a fresh fluid-filled blister, Thom responded, "It is to you for just as long as I'm not somebody else anymore," Ricketts stood with his mouth open until recalling the purpose for his visit. "Where's Mr.—is it really Pickle?"

"I'm afraid so," Thom said.

Thom led Ricketts to the café—that's what they called the bar before eleven, not that the name made it any lighter or less smoky inside or changed whatever was in Dill's cup besides or in addition to coffee.

Ricketts headed back to Dill's corner table. Thom stopped by the tall stool at the side of the bar on which Jade rested. Thom and Jade barely spoke for fear of missing what the deputy and Dill were saying. The golf pro had just remembered that he was socializing with a club member late the night of the murder—bonking someone's wife, Jade translated. It was pretty dark when Dill went outside—he was three-sheets to the wind, Jade offered.

"I'm fifty percent sure it was Troy and the girl out there standing next to a Volkswagen Bug."

"Yellow?"

"Troy or the girl?"

"The car."

"Could be . . . let me think. Yeah, it was yellow. And it looked like maybe he was trying to kiss her, but she kept backing away."

"That's all fine and good, but fifty percent just don't cut it in this business, Mr. Pickle," Ricketts said. "His shyster lawyer will twist it around to mean you're fifty percent sure it might have been someone else. Hear what I'm saying?"

Dill drained the dirty aromatic potion in his cup—"vodka-plus," according to Jade. "Would ninety percent be enough?"

"Now we're talking," the deputy said.

Dill nodded at Jade, who mixed a refresher.

The men's Sunday foursomes were off by 2:00. After that, tee times reverted to first come, first served. Perhaps it owed to the state's three NFL teams playing on TV early enough in the season that none had yet been mathematically eliminated from the playoffs, but the arrival of casual afternoon golfers slowed to where Thom no longer organized foursomes to get them off promptly—singles, twosomes, whatever, could proceed at their leisure. He was toying with the idea of installing an inflatable kiddie pool in the space between the clubhouse and the storage garage when Brett and Jimmy Simms showed up to play a quick nine holes. Each already had some beer onboard—the smell and extra split second to focus were giveaways. Thom put Jimmy's clubs on a cart and returned to the garage to fetch Brett's. Brett followed Thom and, once inside, tendered a plastic Wal-Mart bag. "Twenty-four bucks with the ten percent discount."

It took Thom an extra split second to understand, and he hadn't had a beer—ever. "Hang on a second," Thom said. He didn't carry that much in his wallet, so he took an indirect route back to his corner where he stashed his life savings beneath the bedside crate. He saw no point in advertising its precise location.

He returned with exact change, and Brett said, "I hear you rock the up-and-down out there."

"You mean my *short* game, right?"

"Well, now that you mention it." Brett smiled easily.

So much for the illusion of anonymity. If Brett knew about Thom's game, chances were that others did too, particularly those in Brett's circle—L.T., for example.

When Thom was actually playing, he had never been tempted to boast over a round of five or six under par, despite the magnitude of the accomplishment even for players who enjoyed all the leverage of height and length. First, who would have believed him; then, who would have cared. Mostly, however, the opportunity to go even lower the next time out had always felt more urgent than bragging about rounds already in the book. Finding that extra stroke was what it was all about. Now, however, without that all-consuming preoccupation? Thom proffered the time-worn bromide, "Drive for show; putt for dough," and then, "Without a short game, it'd be tough for a guy like me to play scratch."

"Scratch? No way."

"Better most times. I'd go seven or eight under if I could ever par eleven and seventeen in the same round." Seventeen was a 625-yard monster. Eleven, "only" 550 yards, played uphill, and another swamp guarded the green. Absent a tailwind, Thom rarely reached either green in four, which guaranteed bogies. Since they lay in opposite directions, the chances of a favorable wind on each in the same round were practically nil.

"No shit? Even though you're . . . "

"Even though," Thom said, filling the pause and recalling Mr.

Waldron's "Even though I'm uh." It was interesting how a word left unsaid might convey more than ones actually spoken.

Brett said they should shoot a round sometime. Thom wondered whether he was being patronized. Insincerity hurt every bit as much as scorn. To eliminate any possible misunderstanding Thom moved a shoulder back and forth, rubbed it. "Not anytime too soon. I must have pulled something."

"I know. Ever since you found Savannah, right?"

"How'd you know?"

"Pickle said. Or slurred is more like it." He smiled that easy smile.

"No kidding," Thom said, intending to affirm only that Dill slurred.

"Hey. Me and some buds are hitting the midnight movie in Palatka tonight. It's some show about a hotshot black detective from way back."

"*Shaft?*" Thom guessed. He'd read a book about movie genres, and *Shaft* was featured in the "Blaxploitation" chapter.

"Yeah, I think that's it. You want to come? You're almost on the way. We could swing by at a quarter till."

Thom was unsure why he not only said yes but also did so without hesitation. It must have been because he was sleuthing. Just to make sure, he silently lamented sacrificing an early night to bed, alone with his gloomy thoughts and roaches, in an un-air-conditioned cinderblock hovel. This night, the floor fan would have to make do without his company until later.

Brett showed up at five before midnight in his maroon SUV.

He and L.T. sat in front; two additional behemoths occupied the bucket seats in back. A rear door opened, and it smelled as though they'd been bathing in beer. Thom did not want to die in the vehicle of a drunk driver, but such tragedy only strikes losers, right? Brett was a winner. He exuded control. Invulnerability. Success. He would never suffer such an inglorious demise. All of which meant that, if there were a crash, Brett would most likely escape unscathed, while Thom was almost certainly doomed. No graceful means to back out presented itself before one of the huge fellows stepped out. This one, Thom would learn, was Jamison. The other had lowered a sort of jump-seat between the rear buckets.

"So, you need a lift?" Jamison said.

"Yeah, well, I don't have a car—"

"No, this." Jamison grabbed Thom under the armpits and swung him into the backseat. L.T. laughed loudly without turning around.

Brett eased the SUV out of the parking lot as L.T. lit something. The unmistakable odor of marijuana wafted back. The acrid smoke wasn't uncommon in the Pointe—the burning leaves more closely resembled a natural scent than anything else there. Thom had also caught whiffs out on the golf course from time to time, particularly early mornings when the seniors were playing. He had never partaken. There was the diminished lung capacity common with achondroplasia dwarfism to worry about, as well as Thom's predilection for overdoing escapes, particularly ones readily available, such as books and golf, booze and drugs. All that and, as it happened, no one had ever offered.

L.T. took a big hit and tendered the joint to Brett, who said he was loaded enough already. Thom chose to regard Brett's discretion as a good thing. The guy on Thom's right inhaled. He was variously called Jack or Laser. Jamison reached across Thom as if he weren't there to grab the butt from Jack/Laser. After several long, hissing draws, with everyone but Brett and Thom holding their breath and half successfully stifling coughs, Jamison offered Thom what was by then the barely surviving ember. Thom shook his head and pointed to L.T.

Instead, Jamison took another hit as L.T. turned on Thom. "What the fuck, man. You a narc or something?"

"Drug testing," Thom said, to which L.T. repeated his favorite one-word explanation regarding what might have been Thom's gleeful disposition but wasn't.

Brett looked back over his shoulder. "Pickle drug tests? Ain't that a laugh."

Pickle didn't drug test, and Thom didn't laugh, because only then did he realize how easily Brett could discover the truth from his dad, the BRGC board chair. Jamison put the tiny roach in his mouth and swallowed. Brett watched via the rearview mirror. He laughed and shook his head as his gaze met Thom's. The car stereo blasted hip-hop, and the boys argued at the top of their lungs about who was better, Eminem or the Beastie Boys. Brett shouted something about Lil Wayne, and L.T. yelled back, "Nah, man. None a that gay nigga shit." Thom felt some relief at not being the only object of L.T.'s scorn.

The debate continued as they left the gravel road for the main highway to Palatka. Thom focused on the highway centerline as though he might will the SUV to remain in its lane. Perhaps benefiting from Thom's assistance, Brett piloted the vehicle in a straight line, appropriately stopping and starting on their way into the Putnam County seat. They parked across the street from an old brick theater in a forgotten corner of an otherwise forgettable downtown. Everyone but Jamison piled out. He remained motionless with one eye open, the other shut.

"Lights on and no one's home," Brett observed.

L.T. came over to Jamison's side and shouted, *"Fucking lightweight!"* three inches from Jamison's ear. Jamison turned his head slightly to the other side, the shade still up on one window. Inside the theater, Brett, L.T. and Jack/Laser each ordered a hotdog that had been turning under a heat lamp for an undetermined length of time, an extra-large buttered popcorn with extra salt, and an extra-large coke. Coke, Thom by then understood, was the favored term in Florida for soda of any flavor. Thom requested a medium coke that was actually Sprite and—what else—a salted nut roll. Laser—it was Laser more often than not—promptly returned to the concession line to order a salted nut roll, followed by the other two.

Inside the theater, Thom could only see the top two-thirds of the screen, but he wasn't about to ask L.T. to trade his center aisle seat for a clearer view. The movie's music and clothes were dated. Even so, parts of New York City—the darker dangerous parts— reminded Thom of the Pointe, only taller. No one was likely to mistake Thom for John Shaft, the larger than life black detective with a selective sense of justice and flair for violence. Nonetheless, Thom admired the protagonist's rejection of the status quo and his refusal to submit to others' expectations. Behind all this, the man projected a kind of optimism as though constraints weren't fixed and barriers could be overcome. Thom wasn't sure what to make of that part of the equation.

On the way back to the car, they were having fun with the movie's theme song. When one growled, "Who's the black private dick that's a sex machine to all the chicks?" The others, parodying the backup singers on the classic Isaac Hayes recording, responded in falsetto, "Shaft." Thom added, "Damn right," in his deepest voice, which would never be confused with that of Hayes. The others laughed.

L.T. suggested that one of the white mobster antagonists should've just "capped the nigger when he had the chance." Thus even the movie's hero made L.T.'s shit list. Not that racism distinguished L.T. from many others in Putnam County. In this slice of the United States of America, Jim Crow still resided in a big mansion on a hill. Yet with L.T., it was something more. A person's mere existence seemed sufficient to enrage L.T., with Brett appearing to be the lone exception.

Jamison hadn't moved. Brett voiced relief that at least Jamison hadn't barfed in his car. L.T. screamed, "Fag," into Jamison's ear, and the latter did not stir. As they approached Hollister, Brett announced that he'd drop Thom off first. "Too bad," Thom mumbled. "I'd have liked to have lifted *his* fat ass *outta* the car." Laser burst out laughing. Brett joined in when Laser repeated what

Thom had said.

Back at the BRGC parking lot, Thom jumped down from the SUV more carelessly than he would've done had the other boys not been watching. Brett called, "Thanks for coming, Thommy Boy. Have fun working bright and early."

"Damn right," Thom reprised in the closest thing he had to a bass voice. Brett honked twice pulling away.

Chapter 9

Another busy Monday morning at the BRGC, this one on less than optimal sleep, and Thom still imagined he was feeling a lot better than Jamison. A couple of recent late-night downpours lessened the need for irrigation, which lightened his load. Thom made it to the snack shack by eleven.

"What do you mean he'd be better off in jail?" Thom said to Dyleane. It had barely been twenty-four hours since Dill's revelation that—to a ninety-percent degree of certainty—he had seen Troy and Savannah May alone the night of the murder with Troy forcing himself on the poor girl. Already, according to Dyleane, Troy had been arrested, charged, and spared pretrial incarceration at a hastily arranged bond hearing. Dyleane was still obsessed with the murder, particularly over Troy and Brett. Her nonstop monologues, which oozed speculation and righteous indignation, grated like the edge of a metal spatula screeching across the grill top. Yet Thom wanted to golf, and even he had to admit that solving the murder might well unlock the door to Thom and Moe's world. So he tolerated Dyleane's perseveration, appreciated it even. Thank goodness someone other than Deputy

Asswipe was on the case.

"Did you hear the conditions of release?" Dyleane asked. Thom hadn't. "He has to *keep* going to school—the same school where just about everyone thinks he murdered the nicest, prettiest girl there. And he has to keep working *here*. With Brett Simms playing the righteous victim card in both places to anyone who'll listen, you can guess how fun that's gonna be."

Father Crittenden, Troy's guidance counselor, and Jimmy Simms had each testified on Troy's behalf at the bond hearing.

"Why Simms?" Thom asked.

"I guess to establish Troy still has a job at the BRGC," Dyleane said. "It's all about ties to the community."

"Letting a suspected murderer keep working at the swimming pool can't be all that terribly popular with members. Why would Simms do that?"

Dyleane shrugged, "Hell if I know. The good news is that we can talk to Troy tonight when he comes to close up the pool."

Thom agreed that talking to Troy made sense. But why did it have to include him? Except for Dyleane—sometimes—Thom hated conversation, asking questions, that whole communication thing. The fruit born rarely proved worth the effort. Thom, after all, was already going above and beyond by hanging around with Brett Simms and his friends. Then again, how was Dyleane supposed to know anything about this selflessness when Thom wasn't inclined to tell her?

"So, God, you're telling me I've got to sacrifice the serenity of being alone in order to regain the serenity of being alone? You've got some really warped ideas, you know that?"

"Huh?" Dyleane said, turning from the sizzling burgers on the grill.

"Never mind."

"Excuse me?"

"I mean ever kind. You're ever so kind."

As he was leaving, Thom mentioned the movie with Brett. He climbed on the green John Deere and fired it up in a cloud of blue smoke before Dyleane could express her surprise or start in with more questions.

At the hour when Thom, by then done with mowing, trimming and reconfiguring, would typically have been teeing up on number one, he sat behind the glass counter in the air-conditioned pro shop reading the most recent *Golfing Life* a third time through. He wondered about the necessity of including a how-to piece on curing a slice written by every living teaching and touring pro in every edition of every golf magazine. Sometimes two or three such pieces graced a single edition. He also wondered whether a candy bar and chips from the machine would tide him over until breakfast or should he risk Dyleane's certain interrogation about the movie over dinner. He decided to go up as the snack shack was closing, hoping to pick up dinner just as Troy appeared to avoid the third degree from Dyleane.

The advice for curing a slice ranged from the common sense to lining up swimming pool floaties next to the golf ball, fitting helicopter blades on the club shaft, or smearing Vaseline on the clubface. The latter bit of guidance stopped short of suggesting explanations to his playing partners for why a guy just happened to be carrying around a jar of Vaseline in his golf bag.

"Jeez, people, just strengthen your grip and move your damn hips out of the way."

"Huh?"

Thom looked up to see Dill, glassy eyed and unsteady.

"A slice for God's sake. Move your damn hips," Thom said.

"It ain't always that easy," Dill said.

"Sure it is. Just post those two instructions on a sign at the first tee—'Turn hands over and move your hips'—and you'd cut your lessons in half."

"Just why the hell would I want to do that?"

Dill had a point. Private lessons constituted a prime revenue source for any club pro. When he wasn't busy drinking, he offered them at half-price to women of all ages and shapes, paying special attention to their stance and upper body while their extended arms enhanced cleavage. Any profit from these lessons that might otherwise have inured to the club was blown on booze immediately swilled at the close of class, particularly when the one student out of ten inexplicably accepted Dill's proposition of a few drinks at his dark corner table in the Nineteenth Hole.

"Hands forward and exaggerate an inside-out swing motion if they want to turn that slice all the way into a hook," Thom said.

"Huh?" Dill rejoined.

"Eight o'clock-to-two swing pattern spins the ball inside-out, eh? Voila—no slice."

"You're so damn smart, then just what the hell is this supposed to be?" Dill waved a scrap of paper upon which he himself appeared unable to focus.

"Jeez, Dill. I dunno. A scrap of paper?" Thom said.

"Do I look like your dang secretary?"

You sure as hell don't look like a golf pro, Thom did *not* say. Instead, he accepted said scrap from Dill's wavering, tremulous hand. It contained a phone number.

"Who said you could be giving out my cell number?" Dill said.

"Dill, I don't know whose number this is. And I don't even know yours. I've never called you because I always know exactly where to find you."

"It's Brett-goddamn-Simms, that's who it is. And why the hell is he calling you?"

"He called you."

"But he asked for *you*."

"Probably wants help with his slice."

Brett, in fact, wanted to invite Thom over for Monday night dinner. After immediately accepting, Thom remembered Dyleane's plan to meet with Troy that night. He only briefly considered standing Dyleane up, and briefly considered it again, before telling Brett that he already had plans. Some consolation existed merely from being able to say he already had plans, albeit plans to engage in something he'd just as soon avoid. And never mind that said plans were intended, at least by Dyleane, to prove Brett murdered Savannah May. At least Thom had plans. Thom was most pleased when Brett said, "That's cool, bro. How about tomorrow?"

To Thom's great relief, Troy showed up soon after the snack

shack closed, just as Thom ran out of food to shove into his mouth in an attempt to stymie Dyleane's interrogation. They'd barely had time to review Dyleane's plan to play the good-cop bad-cop routine with Thom playing the good cop, of all things.

"For the advantage of cognitive dissonance," Doctor Dyleane explained as Thom took his time with the last bite of salted nut roll.

Wearing a black Miami Heat jersey and baggy shorts, Troy immediately set about skimming the surface of the pool for the various beetles and fire ants that mysteriously gathered in just a couple of stretches along the walls. He leaned over the pool's edge to snag a fat bug drowning out in deeper water before spotting Thom and Dyleane through his greasy hair.

Dyleane elbowed Thom.

"Oh. Hi there, Troy," Thom said. "Good job with the bugs, eh. So, me and Dyleane here were wondering whether or not you killed that girl."

"Well, that's pretty damn sly," Dyleane said. "The way you plied him with kindness, set him at ease, built up the kind of relationship where he wants to please you with his candor."

"So who the hell's idea was it to make me the good cop?" Thom asked.

"You guys would make a great comedy team," Troy said. "You know, if you were funny."

"Team?" Thom said. "With her? She'd be better off with a dummy who'd parrot whatever the hell she wants, just the way she wants it."

"You said it, not me," Dyleane said.

"Hey, guys." Troy was shaking insects out of the skimmer into the brown grass just beyond the pool deck. "My lawyer says don't talk to anyone. That includes Laurel and Hardy."

"I *love* those guys," Dyleane said.

"Besides, I have to finish here and get home before my ankle bracelet sets off some kind of alarm somewhere," Troy said. "But hey—thanks for dropping by and all."

"Fair enough," Thom said. He'd been up late the night before because of the movie and spent all day outside grooming the course. A little peace and quiet back at the garage sounded good. He turned to leave.

"Damn it!" Dyleane grabbed the back of Thom's shirt collar.

"Damn what?" Thom said. "Him or me?"

"Both of you," she said after the briefest of pauses. "First off, Thom, you're no help at all. Second off—come on, Troy, we just want to help. We know you didn't do it."

"I guess that makes three of us," he said.

"You didn't did you?" Thom said.

"Okay, two of us," Troy said.

"Pickle is claiming he saw you with her in the parking lot that night," Thom said.

"That's why they charged me with freaking murder, Einstein."

"Oh, yeah."

"Were you?" Dyleane said. "With Savannah May that night?"

Troy launched the skimmer across the pool to the opposite deck. The long aluminum handle clattered against the concrete, sounding every bit as brittle and angry as Troy looked. The noise momentarily silenced the early evening chorus of crickets. He took a great breath and pointed at the would-be good and bad cops, but whatever he was going to call them stuck in his throat.

"Well?" Dyleane gently prodded.

"Yes," he said. "Next to her yellow bug."

"What happened?" Thom said.

"She told me she was going to ride her bike across the whole United States someday. How's that for wild? "

"That's it?" Thom said.

"She said she liked wine more than beer. And . . . "

"Uh-huh," Thom coaxed.

Troy shook his head at the ground. "I promised I wouldn't tell. I haven't even told my lawyer."

No one spoke before Thom finally said, "Damn, those crickets sure are loud tonight."

"Troy, she's dead," Dyleane said.

"No shit," Thom said.

Dyleane did not acknowledge Thom. "If she told you a secret, it means she trusted you. That means she liked you. If you didn't do it—"

"I *liked* her," Troy said.

"Okay," Dyleane said. "So do you think she'd care more about her secret now that she's gone than she would about you not going down for something you didn't do?"

"Huh?" Thom said.

After another pause filled by incessant cricket song, Troy said, "She said she liked me. She wished she'd have just said yes when I asked about the dance. But . . . "

"But?" Thom prompted.

"She was gay," Troy said. "You know, a lesbian."

Thom perked right up. "No way! Now we're getting somewhere."

"Will you just shush," Dyleane hissed. Then to Troy, "So that's why she turned you down—you *and* Brett?"

"Me, yes. She couldn't stand Brett. He scared her. She said his new girlfriend did too."

"Cheri? Me too," Dyleane said.

"And even Cheri's mom," Troy said. "Her mom holds all these parties and comes on to half the guys. Since it was her senior year, Savannah figured it was time to come to terms with who she was. She wanted to quit pretending. That and how she was going to get out of Putnam County if it was the last thing she ever did. I was the first kid at school she told, so she made me swear." He appeared lost in the memory.

"Who would've guessed at how she'd finally get out of this damn county," Dyleane said.

"She was looking at colleges up north that had majors in gender studies, sexuality, that kind of stuff," Troy said. "Where she could learn more about it, about herself, make friends just being herself, without being scared shitless by the rednecks. She looked so damn happy."

"She just wanted a second shot, didn't she," Thom said.

"Then she smiled and gave me a big kiss. You know, on the cheek."

More silence. Thom couldn't tell who was closer to shedding tears just then, Troy or Dyleane. He sat on the edge of one of the plastic recliners that Troy had so neatly lined up. Maybe that's just how life was. People who don't fit in don't get second chances. Not Savannah May. Not Moe. Not him.

"Sheesh. I'm not sure which of you two is closer to bawling," Troy said with a little smile.

"I was wondering the same about you boys," Dyleane said softly. "Then?"

"I said I'd better be going. It was practically midnight. She said she was going to hang for a little while before going home. It didn't seem odd at the time. There was some pretty cool lightning—you could tell a storm was brewing. Then she kissed me again and we hugged."

Turned out it was Thom who broke. Until then, the only Savannah May he had known was a corpse that looked more like his mother than a vibrant young woman on the verge of stepping out and making a new life. She'd had a place to go. She had a ticket out. She *was* getting a second chance. Then she was dead, lying there with a goddamn hole in her heart where all the hope spilled out until there wasn't any left. Dyleane touched his shoulder. Thom shook free and took off running—awkwardly, jerkily, but running still—back to the garage.

Chapter 10

Thom had only recently looked forward to meeting Dyleane, getting closer to Dyleane, kissing Dyleane, and now he dreaded seeing Dyleane. What was it about that girl? He feared her questions about his bawling the night before, about the movie and sandals before that. He feared her response to news of him dining at Brett's house later that very night if, of course, he chose to tell her. All fear aside, the stark truth was that he still had to eat. Thus, after giving Dill notice of his meal break with a rap on the window next to Dill's dark corner table (and Dill's profane response), Thom headed up the back pathway to the snack shack.

He found breakfast sitting on the sill of the serving window. He picked up the tray and turned toward the clubhouse, appreciating Dyleane even more for understanding his need for solitude so soon after his most recent breakdown.

Before he'd taken a second step, however, Dyleane called, "Savannah didn't say she'd never told *anyone* about being gay."

Okay, sure, Dyleane had some quirks. This morning the quirk was completely ignoring what Troy had said just the night before.

"Listen," Dyleane said. "She said she hadn't told anyone—at

school. That doesn't mean she'd never told anyone else who wasn't at school."

"So what, Dyleane? What if she had told someone else? She still wanted it kept secret. It's not like she was blabbing it all around. I mean, who would?"

Dyleane fired another one of those metal-melting looks right through the serving window.

"Oh, for God's sake." If Thom had not been holding a tray of food, he'd have waved his arms for emphasis. "You don't think I'm a bloody expert about what it's like being a freak? A freaking four-foot seven freak? That if I could, I'd damn sure keep secret how I'm a foot shorter than everyone graduating middle school? And stop with the look already."

But she didn't. Thom wanted to stare right back like she deserved, but he felt about ready to begin crying like a damn baby again. He turned, kicked a stone, and walked away stifling a scream and struggling not to limp because the damn rock had caught his big toe just wrong.

Eating was a serious affair in the Simms home. Mr. Simms was already waiting at the head of the table by the time Brett arrived, freshly showered from football practice, having picked up Thom on the way. Brett hadn't warned his mom about bringing home an extra mouth to feed, but that didn't seem to present a problem. Over Thom's meek protestations, silenced by Mr. Simms's "Just sit down so we can get started," Thom sat at Mrs. Simms's place. A tall woman with black hair who regularly golfed and swam at the BRGC, she said, "If it weren't you, hon, it'd be L.T." Thom would learn that L.T. practically lived with the Simms. His clothes filled the dresser and closet of one of the guest rooms. Mrs. Simms's place setting seemed superfluous anyway—she was constantly passing platters of meatloaf, gravy, potatoes and green beans slathered in brown butter, refilling glasses of milk, and asking if everything was all right.

Only upon hearing an acclamation of satiation did she set down a plastic tub full of fried shrimp from a previous meal alongside cocktail sauce faithfully concocted from ketchup and jarred horseradish.

"They just go bad if someone don't eat them," she said. These leftovers merely preceded the spice cake and peppermint ice cream (Mr. Simms's favorite) and more milk.

She wouldn't truly sit down and eat until all the other dishes were cleared.

Dinner for Thom at the Simms home proceeded similarly the next two nights, except that L.T. brought the number for Mrs. Simms to wait upon to four. Mrs. Simms doted on Thom, likely because he was the only one who took time between bites to compliment the food and say thank you. Thom sensed she wanted to pat his head and was very grateful that she did not.

Brett owned all the newest implements of video gaming, which Thom had never seen outside of ads in glossy golf magazines. After dinner, with the parents in a different part of the house, he mostly watched Brett and L.T. spar. Brett preferred sports such as football and basketball. L.T. leaned towards combat games, the bloodier the better, particularly those he could replay in slow motion to fully appreciate an especially gruesome decapitation or disembowelment. To the surprise of all three, Thom proved adept at jai-alai. Jai-alai vaguely resembled the game of squash, if squash were played on a much larger court and with scooped out tusks instead of rackets that hurled the ball over a hundred miles per hour while betting patrons screamed hysterically as though this might better secure their wagers. Brett assured Thom that jai-alai was a real sport and that people actually played it down around Miami. "At least, they used to," he added.

"Gay," L.T. said.

"How about a round of golf?" Brett said.

"God, no," Thom said, dropping the game controller as though it were electrified.

"No, on TV—I've got a new golf card," Brett said.

"Yeah, well, nah, not right now." Thom forced a chuckle. "I'll stick to the real thing."

"How's your shoulder?" Brett asked with a thin smile.

Thom moved a shoulder twice in a circle, hoping after the fact that it was the same one he had previously indicated. "It's taking longer than I figured, but it's getting there."

L.T. also enjoyed pontificating upon which women he would fuck, ravage, do, or plow. Particularly plow. Game characters, models from the swimsuit magazines left lying around, girls at school. His attractions seemed as indiscriminate as the intense distain he harbored for everyone but Brett.

"I'd totally do that black bitch up at the club," he offered.

"The one with the frying pan?" Brett said.

"I'd plow her till she knew who had the real soup bone in this here butcher shop."

Brett turned to Thom and rolled his eyes. Thom gazed at the big screen where L.T. had paused the video just as some guy's guts were splattering apart in graphic, colorful detail.

Chapter 11

Gram McDougal had been Dill's caddie during Dill's six years on the PGA Tour. Living up in Jacksonville, barely an hour north and east of Hollister, it was no surprise that Gram would drop in every now and then. Dill and Grammy would play a round and drink. Or drink, play and drink. Or as often as not, drink and drink while they talked about golf, then drink some more. That Friday morning, just as Thom had stood by and watched the final seniors organize themselves and tee off, Dill approached Thom to announced that Gram would start "helping out" around the clubhouse and golf course.

"Say what?" Thom said.

"It's not like you've been all that reliable lately. I need someone round here I can depend on."

"I took two days off after the murder. That was two weeks ago. They were my first days off since I got here. That includes Christmases, Thanksgivings, birthdays. And the Azalea Festivals. If it weren't for me, you couldn't even go." Dill's benders during this statewide gathering one weekend each March in Palatka were notorious.

Gram stood behind Dill, seemingly contemplating a spot in the cloudless sky. Perhaps it was something about this nondescript spot that inspired a smirk.

"Don't you worry your little self about the Azalea Festival. Everyone deserves a day off now and then." Dill did not pause to appreciate the irony of this last statement. "Besides, what the hell do you even know about golf?"

One thing Thom knew was how to run a golf course. For marginal room and board, plus five fins under the table each week —that's fifty bucks in Yank English—and the occasional tip, Thom took tee times, ran the driving range, fetched clubs, brown-nosed the few members who were at least half civil in return, and sold balls and tees along with the occasional set of irons. That's when he wasn't mowing, manicuring, cleaning, and keeping the greens green. What did Dill do? When he wasn't drinking, he offered half-price private lessons to women wishing to cure a slice and risking far more in the process.

Thom might also have informed Dilly Pickle that he could kick his ass on the golf course every day and twice on Sundays. Except that was then, this was now, and now he couldn't even swing a club.

At night—just about every night, according to Jade—when the Nineteenth Hole was jumping and Gram was around, he and Dill recounted Dill's final-round albatross at the Greater Jacksonville Open. The former caddie functioned as Dill's backup chorus, following an imaginary ball through the air and jumping with excitement when it rolled into the imaginary hole.

Why Gram? According to Jade, who had heard all their self-aggrandizing yarns dozens of times, it was not a bastardization of a proper name such as Graham, nor anything having to do with a cracker. Rather, it was Gram's propensity to take care of his golfer as might a grandmother. He never hogged the limelight, always had a spare smoke and a light, took care of clothes at the nearest laundromat when on the road, and was known to produce cookies out on the course. Even Jade didn't know his real name. Anymore, Gram looked frailer than most grandmothers, even the really old ones, and likely never worked as hard. He primarily functioned as Dill's courtier.

"Just keep kissing your best buddy's daddy's ass," Dyleane advised when, later that morning at the snack shack, Thom voiced concern over suddenly having a co-assistant and the possibility of being replaced altogether.

"What—wait, how did you know?"

"L.T. told me."

"Wha—L.T.? You guys, like, talk or something?"

"He's got Library Assistant first period. I saw him when I checked out books on the way here."

"L.T., in a library, with books?"

"Uh-huh, lots of books."

"He can read?"

"I said some of them were for you. He said to let him know what you thought when you were finished with them. You didn't expect that, did you, Shaft?"

Once again channeling Isaac Hayes, Thom offered up a

halfhearted "Oh, baby, baby." He added, "Thanks for the books." They included a biography and two mysteries and constituted her second weekly delivery, for which Thom was extremely grateful. His thanks did nothing to soften Dyleane's glare. "Come on. How else am I supposed to know what's happening—what happened? I'm gathering intel." Accordingly, he summarized his impressions of Brett and L.T.

"And?" Dyleane said.

There wasn't much to add other than Brett couldn't be a murderer, but L.T. sure as hell could. "Uh, Mrs. Simms is a pretty good cook?"

"What else does she do besides stay home, take care of her husband and your BFF?"

"Here it comes. It's like you're jealous or something. Not, you know, jealous jealous but . . ."

While Thom prepared for the inevitable, "No, I don't know," Dyleane actually said, "Maybe I am."

"Am what?"

"Jealous."

"Really?"

"Jealous jealous."

"Huh?"

"In case you haven't noticed, Mr. Loudon, neither of us fits in all that well around here."

"I noticed. Noticed noticed."

"I don't have any real friends at school. I hardly ever see my mom. We keep all the doors and windows locked in case her old man comes around. A home-cooked meal at our place is a bag of Doritos that aren't soggy yet." Dyleane folded her arms and turned away.

"Your mom's old, old man, right?" Thom said.

Dyleane turned back. Tears tracked her flushed cheeks. "You're my friend, Thom. My best friend."

"Except maybe L.T."

Dyleane did not rise to the bait as Thom was expecting. Hoping? Instead: "I see *you* every day. It's like I see you go off to work each morning, and then you come back from work all dirty and sweaty. Like you're my family."

"Dyleane." Thom slid off the chair.

Dyleane raised a hand. "Wait."

"Dyleane, I—"

"No. I—just go. I'm okay. Go."

"You sure? I could . . . " But Thom wasn't sure what he could.

"We'll talk. Just not now."

Thom didn't look back when the door closed behind him. As soon as he passed the live oak on the back pathway and was safely out of sight he heaved a large sigh. A red squirrel watched from an improbably long limb of the ancient tree that gracefully swung down from the trunk and nearly touched the ground before arching back up again. Dyleane hadn't given him an opportunity to say he'd been invited to Interlachen High's football game that night. And it was possible that he'd just been getting around to mentioning it.

Thom scrubbed the range of practice balls and was getting

ready to wash up when he saw Gram engaged in a lively discussion with the three caddies still holding out for a Friday afternoon job. Members did occasionally choose to start their weekends with a quick nine holes after work, sometimes finishing after sunset.

"Hey, Grammy," Thom called. "I'm taking off the rest of the day. You'll handle things around here, right?"

Gram looked up, squinted in apparent contemplation of this request, and broke into a crooked toothy grin. "Ah, hell. Ain't no one gonna be playing in this heat after a hard week's work. Ain't that right, boys?" While the caddies to whom he'd directed the question did not seem to agree, Gram pressed on: "I figure if they that gung-ho to kill their own selves, they got no problem getting down their own damn clubs."

A proper request lodged with his co-assistant, Thom walked up to the pool showers with a fresh change of clothes in hand. By using the front path and approaching along the far side of the pool, Thom remained out of view from the snack shack.

Mr. and Mrs. Simms picked Thom up at 6:45. He rode alone in the back seat of Jimmy Simms's four-door pickup, branded on each side with:

SIMMS

Building & Supply

Since 1969

From a distance, the stadium rose as an illuminated apparition from the swampy dusk. Inside, the lights were surprisingly effective at banishing night, if not the swarms of mosquitos that turned out at the prospect of an all-you-can-eat buffet. The commotion caused by Mr. Simms's entrance enhanced Thom's invisibility. Everyone they passed on their way to seats near the fifty-yard line, about halfway up, stood and leaned over to shake Jimmy Simms's hand. This slowed Simms enough for Thom to keep up. It helped that the stadium steps, while numerous and irregularly spaced, were shallow. There was plenty of "Hope the defense shows up tonight," and "This would be a big step toward the playoffs," along with other sporting platitudes. Thom welcomed the relative anonymity among so many people. Less clear was whether Mrs. Simms enjoyed the status of an afterthought.

Mr. Simms continued drawing attention to himself during the game, yelling at the refs, dramatically bemoaning the occasional drop of one of Brett's passes, even ones an NFL receiver might have had trouble with, and standing to applaud the more frequent completions. Thom had never watched a whole game of American football. He had previously seen only portions of games where, on TV, downtime was covered over with commercials and canned filler. To his untrained eye, Brett clearly outplayed his counterpart on the other team, but there sure was a lot of standing around. Thom even came to appreciate the vital role played by the left tackle in protecting the quarterback when he dropped back to pass (after confirming with Mrs. Simms the difference between offensive tackles and guards). When the quarterback faded back to throw, his entire attention was downfield. It was easy enough for him to see who might be attacking up the middle and to his right, because that's how he was turned. Unless, however, he had eyes in the back of his head, he was a sitting duck for any defensive player coming from the left side. And taking an unexpected hit in the back from one of those rushing bulls could easily put him in traction for the next month. Thom overheard Mr. Simms and one of his sycophants discussing how the other team's standout player, number fifty-four, a boy who possessed a couple of major school scholarship offers as did Brett and L.T., played right-side defensive end for that very purpose.

Thom then understood why L.T., labeled as such because he played the critical position of offensive left tackle, was so invaluable. L.T. protected Brett from being hospitalized by the likes of number fifty-four. Thom found the play-to-play battle between L.T. and fifty-four the most entertaining part of the slow-moving contest. They fought like two pipefitters mucking it up against the corner boards in an overtime Stanley Cup game. L.T. never once allowed number fifty-four any closer to Brett than an arm's reach.

At halftime, while Mr. Simms continued to glad-hand and exchange inane comments about the game with other parents and fans, Mrs. Simms promised Thom something from the refreshment stand. Thom said it wasn't necessary, and she said it was nice to do for folks who show some appreciation. She returned with frosty malts and hotdogs. They ate the ice cream first because the hotdogs weren't about to melt even on this warm, sticky evening.

Before Brett was replaced late in the third quarter, with Interlachen up by thirty-five points, Mr. Simms screamed indignantly when the opposing team's fifty-four was flagged for roughing the passer—he'd dealt Brett an innocuous push a second after Brett had thrown another pass. Mrs. Simms observed quietly for Thom's benefit alone that Brett and L.T. had been trash-talking fifty-four all game long. This had been clear to Thom as well.

The Simms and Thom waited for Brett to emerge from the home locker room alongside other family members and girlfriends. He was the first player out and so basked in the cheers and applause that may also have been intended for boys trailing right behind him. His attempt to give Mrs. Simms a peck on the cheek was intercepted without much resistance by Mr. Simms, who pumped his hand, pounded his back, and messed up his hair to the extent possible with a crew cut. He whooped a couple of times for good measure.

As the locker room emptied and the initial excitement died down, Brett turned to Thom. "Stick around a few minutes and I'll give you a ride to the team keg." Mr. Simms squinted. Mrs. Simms said, "Are you sure?"

"Sure. Why not?"

So it was that Thom once again found himself in the back of Brett's SUV, this time sandwiched between L.T. and Laser—it was definitely Laser, at least for now. A faux leather bota bag hung from a yellow cord around L.T.'s neck. He held the opening a foot from his face and squirted red wine in his mouth without spilling a drop. A short brunette with pectoral attributes reminiscent of the Canadian Rockies sat up front. She dished on the other team's players, uniforms and cheerleaders more enthusiastically than did the football players. She also produced a small wooden pipe, lit its pungent contents, and passed it to Brett. Thom, once again, did not imbibe. The smoke, however, represented a marginal improvement upon the supermarket aftershave and perfume that was thick enough inside the SUV to fog windows. Repacked twice, the pipe made several circuits before they reached a house that sat on the shore of a large lake over a mile north of the main highway.

The home's polished log-cabin exterior invited a rustic impression. However, the two above-ground stories topped by a loft, along with blazing lights inside and out, picture windows all the way around, decks, balconies, porches and a three-car garage detracted from any such pastoral humility. A bonfire roared on the strip of man-made sand beach between the lush green lawn and water. Hip-hop blared from speakers with enough bass to detach retinas and dislodge fillings. Most of the boys had on t-shirts, shorts, and sandals. The girls wore skirts or shorts; still others sported pep club and cheerleader garb from the game. Many were smoking. There wasn't an actual keg in sight, although a couple of sawed-off oil drums were packed with ice, beers, hard liquor, and a few cokes. Thom waded into the crowd surrounding the drums and unburied a can of Sprite from the crushed ice. He escaped the turned heads and smirks to stroll along the shoreline. But for a water oak and several palms that bordered the far edge of the lot, beyond which grew a jungle of trees and shrubs, he was alone. Or so he thought.

"Ya want me to touch that up for ya, little feller?" came a voice from behind.

"What's wrong with your voice, Jamison?" Thom said.

"You've never heard of John Wayne—the Duke?"

"Maybe." Thom had heard of the actor yet had never actually seen a John Wayne movie. "But hey—it's nice to see you standing." Even then, Jamison's posture didn't hold much promise for remaining upright as the night progressed. Perhaps the bottle of Jack Daniels in one hand was throwing him off balance.

"Just trying to be neighborly," Jamison said.

"Gay," said the tall blonde girl at his side. Her name turned out to be Jody.

"Do you even know anyone here besides us guys from the movie?" Jamison said.

"Has Dyleane been by?" Thom asked.

"Who?" Jamison said.

"That black chick Cheri pushed down the stairs." Jody said. "Hell no, and I don't 'spect she will."

"Cheri?" Thom said.

"Cheri Hogan, Brett's girlfriend," Jamison said, apparently trying to be helpful. "This here's her mom and daddy's place."

Jody rolled her eyes. "You rode here with her, duh."

Thom held out his hands, emulating large breasts. Jamison nodded. So that was the little shit who broke Dyleane's tooth and scared Savannah May. Thom had seen Cheri before at the BRGC. She typically hung out with a gaggle of girls, mostly slim and blonde, who, if they noticed Thom at all, apparently did not feel it inappropriate to giggle as they passed. He felt irritated that Dyleane hadn't pointed her out.

"I thought Brett liked Savannah May," Thom said.

"That's so yesterday," Jody said. "He ended up taking Cheri to Fall Formal. Let's just say she wasn't too hard to convince."

"And man did *they* tear it up," Jamison said. "Cheri's been all wet for Brett since forever. He asked her to the Formal about thirty seconds after Savannah turned him down. And ain't they been all lovey-dovey ever since." He and Jody laughed as they wandered not so much aimlessly as without much aim in the general direction of the fire.

Thom contemplated the lake's sapphire-green tranquility. The faithful reflection of the night sky on the water's glassy surface obscured any demarcation between Earth and space. A few girls and fewer boys danced in the sand near the fire, while the others milled about in groups, small and large. Thom steeled himself with a long pull of Sprite and approached a group that included L.T., Jamison, Jody and Laser—he was still Laser. The yellow cord dangling from L.T.'s bota was long enough to reach around his stump of a neck and under one massive arm with plenty of slack to spare. A string of red wine stretched a foot and a half straight from the wine bladder to L.T.'s gob.

"Awesome party," Jamison said.

"Way turnt," Laser said. "I can't believe how cool Cheri's old lady is to buy all this beer and shit after every game."

"Every game?" Thom said.

"Every home game," Jamison said.

"Even the night of the murder?" Thom said.

"Huh?" L.T. said.

"The night—well—you know," Thom said.

"Fuckin' eh," Jamison said. "That was the night half the party ended up all sweaty and naked."

"Shut up," L.T. said.

"We got so wasted we couldn't even remember—" Jody began.

"You guys deaf?" L.T. said. "Shut up."

Jamison and Jody wandered off again, this time in the general direction of the barrels. They had already polished off the bottle of Jack or sat it down somewhere they couldn't remember. L.T. stared down at Thom.

"So, uh, pretty good party," Thom ventured.

With but a sneer in response, L.T. walked away, followed by Laser. Had Thom been too obvious? He found out five minutes later while standing by himself near the water oak and palms, thinking he should call Dyleane for a ride home. He had her number in his wallet. He'd have to borrow a phone—and Lord knows every kid at the party but Thom had one of those, and most were out and in use. More than once it was apparent that people near enough to carry on a conversation were exchanging texts.

"You're coming with me, punk." L.T. was dragging Thom by his upper arm before any thought to resist materialized. Thom made eye contact with one girl before L.T. pulled him into the jungle beyond the palms. With a brown bottle half raised, she watched with neither hope nor no hope but rather the idle detachment of a person watching a big fish eat a little fish. Others must have seen but none interfered. Thom grabbed at a sapling's trunk as he was hauled deeper into the brush. L.T. merely gripped tighter and pulled harder at the brief increase in resistance.

"You're breaking my arm," Thom shouted.

"Tough shit," L.T. replied.

L.T. finally dropped Thom at the edge of a tangled patch of saw palmetto. The plant was a bloody menace despite its apparent ability to stop cancer, grow hair, and shrink prostates, powers regularly extolled upon in the backs of golf magazines whose last pages were packed with little black and white classifieds. The edge of each green bayonet could slice through flesh more like a jagged razor than a saw.

"You ask a lot of questions for a faggot," L.T. said. "Maybe you oughta think about keeping that little mouth shut." He'd swung the bota around so that only the yellow cord was visible in front.

Thom hadn't practiced lying since Mr. Waldron busted him about his age, but then L.T. didn't look half as bright as Mr. Waldron. Even so, "What questions?" was the best Thom could muster.

"About Brett and the party that night the perv bitch went missing."

"Huh?" That part was sincere. "Went missing? What the hell are—"

"That's your problem, Loudon, you're always asking questions." That was Laser—Laser it was. The music played so loudly Thom hadn't heard him approach even through the thick undergrowth. Laser picked Thom up and practically tossed him at L.T. "Looks like someone's gotta teach you about keeping your nose out of other folk's business."

L.T. picked Thom up and threw him towards Laser. Laser

threw him back at L.T. "This is easier than a damn medicine ball," Laser said.

Except medicine balls don't have feet, and one of Thom's stuck in L.T.'s crotch partially by accident when Laser threw him back. L.T. screamed and dumped Thom into the palmetto patch. Something sharp scored Thom's neck. Thom jumped to his feet, looking for a way to run, which was when L.T. nailed him with a quick shot to the face. Thom went back down, and someone kicked him in the ribs. He curled up anticipating the next kick, which landed toe-first near Thom's asshole—probably L.T. aiming for Thom's balls in revenge.

"Whoa, dudes."

"Just in time, Brett-o. We're just starting to get down," L.T. said. He kicked again, striking the back of Thom's upper thigh. Fortunately for Thom's balls, L.T. lacked the precision of a competent placekicker.

"I said talk," Brett said.

"The punk fag didn't want to talk, man. Just ask more questions," L.T. said.

"There's bongs in the boathouse," Brett said. "I got this from here."

"What now?" Thom said when the other two were gone.

"What ought to be, little man?" he said.

Someone *ought* to say that beating up a person nearly two feet shorter was wrong. Those guys were the punks, not Thom. "Fuck you, Brett-o."

Brett smiled and offered a hand.

"I said fuck you." Thom struggled unassisted to his feet. L.T. may have had bad aim, but his kicks were definitely going to leave a mark. Blood flowed freely from his nose. He felt the sting on his neck—more blood.

"Palmetto?"

"What's it to you? I'm out of here if, you know, it's okay with *you* punks."

"I don't blame you for being pissed. They just got a little excited. L.T. is like that. Come on up to the house to clean up first." He took a couple of steps. "Come on. 'Sides, how do you think you're getting home?"

There was that. Thom followed Brett out of the trees and up a little rise to the road. They skirted the edge of the front lawn to the main entryway, avoiding the crowd down by the lake. Thom still heard the revelers, louder than ever, shouting and laughing over the music. Brett walked in without knocking. All the lamps, track lighting and ceiling lights blazed. Voices and canned laughter emanated from a television in the next room.

"Fay," Brett called. "Ms. Hogan."

"Is that you, Brett dear?" The television noise diminished in volume. "Are you alone?" Click-clacks from long-heeled sandals on the hard floor announced her approach.

"Yeah, well, I gotta friend here who, uh, stumbled into something down by the water."

Fay Hogan appeared. This was the lady who had creeped out Savannah May. Thom had also seen Fay Hogan coming and going from the pool. She may even have played a round or two with

Cheri and, Thom assumed, Mr. Hogan. Before then, however, he couldn't have placed either's name. She was considerably taller than Cheri, especially with heels. Her hair, an unnatural orange, was up in pigtails. She wore a wraparound dress typically intended to cover a swimsuit between the parking lot and pool, only Thom wasn't sure what, if anything, she had on underneath. He guessed it might not be much by her smile as she sidled up to Brett's side.

"Why, I know you—from the golf course, right?" She raised eyebrows that appeared to be more paint than actual brow. "And bless your heart, but whatever it was you fell into might just about have busted your nose. And it scratched you pretty good on that shoulder too. Is something going on out there you need to tell me about, Brett honey?"

She touched his arm softly, caressed it.

"Nah, Ms. Hogan. Just some roughhousing got a little out of hand. You know how things get after a big win. Ain't nothing to be concerned of."

"It's okay to call me Faye with others around. And you know I don't need no trouble going on out there, what with Jerry being out of town and all." There was already trouble enough in those eyes. "Well, let me take a look at you. My, my, my." She my-myed a couple more times before directing Thom to the hall bathroom with instructions to wash up and use the antibiotic ointment from a sink drawer on his neck.

Thom did as he was told. He turned off the water and heard them laughing. When he came out, they were standing close, each with an arm around the other's waist, swaying perhaps to the beat of the music outside.

"Well, don't you look better already," she said. Being addressed as a child at once fueled Thom's indignation and robbed it of some of its righteousness. Ms. Hogan gently undid herself from Brett and left the room, walking as though she knew she was being watched. She returned a moment later with a sandwich baggie full of ice from the refrigerator door and a University of Florida Gator t-shirt. "Here you go, dear. Put that cold pack right over that nose of yours. You already got a bit of a shiner. And that shirt, well, Cheri don't need it anymore, does she? Now that Brett's going to Florida State, she's a Seminole. It's good you and her are about the same size. And you might as well use that one you're wearing to sop up the new blood. It don't look like that rag's gonna be good for much anything else now. Okay then, can I get you boys a little something to eat or drink?"

Brett said he'd really love to stay but that Thom had to be going, and he'd better get back to keep an eye on what everyone else was up to. Ms. Hogan allowed as how that made sense, albeit without much conviction. Brett and Thom exited the front door and stood at the top of the wide red-pigment concrete steps.

"How're you figuring on getting home?" Brett said. "I can give you a ride, but it probably won't be for another few hours."

Thom demanded Brett's phone to call Dyleane. Brett relayed directions that terminated at the corner of Cabin Ridge and Laker Roads. When Thom hung up, Brett instructed him to walk one block down and another over.

"Why?"

Brett pointed. "Because Cabin Ridge and Laker are two blocks over. In case you ain't heard, Cheri and Dyleane don't exactly get along all that well. It's for the best if Dyleane don't come too near."

"Sure."

"And I'd appreciate it if you didn't go into a lot of detail about tonight's little get-together. You know, whose house it's at, what the kids are doing. Some of the town's tight-assed citizenry might get all puckered up if they knew."

"You okay with Mrs. *Brett Honey* in there?"

Brett smiled. "Yeah, she is a problem. There's more jealousy in that house than laminate floor. If Cheri ever caught me messing with Faye, I wouldn't need Life Flight so much as a body bag."

Cheri must have some spunk; Mrs. Hogan, too. Perhaps it was projection, but Thom saw anger in any such abundance of attitude. For some, life wasn't about getting along, even if they occasionally went through the motions. It was about getting ahead and even more about getting even.

"Any more questions before you go, Thommy Boy?" Brett wasn't smiling anymore.

Sure. Was Savannah May at that party the night she got stabbed through the heart? That same party you're lying to cover up? "Me? Why?"

"Yeah, well, sorry about those guys."

Thom made it to the anointed meeting place. He hurt all over —his face, neck, thigh, ass. Even two blocks removed from the party, he could make out a girl calling someone "queer," a guy screaming "blunt," and the rumbling, throbbing bass that dominated every song. Thom knew enough about rap and metal to understand that the best songs possessed strong rhythm and rhyme even when the lyrics were otherwise unintelligible—ofttimes, the more unintelligible the better. Even the tunes played over and over on the rock and roll oldies station to which Dill had practically glued the pro shop radio adhered to this formula. Thom preferred silence. Other sounds naturally present were tolerable, whether the songs of a robin (which in Putnam County were sung year round) or the revving of a smoke-belching garbage truck motor as its extended pincers raised the loaded dumpster parked between the clubhouse and storage garage. Thom could turn off neither, so they just were. He, after all, was a reader. He used to be a golfer. If either pursuit had to be attended by music, something more along the lines of compatriot Gordon Lightfoot's "Canadian Railroad Trilogy" was preferable to party music that plunked the listener's ribs like fat piano wires. Even Lightfoot's ballad about the big ship that sunk before it reached Whitefish Bay would do—never mind that the actual wreck might lie in American waters.

Dyleane's was the first car Thom saw. He had just finished switching out his bloody, gray t-shirt for the blue Florida one when he spotted her headlights coming up the street.

He climbed into the rusty little two-door and clanged shut the door. Dyleane immediately threw hers open, which turned the dome light back on. Thom had been holding the old shirt against his nose; he used the light to see if it was stained with fresh blood.

"What in God's name happened to you?" Dyleane screamed. It wasn't loud, but its intensity made Thom jump.

Thom described the football game, the halftime frosty malt, and finally how Brett saved him from being stomped to death by L.T., glossing over the fact that he had known about the game that morning and hadn't told Dyleane.

Dyleane's mom was already asleep at her home, Thom's stuffy and all too intimate storage garage didn't strike Thom as appropriate, so they retired to the BRGC pool. Only the floodlight between the men's and women's locker rooms remained illuminated, and it was swarmed by moths, mosquitos and flying beetles nearly the size of golf balls. Troy had already been there—the recliners on either side of the pool were uniformly spaced and neatly aligned. The clear-water chlorine smell competed with the richer green odors emanating from just beyond the floodlight's reach. Either aroma beat the heck out of teen-quality aftershave, cigarette smoke and spilt beer. Thom shivered a bit at the recollection and was thankful for the used t-shirt that smelled freshly laundered. Nothing, however, competed with the cyclic sawing of crickets, occasionally interrupted by an otherworldly outburst away off in the woods from something that Thom simply didn't want to know about.

"And L.T. called Savannah May a pervert?" Dyleane said. "Do you think he knows about her being gay?"

"'Perv,' technically speaking. Like saying the whole word implied too much disgust to bear. The 'went missing' part was weird too," he said. "If he did know about her, you know, it wouldn't have been a good thing—not for her, anyway. To him, anyone the least bit unlike him is gay or a fag or an N-word. As far as I can tell, that includes pretty much everyone except Brett. He's a real piece, that one."

"Yeah, Thomas Loudon, don't it just suck when someone is so judgmental about another's personal characteristics? Like, say, calling someone a freak for something they have no control over."

"I am *not* judgmental. And I never said it was about good or bad, or right or wrong. It's just—just normal and abnormal."

"Oh, and you're all about celebrating the abnormal, the different—the 'special'—among us, right? Of course, you're not passing judgment. Oh my no, not at all." She turned to look Thom directly in the eye. "Will you just listen to yourself?"

"Look, Dyleane—how can I be judgmental against myself? I am abnormal. Fucking abnormal to the tune of four-foot seven."

"And a half," she said, rolling her eyes as if she'd heard it all before, which she had.

"Wouldn't life be better with just normal?" Thom insisted. "Where no one has to wonder about the other? *The* other. Where I don't have to walk in anybody else's shoes, nobody has to walk in mine, 'cause we're all wearing the same ones? Where there isn't any 'I'm the way it's supposed to be and you're not?'"

"Hell *yes,* it would. But *you're* the one who insists on dividing. Wouldn't life be better if people ignored color, money? Your darn shoes? Who Savannah May was and wasn't attracted to? Height? Understood that differences are just differences? Not normal or abnormal, good or bad. They just are. It's the people who make all those divisions, they're the ones who end up bitter and dying of jealousy—you know that, right? Wouldn't it suck if some old white guy—no offense—"

"Huh?"

"—chose what normal music was, and we couldn't listen to rap or jazz without being abnormal?" She air-quoted 'abnormal.' "Damn it, Thom—with an *h* and *a half*—you aren't even listening!"

"I am too. White kids listening to nothing but white rap is totally abnormal."

Dyleane nodded because that was irrefutable. Thom conceded that the "*h* and *a half*" was a little bit funny. They sat for a while.

Then out of nowhere, "Don't you get it, T-*h*-o-m-a-s and a *half*? Those are exactly your ways of trying to be normal—you and your *h* and *a half*. You're the one separating the world into tall and short people, *h*s and no-*h*s, and you're doing your best to fit in with the tall ones and avoiding the *h*-less. You're dying inside from the divisions *you* are making—that *you* are buying into and only perpetuating. Because you can't get it out of your mind that, yeah, maybe you *are* different."

"Ha! You said it, not me."

"But that's not normal or abnormal. Not good or bad. Dang it —different *is* normal. I don't see abnormal when I look at you—I see you. And that sure as hell better be how you look at me." Thom looked at Dyleane without speaking. She added, "You still don't get it, do you?"

Of course Thom 'got it.' He understood far better than Dyleane. Yeah, being black in Red Neckia couldn't be a piece of cake, not even chocolate cake. But she could still go into stores, cafés and parties and usually see people that looked like her. Some dumb fuck might say something ignorant, but at least she wasn't all alone. No Florida politician had introduced a law making it easier to demean and hurt black people—not recently anyway. Unlike the yahoo, the tall yahoo, who introduced a bill in the Florida legislature to legalize dwarf tossing—for "their" own good, he'd said. It would help "them" get out more, he'd said.

Dyleane had never had to use her hands to help climb up stairs with people behind her laughing or, more likely, getting all pissed off at the grotesque freak slowing them down. A freak so different that empathy was completely out of the question, and even sympathy was a stretch. Dyleane did not understand. How could she?

Dyleane took Thom's hand and squeezed it. "*N'est-ce pas?*" she offered. She was almost completely reclined in her tank top and shorts, one knee up, looking at Thom, smiling. She gazed at the stars, still smiling. Still holding Thom's hand. He caught a whiff of her perfume, what little scent was then capable of negotiating the dried blood packed in his nostrils. Dyleane smelled like flowers, nice flowers, not flowers soaked in cigarette smoke.

No, not *n'est-ce pas*. She still didn't understand. But, well, just then, all that philosophical stuff suddenly didn't seem so important.

Chapter 12

Thom awoke Saturday morning to someone pounding on the storage garage's only door. In only the Gators t-shirt and boxers, he opened it a crack. Dill pushed it the rest of the way open and stepped inside.

"Where was you at yesterday?" Dill demanded. "The Higginses stood around fifteen minutes waiting for someone to help with their clubs before they found me. And you can bet they was pissed. You think you can just take off like that without letting anyone know?"

"Are you finished, Dill?" Thom said.

"Just catching my breath, boy. You're making me look bad. And furthermore—" Dill scrunched up his eyes and nose in an apparent attempt to focus on Thom's battered face. "You don't look so good yourself. You ain't particularly well suited for fighting, if you catch my drift."

"I asked Gram—you know, my co-assistant—to cover for me just this once because I was at Brett Simms's football game as the special guest of BRGC Board Chair Jimmy and Mrs. Simms." If that didn't outright kill Dill's morning buzz, it inflicted a mortal injury. "And I just kind of fell into something after the game."

Dill observed that Thom ought to be letting him "in on anything of that sort going on round here. Otherwise we gonna maybe be making some changes that you ain't gonna might not care for." He turned to depart, although he looked as if he didn't really know where to go. Thom had been running the damn joint for three years without Dill having a clue what was "going on round here."

One advantage of going unnoticed for so long was that no one notices when suddenly the unnoticed wears cheap, overly-large sunglasses retrieved from that part of the lost-and-found pile that no longer merits notice. Thus no one noticed the black eye the Jackie Onassis shades disguised. In a similar vein, Thom's ass and thigh muscles took little notice of the three ibuprofen he washed down first thing with a Sprite from the machine. Thom, however, most certainly noticed those muscles with every step and squat.

Saturdays were the busiest day of the week, particularly during the slightly cooler autumn days when FSU, Florida, and any number of other state football teams were either idle or playing at night. Despite his injuries, Thom still fetched, loaded, sold and announced foursomes as Saturday mornings demanded. Thom was hurrying inside to sell a three-pack of unblemished Titleists, at least one of which the dink would lose in the water and another he'd almost certainly cut nearly to its core with a thinly hit fairway iron, when he passed Dill and Mr. Simms.

"Ah hell, it's not like that girl never heard them words before, I'll tell you that much," Dill said. "There weren't no need to get all hysteric."

"We're just lucky I still stock that shade of off-white down at the B & S," Simms said. "That one's got a touch of blue pigment in it. Even so, it'll take a couple, three coats to cover. I'll just have L.T. paint the whole damn building while he's at it. It's due."

"Now ain't that L.T. a good boy," Dill said. "How'd you get him here so early the morning after a big game?"

"He spent the night at our place like he does. Brett won't have it no other way. They're like twins, those boys are. He was already up when I got that crazy girl's call. He couldn't a got more than an hour or two in the sack, I'll tell you that."

"Dill," Thom said. No recognition. "Dill," he repeated. "You ring up the balls for Dr. Wallace, okay? I've got to take care of something."

"Huh? Since when do you—"

"Or maybe Gram can handle it. He's around here somewhere, right?" Somewhere still around bed in Jacksonville was more like it, but Dill must already have known that.

Thom found Dyleane and a shirtless L.T. lounging in standard BRGC white molded-plastic chairs on the poolside of the snack shack. A single coat of shiny paint, still wet, failed to cover what had been scrawled with black spray paint: *GET PLOWED NIGGER BITCH.*

Dyleane's calm façade crumbled slightly when her eyes met Thom's. She stood, silently inviting Thom's embrace. With his head resting upon Dyleane's breasts, Thom turned to see L.T. grinning like the sociopath that at least Thom understood him to be.

"You okay?" Thom asked as he and Dyleane parted.

"No—yes—well, not at first. Thank goodness Mr. Simms and L.T. got here so quick." Gesturing at the wall without looking, she said, "Just getting it covered a little really helps. I'll bet Mr. Simms thinks I'm crazy after I called him this morning." Dyleane permitted herself a small smile. "I might have been a tad bit hysterical."

"I'll bet he doesn't," Thom lied.

"Nice shades," L.T. cackled.

Dyleane's smile turned less natural as she resumed her seat and said, "They lend an air of mystery." She offered to grab a chair for Thom, the only party left standing.

Thom ripped off the glasses and stepped toward L.T. "Yeah, well—"

L.T. didn't flinch.

"You look famished," Dyleane said, standing so as to halt Thom's advance and then leading him around the corner towards the shack door. Thom didn't think about smiling at L.T. over his shoulder until it was too late. The satisfaction derived from Dyleane's preferential treatment and then rubbing it in might have helped banish the image of L.T.'s obvious contempt for whatever threat Thom might pose.

"It was L.T. who wrote that stuff," Thom hissed. "L.T. You know that, eh?"

"I don't think so," Dyleane said.

"I heard him at Brett's. It's exactly how he talks. The very same words!"

"About *me?*"

"Of course not," Thom lied yet again. "About every girl."

"You didn't hear him when he first got here. I was a mess and he said he understood. Like he really meant it."

"I'll bet he did."

"I think he did, Thom. Honestly. He said some things that really rang true."

"Such as?"

"Like he understands what it's like to stand out, to be different. Different in a bad way, the way you say the word." Dyleane glanced at the windowless wall, on the other side of which hateful words were written and L.T. was resting. "Let's talk about it later," she said.

"Dyleane, that's the guy who tried to kill me last night."

"Because your buddy told him to."

Dyleane immediately set about preparing Thom's breakfast, a task that typically did not require the full measure of attention she was then devoting. As she set the nut roll and saucer with extra garnish on a tray next to the double cheeseburger and fries, Thom said he needed to get back. He slipped from the shop's single chair. Dyleane took Thom's face in her hands. Her fingers were damp and chilly from the pickle slices, her breath slightly foul from the residue of fear.

"You are still my best friend and family, Thomas Loudon." Gently, slowly, softly, she kissed his swollen eye and then the bridge of his broken nose. As seemed to be his want that morning,

Thom did not think to take Dyleane in his arms to return the sensual kisses until the moment had passed. Or perhaps this show of genuine affection so discombobulated him that any such thought instantaneously fizzed into nothingness like the tiny bubbles topping his Sprite.

Dyleane offered him the tray. "Thanks," Thom said.

"Anytime," Dyleane said.

L.T. looked up as Thom rounded the corner. He was shaking a gallon paint can in his small hands and big arms. "It's sure a fine morning," L.T. said, smiling and showing no sign of exertion. "Fine, fine, fine, eh, slick?"

"Hey, Rembrandt," Thom said, nodding towards the building, "You missed a spot."

Dyleane, who had followed Thom outside, forced a laugh. L.T.'s grin was cold, sharp.

Autumn was approaching in North Central Florida. Leaves would fall from deciduous trees at an uneven pace, so uneven that certain oaks would not shed theirs until the buds on others had already blossomed. The big yellow and green leaves of popular shrubs had taken on hues of orange and brown. The soupy early morning humidity and ground fog veiled rather than intensified the sun's radiation, coated every surface with dew rather than heat.

Temperatures might still climb above ninety by mid-afternoon, but the sun passed a little lower in the south. The days were a little shorter, the nights a little cooler. Some Putnam County residents claimed this as the nicest time of year.

Thom? At night he aimed the big square fan, always on high,

slightly to the side of the mattress. The cool morning air might even bring a smile, might even cause him to don a tattered gray University of Alabama sweatshirt rescued from the lost and found for warmth until the midmorning sun rendered it excessive. Everyone in that community so despised the University of Alabama that the sweatshirt also insulated Thom from unnecessary human interaction not unlike audible flatulence.

Autumn back in the Pointe heralded a damp, callous cold that cut through sweatshirts like Thom's, as well as jackets and even winter coats. The wind raised clouds of dust born from millions of dead leaves void of moisture and tired to the point of disintegration. Leaves that, when the wind also blew sleet and the first heavy, wet flakes of snow, emitted a rich, rotten aroma from gutters where they had drifted into ankle-deep piles.

Thom missed that earthy autumn scent of compost, but not the gristle-piercing wind. And certainly not the Pointe or the number-two flat. For that was not home; it could never be home. Thom therefore would never feel homesickness for the place he was raised.

The same part of Thom's heart that rejected any such notion of home up north also refused to buy fully into the glory of Florida's autumn amidst her lakes, forests and pastures. That recalcitrant portion of Thom's soul guaranteed that Thom would never truly settle anywhere, that he would remain homeless, a homelessness that shielded him from commitments sure to be dashed, protected him from the risks of intimacy. But a homelessness that, when storms brewed not merely around Thom but within Thom, also left him wholly exposed to the harshest elements—inside and out.

The arrival of autumn, with its longer shadows and cooler temperatures—by Florida standards—also meant the appearance of two or three white plastic chairs in the space between the clubhouse and the storage garage. The location offered a choice between sun and shade thrown by the garage's north wall. The seasonal cool helped keep at bay the rankness escaping the dumpster some thirty feet away. The chairs were out of the way and yet offered a view of the clubhouse entrance and approaching golfers.

Upon his return from the snack shack, Thom claimed one of the chairs ostensibly to eat breakfast. Dill was managing the Saturday morning traffic well enough to avoid any major snafus. Thom had managed only a few fries before Jade appeared with a freshly lit cigarette to take the other chair. The chair did not collapse under Jade's bulk but might have grumbled had it been able. "Cheap ass pieces of shit, these chairs," she observed.

"God, that's an ugly habit," Thom said as a cloud of smoke gathered in the still, sunlit morning air.

"Ain't a habit," Jade said.

"You smoke all the time. And you blow it out of your nose."

"I smoke because I want to, not because I have to. And I ain't never heard no such nonsense about nose smokin'."

Lifting the tray laden with food an inch off his knees, Thom said, "You know it's illegal to smoke in a public place where people are eating, right?"

Jade waved a hand at the clubhouse. "Tell that to them in there. That's why I come out here for fresh air."

Conversations such as these convinced Thom that a certain

effrontery might run through Jade and Cory's shared genetic material.

Which is when Jade turned and caught sight of Thom's face. "My Lord, child. Please tell me you wasn't the only one in that fight what got all beat up."

Thom's first bite into the candy bar confirmed his fear that a front tooth had been knocked perilously loose.

"Who done that to you?" Jade persisted.

"Brett Simms's henchmen, L.T. and Laser." Thom described being used as a medicine ball and a punching bag before becoming a kicking dummy.

Jade took a long drag and blew smoke, thoughtfully, from her nose. "Them boys always been civil to me, mostly. But I can see where that L.T. might react some if'n you kick him in his manhoods."

Jade undid the dressing of paper towel and scotch tape Thom had applied to his neck that morning. She said she'd fetch some real bandages and alcohol wipes stocked behind the bar. Upon her return with a new smoke dangling from her lips, Jade cleaned and dressed Thom's palmetto wound without dropping an ash anywhere near the laceration.

"I need a favor," Thom said.

"That would be *another* favor," Jade said. "And I'm assuming a small one at that."

"I'll repay it. Next time you need initials carved into someone's boobies you just let me know."

"Oh honey, you got potential, no question about that. Your

heart is a vessel of doom. Well, okay, maybe just a shot glass of doom, but it is dark, dark, dark all the same. No question, none whatsoever."

"I need to get someone drunk."

"You? I think you better off just paying for it. Otherwise, she'll have to get so drunk she ain't gonna be of any use."

"It's a he."

"TMI, honey. T-M-I."

"What's the employee discount on a fifth of Jack Daniels?" There wasn't an employee discount on anything, officially. But then Thom was only supposed to receive one double cheeseburger a day. Thom hoped this spirit of employee camaraderie extended to booze, particularly when it was at the employer's expense, not the employee's.

"I'd be contributing to your delinquency," she said. "You're not only a minor you are an itsy bitsy minor. There's gotta be extra laws against that."

Thom explained it had to do with the murder and with his growing mental instability. Jade acknowledged that the second issue was indeed a cause for concern. After an, "Ah hell, ten bucks —I'll charge the difference to Dill's account and no one's the wiser, especially Dill," Thom asked if she knew how to get hold of Brett's buddy Jamison. "I got all them boys' numbers. He'll be by."

"Tell him I got him a surprise."

Sure enough, that evening just as Thom was turning on the fan in the garage in preparation for a good night's sleep, perhaps even one in which every dream did not involve kicks, bayonets growing from the ground, or naked dancing skeletons with orange pigtails, someone knocked. Jamison already had a drink or two under his belt. "Wazzup, Thommy my man? Jade says you got something I might like."

Thom explained that he had just come into possession of a fifth of Jack Daniels, which was more than he needed. Hell, a mini bottle was more than Thom needed. Jamison required no convincing. They retired to a bench set alongside the elevated first tee. The buzzing fluorescent lights in the nearby main parking lot cast shadows that faded about halfway to the fingerling swamp guarding the green. Jamison's sips gradually turned into drinks and then gulps, and became more audible as the whiskey disappeared. Thom drank so as not to appear unsociable. He noticed the improved flavor after a few nips. They discussed the football team and Jamison's girlfriend, Jody, and Jamison soon began to ramble. Thom should have quit drinking when Jamison's ramblings almost began making sense.

Thom asked, "So why does L.T. get to tell people when to shut up and stop asking questions?" When this didn't seem to strum any cerebral cords in Jamison, Thom added, "Like when we were all were talking about what a kickass party Cheri's mom was throwing and he ordered you guys to clam up."

"That's just L.T., man. And 'cause Mrs. Hogan is running for school board."

Silence.

"And that's relevant because?"

"She's promised to carpet the stadium with new synthetic turf like they got in all those fancy-ass, big-time stadiums and totally build a new locker room for the home team. These big lockers and iPads—it'll be better than FSU. Maybe even a juice bar."

"A juice bar?"

"No shit, man. And guess who gets to sell all them materials to the school board without no bids or nothing?"

Thom thought. "I got nothing."

"Jimmy Simms, duh. Brett's dad. Sweet deal, right?"

"A conspiracy made in heaven. And so it might not look so good if she gets busted for throwing beer and pot parties for Brett and his buddies after all the games?" Thom said.

"Zactly. Except that all the main voters' kids go to those parties."

Silence.

"Which makes it worse?"

"Are you gettin' drunk or what. Here." Jamison grabbed the bottle—putatively for Thom's own good. "What parents in their right minds is going to care that someone else did something nice for their kids that keeps 'em out of trouble?"

"Dude, you nailed it," Thom said, struggling to make sense of what apparently sounded logical to his drinking partner. "That's gotta be it."

"Fuckin' eh."

"So she throws these totally rad parties after every home game? Every home game this year?"

"Yep. Every one. Even some road games if we get back early enough."

"I heard the party after the first game was, like, the best ever."

"Dude, that *was* the best ever. Like, it was the first time in months where we all got together and seen each other. Pretty much the whole entire high school went. And you could totally tell. It's where I first hooked up with Jody." Jamison fairly radiated rapture and yearning.

"Oh, wow, and that was the same night Savannah May got stabbed," Thom said.

"No shit."

"Was she at the party?"

"All the cheerleaders were, man. Even Alicia for a little while." Alicia must be black to merit special mention. "It's practically part of their job."

Thom reclaimed the bottle and held it to the stars. "Well, Savannah May, I hope that last party was a good one." He took a slug.

"Oh yeah—pure dope." Thom had no idea what Jamison was talking about, but he was getting the rhythm of this game of riddles.

"Dope?"

Jamison grabbed the bottle. "Fun, man, lit, for fucking everybody. Even Savannah had some beers—Jody saw her. And Savannah practically started a fight flirting with Brett. Whoa, man, you shoulda seen Cheri. She had on this smoking halter-top. Them lunkers was practically jumping outta the boat. She sees Brett and Savannah doing the slow-dance thing and totally loses it. It was almost a goddamn chick fight."

"You remember all this stuff that clearly?"

"Dude—like, it was still early."

"Of course."

"Then Savannah backs off like it's no big deal. She was just trying to have some fun. It was kind of different for her because she didn't usually party all that much. But she was dancing with a bunch of guys. She even danced some with Alicia. They were totally getting down—I remember that. You shoulda seen L.T."

After silence failed to induce further explanation, Thom said, "Why?"

"See, her and Alicia were tearing it up when L.T. comes stomping by like he actually had somewhere to go, right? But he's already got that wine bag around his neck, that one he always does, so where else does he need to go? Savannah reaches out and claps his ass a good one, like, she even gives it a squeeze."

"Did he squeeze her's back?"

"Hell no. He acts like he's all insulted or something. Like he's tired of getting felt up by hot chicks." Jamison gave a hoot before adding, "*Not*," and hooting some more.

"Did Cheri rip Brett a new one? She looks like she could if she wanted to."

"No shit, man, but not until later. I remember Brett going inside, like maybe he figured it'd be safer in there. Cheri stayed outside and started flirting and dancing with whoever. She even came over to me and started shaking it. Which was just fine by me, know what I mean? But me and Jody were just sort of starting to get close, and Jody didn't exactly dig it."

"She's got something to jiggle all right."

"That's why Jody wasn't all that thrilled, duh. Anyway, at some point Cheri goes up to the house, and that's when the fireworks really started. Brett and her were screaming at the top of their lungs for, like, five minutes straight."

Thom nodded as if that was only to be expected. "What were they saying?"

"No way to tell, man. The music was like totally cranked. It was amazing you could hear them at all."

"Thanks for telling about all that. I never made it to high school, and I'd never even been to a big party like that until last night. All things considered, that once may be enough."

"I'm not sure I should mention it, but that's one hell of a black eye. It's kind of screwed up what happened, man. You know, in my opinion."

"Mine too!" They laughed, passed the bottle. "How long did Brett and Cheri go at it like that?"

"Dude, I told you: five minutes. I didn't see either one after that. I'm thinking they spent some time in Cheri's room making up—know what I mean?"

"Oh yeah, I know what you mean." Thom didn't really, not the details anyway, but he also didn't feel like confessing his naïveté just then. "How long did Savannah May stick around?"

"I don't know, man. That's when me and Jody started getting really tight. Over by those trees, remember?"

"All too well."

"I saw her and L.T. talking at one point. She was being all nice, like maybe she was saying she was sorry or something. She even took a shot off L.T.'s stupid wine thing—he squirted it into her mouth from, like, feet away."

"Bet that gave him a woody."

"He's weird, man."

"Which means?"

Jamison stamped his foot in exasperation. "Which means he's weird. It was like he was pissed off or something, like he didn't like it. As if anyone else half that fine had ever paid him attention before that."

"Right."

"Anyways, me and Jody was going at it real good when L.T. comes up and screams something obnoxious in my ear. He's always doing that shit like it's really hilarious. Did he pull anything like that in Palatka at that movie?"

"Twice."

"That mother. Anyways, he says something about going out for more wine and takes off, which meant I had to find my own way home. Jody had her old truck, so that was cool. I don't know when Savannah left—then again I had my hands pretty full just then, if you know what I mean."

Thom again pretended to know. In the midst of trying to make sense of everything Jamison had just said, he wished he didn't have to pretend. But maybe some things are just not meant to be—never ever to be. He felt morose. He indulged another pull and forged ahead.

"Why's L.T. call everyone a fag?"

"Cause they are, man."

"Everyone?"

Jamison stood as if he were leaving. Then he sat back down and took a swig. "I wouldn't fuck with him if I was gay. Last spring he beat the crap out of Hank Tooley 'cause he's gay. I mean, it's like Tooley always took girls to dances and stuff, but L.T. figured he was a fag, so *boom*."

"Boom."

"You don't fuck with L.T., man. And when him and Brett are together—"

"You mean like always?"

"Damn near. They bad enough by themselves, but when they get together, you don't fuck with either of 'em. It's like Colossus and Kitty Pryde."

"Say again?"

"Dude, ain't you never seen the X-Men? Except Kitty's a girl, and they're both like—"

"Guys. Got it."

The subject turned towards the meaning of life and which girls Jamison knew put out—inferring firsthand knowledge but never coming right out and claiming it. Thom surrendered the bottle once and for all when it was barely a third full and never once hinted at firsthand knowledge.

Chapter 13

Hungover as hell, Thom had little choice but to ask Dill to take charge of the Sunday morning agnostic duffers until he managed to get—and keep down—solid food.

"You want some Tabasco on that burger, Slick?" Dyleane said.

"Oh Lord, Dyleane," Thom winced. "Don't call me that."

"Sorry," she said.

"How'd you know I wanted Tabasco?"

"It's how my mom's old man medicated his hangovers. Till he gave up on that approach and just stuck with drinking. And not just that hair-of-the-dog-style drinking, either. He'd say, 'Can't hangover what ain't never been over,' or some such nonsense as that."

Thom slowly shook his head.

"Oh, right, my mom's *old,* old man."

Thom continued to shake his head.

"Oh—the hangover—how'd I know?" Thom nodded. "It's obvious with you white people. Your eyes get kind of sunk in and teary. Your face goes all gray, the skin I mean, gray, like something dead that's starting to smell really putrid and rotten. And you're always nodding your head back and forth, up and down, looking like you're trying to swallow down whatever it is that's trying to come back up."

"Got it."

"You can see in your sickly eyes how the world is all blurry, spinning around like—"

"*Okay.*"

Thom slathered Tabasco over his fries and burger in lieu of ketchup, with extra salt. He was halfway through the burger and second large Sprite before feeling steady enough to fill Dyleane in on the additional information from Jamison courtesy of the Jack. He pocketed the candy bar and left with thoughts of relieving Dill in the not so distant future.

Thom retired to a chair set between buildings. He'd just recover from the walk and then resume his duties. Feeling more optimistic about his chances of survival, he unwrapped the candy bar, bent off a bite-sized piece, and fed it to his molars for fear that the damn loose tooth in front might pull all the way out with a more direct approach. Corey walked by and stopped when he saw Thom. He pulled a pack of Salems from a shirt pocket.

"Where'd you get those?" Thom said.

"Stole 'em from my mom's glove box, and boy is she going to be pissed."

"Can you blame her?" Thom said.

Corey lit up and exhaled a plume aimed directly at Thom. "I could always blame you," Corey said. "You obviously doing something what stunts your growth."

The smoke constituted a definite threat to Thom's perilous relationship not merely with his immediate surroundings but also the recently consumed burger and fries drenched in Tabasco.

"You look like crap," Corey said. "What the hell you been up to now?"

Still engulfed in smoke, the image of crap wasn't helping.

"Here." Corey proffered an envelope. "Mom found it in a load of mail that's been piling up back by Dill's table. Damn past-due collection notices and everything." The return address read Provincial Correctional Services. "Who is it you know living in the joint? And what do you need prisons for up there? I thought you folks in Maine was all the time so sweet and nice."

"Canada."

"Whatever."

"Jade didn't tell you?"

"She don't tell me shit."

"Maybe because you steal her cigarettes."

"Maybe because you steal her cigarettes," Corey mimicked.

"It's none of your business," Thom managed. He stuffed the envelope in a pocket.

"Be that way, man. Guess it's none of my business who I saw in town yesterday night."

"Guess not," Thom said, by then hoping that calming breaths would work on a roiling stomach as well as it purportedly did on the yips. Only instead of smelling the cake before blowing out the candles he was inhaling second-hand smoke.

"He was coming out the Acorn Tavern. That man was carrying

a full load he was."

"Which describes pretty much everyone coming out of that dive," Thom said. The Acorn Tavern, the only functioning concern among a stretch of derelict structures a block off the main highway, enjoyed a certain reputation.

"True that," Corey said. "But this one weren't no taller than you, and he was *still* carrying a full load. But that look on his face? It was mean just the same, all pissed off at whatever and whoever. Just like you, man."

So much for calming breaths. Thom briefly considered the necessity of interrogating Corey to make sure this wasn't another of his gags. He had but an additional half second to wonder whether Corey's prior reports of seeing Thom's old man were gags after all before his most pressing thought turned to reaching the dumpster before hurling. Which he soon realized was silly, because even a tall man could barely see over the trash bin's edge and he'd need a ladder to puke inside it. The odor of whiskey merged with that of the stomach acid and undigested breakfast splattering the greasy concrete beside the big container. The fundamentally vulnerable feeling that accompanies uncontrollable puking soon gave way to guilt—there was no way he could return to clean up his mess. Not today; maybe never. He would, however, warn Dyleane against any unnecessary trips to the receptacle that, even on good days, still reeked of rotting food and rancid grease. Thom wiped his face with the Alabama sweatshirt and returned to the chairs. Corey was gone, as was the remainder of the salted nut roll Thom had left on the arm of his chair. A cigarette butt floated among ice cubes on top of his Sprite.

The chunder spew helped. A nap would have facilitated an even fuller recovery. Yet, at just sixty or seventy percent, Thom bought a coke from the machine, and set off to relieve Dill. Thanks to Corey's report from the Acorn, he already knew what the letter in his pocket would politely explain: His dad had been out of jail for some time now; they couldn't disclose where he currently resided, even if they knew, due to privacy laws.

That afternoon at supper, Thom remembered the letter and handed the crumpled envelope to Dyleane. Dyleane opened it with a small paring knife, extracted the single-page, flattened it out, and read. Her mouth fell open.

"Don't bother," Thom said. "I already know what it says."

"You—but how?"

"Corey saw him staggering out of the Acorn last night."

"Corey did? Even if he isn't yanking your chain again, how would he know it was your father?"

"Dyleane, I told you. I've felt it, felt him. Even saw him right there on the tenth green that time in the storm less than two days after the murder."

"But how did you know he never even *went* to jail?"

"Say what?" Thom snatched the letter from Dyleane.

Dear Mr. Loudon:

Neither provincial nor federal officials have any record of one Mr. Donald Thomas Loudon, formerly of Pointe-Saint-Charles, Quebec, having been arrested, detained, or incarcerated at any

Canadian governmental correctional or holding facility at any time during the past five calendar years.

> *Remember,* **"Never Skate Before The Ice Bears Your Weight!"**

> *Sincerely . . .*

Thom wadded up the page and barely resisted throwing it into the deep-fat fryer. "I figured he was out. Of course he's out. But he never went in? Didn't even get arrested?"

"You said you called the police right after, right?"

"The Royal Canadian goddamn Mounties. Like an hour after I ran off and talked that trucker into smuggling me over the border. Maybe less than that. I used his phone after he dialed 911 for me. The guy knew dad so he understood."

"You use that too—911? Bet you stole it from us."

"Right, just like hockey."

Whatever the origins of 911, Thom used Dyleane's phone this time, and dialed a number handwritten on a card he carried. A woman answered, asked Thom to wait, called out, "Sugah, it's for you again," and a moment later: "Trooper Laboda here."

"You know my dad wasn't in jail the night Savannah May was murdered, right?"

"That you, Thomas?"

"Well?"

"In fact, I do. Neither were you, and your police up there would love to talk to each one of you about that dead body they found in the apartment."

"About what? That *body* was my mom and that *bastard* is the one who murdered her. Just like he murdered Savannah May. What's there to talk about?"

"All they have is an anonymous call about a murder and the caller's claim that the victim's husband did it. Oh, and the corpse —they had that too. But no weapon, no witness, and no husband *or* son."

"He ran," Thom said.

"So did you."

"But—"

"Whoa there, son. I saw you that morning on the golf course. And while I may not measure up to your exalted constabulary up north, I know a man who's in no proper condition to lie about something like that. Especially a lie that made as little sense as yours did just then."

"That doesn't make sense. If I was in bad shape, then of course my lie wouldn't—"

"I know what I'm saying here. You're pushing your luck by arguing."

"He's in town."

"Where?"

"Corey saw him, Corey Jacks. Coming out of the Acorn Tavern last night."

"Jade's boy? Why's he hanging 'round the Acorn?"

"How the hell should I know? My dad is here. Someone's gotta go get him. He's a double murderer."

"I'll let Deputy Ricketts know. He's our man following up on what few leads we got so far."

"Him? He's a total—"

"*Thom.*"

"Huh?"

"I also know you're not here all legal-like. So don't you go giving me or the good Deputy Ricketts any reason to do something about your lack of immigration documents."

"Ricketts knows?"

"Well, let's just say he *should* know from everything we looked at and all the interviews. But I can't say it's quite sunk in yet that a white boy could still be an illegal. Know what I mean?"

"Got it," Thom said. They disconnected.

Dyleane had bent over, a hand on Thom's shoulder, to eavesdrop. She accepted the phone and straightened. "Tomorrow's your busy day, right?"

"Monday, yeah."

"Can you get away to come up here at noon? We need more information about their investigation, and I just may know how to get it." Before Thom could respond, she bent, put a hand behind Thom's head, and kissed him on the lips. Not a long kiss but enough there to register *HOT* on Thom's never before used passion meter. "No offense or anything," she said, "but your breath's as rank as what's splattered down by the dumpster."

Thom stayed awake that night a little longer than usual after turning on the fan and shutting off the lights for reasons that weren't anyone else's darn business. It was one of those times he was grateful the storage garage did not have windows. In lieu of the lingerie magazines under his mattress, Thom contemplated the feel of Dyleane's lips on his. Her smell. *His* smell, damn it.

He fell asleep with a smile yet awoke, per usual, at 3:30 a.m. Before the murder, he'd sleep as deeply as the Northwest Passage, only to awaken between three and four. Since the murder, he often had trouble falling asleep at all—and even then it was fitful—before waking up between three and four. A person could set a clock by it. But the only clocks in the storage garage were the digital clock radio on the crate next to Thom's mattress that didn't get radio reception and an electric one, with actual hands, even a skinny red one for marking the seconds, which sat on the workbench nearest the entryway. It was one of those quaint devices that used to clock hourly workers in and out. Even the loading docks in the Pointe where his dad occasionally worked had gone digital. Thom had never seen anyone at the BRGC clock in or out, nor even found one of the timecards they might use. Nonetheless, every sixty seconds, when the second hand completed another circuit and pointed straight up, the big hand advanced one minute with a *click*. Thom never noticed those clicks during the day, even on a quiet day standing right next to the damn thing. It was as if they only happened at night and then loudly enough to hear in the back corner over a fan's white noise. Each *click* announced another sixty seconds of sleep lost, and warned of another golfless day a minute nearer.

At such times in the past, Thom might mentally play a perfect round right there at the BRGC. He'd gauge the wind, shape shots, hole out chips, add an additional twenty-five yards to every drive, all to put him on pace to shatter the course record for eighteen holes—except that he always dozed off before reaching the eighteenth hole. Since finding Savannah May, however, where even the thought of playing golf invited panic, dream golf evolved from sedative to a guaranteed nightmare. *Click*

Or he would conjure up the most incredible holes on the most exotic landscapes. This once had consistently put him at ease. Even though the practice had lost its calming effects, at least it did not herald the cyclones of doom that now accompanied any thought of playing those holes. Thus pretend designing was slightly more benign than pretend playing. Unless, of course, corpses wearing bloodstained orange robes and yellow blouses appeared and every imaginary foursome included his son of a bitch old man. *Click*

And just who was he kidding about Dyleane and the kiss? At the party after the football game he'd seen plenty of those high school girls hugging, air kissing, pecking each other's cheeks. When they kissed a boy, really kissed a boy, it was slow and natural; there'd be eye contact; it was rhythmic, mutual, savored. The image, the feelings, they lingered in the air like the rolling reverberations of distant thunder. Dyleane and Thom were friends. There had existed a time when such a friendship, in itself, seemed extraordinary. Now? Wooptie-do. Thom felt dumber than a stump for imagining that her peck meant anything different. The only real lovers he'd ever known were books and, formerly, golf. *Click*

At least he still had books, thanks to Dyleane. Of course it was Dyleane. He'd never asked whether there were any about Mo Norman in the Interlachen HS library. He feared that Dyleane would say no, and then he'd know for certain that nothing about his spiritual mentor remained within reach. Not knowing meant that maybe it did. As it was, Thom could no longer share Moe's world. He didn't even have the damn ball anymore. He had to believe that Moe was nearby, if only in a book. As for that other lover, he hated that Savannah May's bloody corpse had stolen it away. *Click*

And, just for good measure, *Goddamn his mother and Savannah May.* Why did his mom have to push his old man so hard? Just scramble up a few eggs, brew a pot of coffee, and she and Thom could have retreated back into the bedroom to live and, okay sure, probably fight another day. At least there would have been another day. And why the hell did Savannah May have to hang around the BRGC after Troy left? She wasn't a party girl, it was late, and a storm was brewing. She couldn't just go home to get a good night's sleep? *Click*

Golf had been a friend, a lover—or so he supposed, never actually having had a lover. Golf wasn't like people, wasn't like so-called friends. Friends who were there one day, gone the next, sometimes even threatening to beat you to a pulp before they left. A person had stolen golf from him. Not, of course, Savannah May, damn her anyway. Her murderer—he was the thief. Who was that murderer, that thief? Thom trembled at the possibility that golf, now having abandoned him, might have taken the murdering thief as a lover, might have cuckolded Thom. That human, whoever he was—Thom would find him, goddamn it. Then what? He'd make the murderer take his filthy hands off her, permit her return to someone who cherished her, exalted her. She was what Thom wanted. Needed. Screw all those lame ass humans. If they needed each other, fine. That was their weakness, their loss, not his, nosiree. If Thom ever recovered his real friend and lover, he would never again need or depend upon anything or anyone else. *Click.*

Thom had to find the murderer . . . *Click—*

Chapter 14

The absurdity of Dyleane's noontime plan struck Thom the moment he saw Putnam County Deputy Sheriff Howland Ricketts approaching the BRGC snack shack with a determined waddle. This Monday was gray and drizzly, and it wouldn't break seventy degrees, which represented a significant weather event for mid-September in North Central Florida. The precipitation and stifling humidity obviated any need for dragging around thick black hose and twenty-five-pound sprinkler heads to irrigate the course. It diminished any urgency for changing hole locations. No one would play that Monday. Before the murder, this would have been a perfect day for Thom to go thirty-six, maybe fifty-four holes. While wet fairways might shorten his already distance-challenged drives even further, Thom's precise short game only became more so when soggy greens dampened the potential of unexpected bounces and unkind rolls.

Dyleane and Thom stood outside under a slight overhang next to the take-out window. "So where's this disturbance y'all called about?" Ricketts said.

"Oh, well now, Deputy Ricketts, we may have overreacted a

bit," Dyleane said in a syrupy drawl. "Turns out it was just some golfers, you know, a couple of fancy big-time lawyers from Palatka arguing over some court case." Then she lied some more about having tried to call back headquarters to cancel her request for assistance and getting a busy signal.

The cop eyed the damp, empty course. He rested a hand on his bulky utility belt equipped with everything from a loaded gun to roller skates for all Thom could tell. Then he fixed Thom and Dyleane with a stare clearly intended to strike subservience into their hearts. "Y'all know, doncha, that I got lots more important things to do than answerin' false alarms all the way out here—and in the pourin' rain to boot?"

His stare settled on Thom until Dyleane said, "We're real sorry about that, sir. Know what? I was just about to cook up a fresh batch of fries—all steamy hot on the inside and crispy on the outside. How's that sound?" Thom had never heard Dyleane so chipper and folksy, even for Dyleane.

"Don't mind if I do, ma'am."

"You want something to go along with those fries, officer?"

"You ain't got no more of them chilidogs back there, do you?"

"Well, now that you mention it, I believe I do. And one just happens to have your name all over it."

"Well, ain't that a deal?" he said as Dyleane practically fairy-gamboled inside to start cooking.

"Well, ain't it," Thom said. Ricketts glared at Thom only slightly less malevolently than before. "Look, Deputy Ricketts, as long as you're all the way out here, and as long as I'm not a suspect anymore," Thom paused to ensure there existed no difference of opinion regarding this last stipulation, "mind if we ask a couple of questions, you know, about the murder?"

"That's po-lice business, boy. Not much I can say about an ongoin' investigation, doncha know?"

"It's just that after finding the body and fully cooperating with you guys, I've been having kind of a hard time. It's making me a little crazy—doncha know?" Thom accepted Ricketts's momentary silence as an invitation to continue. Of course, the Putnam County deputy was just as likely focused upon the explosion and ensuing steady gurgle that followed Dyleane plunging a basket full of frozen potatoes into the deep-fat fryer. "Like how about the footprints in the sand trap? They must've told you something."

"Well now, you'd a thought so, wouldn't you? But it rained like hell a few hours before sunrise. Yours were the only ones we could see plain enough since you made 'em later than everyone else. I told the state boys they weren't gonna find out nothin' from those ones what you could just barely make out."

"Well, at least they showed I couldn't have been the murderer, right?"

"Or that you came back to the scene of the crime. You'd be amazed how often that happens."

"How often?"

"Now just how the hell should I know that?"

"Well, you said I'd be—"

"You gettin' smart with me, boy?"

"I wouldn't dream of it."

"All right then. But those state boys, they still got out all their fancy equipment, measured, took pictures, and made casts anyway —of what I'll never know. And you know what they got back?"

"No," Thom said, forcing his eyes wide with wonder.

"A whole lotta nothin,' that's what they got."

"Just like you said."

"Sure enough. How you gettin' along in there, little lady?"

"Just fine, Deputy Ricketts, just fine. You can't rush a good chilidog, now can you?"

"S'pose not. Least ways not one with them chopped onions and melted cheese, right?"

"So you couldn't tell if there might have been, say, two or three people that night or how big they were or what kind of shoes they were wearing?" Thom said.

"I already told you them state boys was just pissin' in the wind, didn't I?"

"Still no trace of the knife?" Dyleane called from inside as she set the fries and chilidog on the window ledge alongside a large coke.

"Well now, don't that look like a meal fit for a king?" Ricketts said.

Dyleane rejoined the men outside. "The knife?"

"No thanks, young lady. I always say that any eats worth eatin' is best ate with your fingers. And this here's some mighty fine finger food."

Dyleane pressed her teeth together in what approximated a smile. "No word about the murder weapon?"

"Nothing," Ricketts said, although with a mouth as full as his there remained some room for interpretation.

"Nothing? How could that possibly be?" Now Dyleane was the one forcing her eyes wide with wonder.

A moment passed before Ricketts could manage anything more than a grunt—it didn't help that he kept shoving in fries alongside half-chewed bits of chilidog. "Well now, I s'pose we coulda sent divers into all that swamp around here. You know, if'n any a them divers wanted to be gator bait."

"No, sir, we wouldn't want that," Dyleane said. "How about fixing a time of death?"

"That's where it gets a little bit tricky, don't it? The drop in temperature just ahead of that monsoon, it lastin' who knows how long at this precise locale, the body itself bein' half submerged for a while in that water down there? And her losin' all that blood all at once . . . well, coulda been as early as midnight and as late as three."

The air grew thin and Thom's breath short at the image of Savannah May lying in a sandy pool of bloody water.

"Didn't you guys find *anything* that helps?" Thom managed, abandoning the pretense of wonder.

"Well, what do *you* think?" Ricketts queried.

"How the hell should I know? That's why I'm asking." Thom reasoned that Dyleane's ability to tolerate this man's ignorance without screaming merely confirmed that he and she would never amount to anything more than casual friends.

"Well, if you gotta know, she'd sure been whorin' around

some," Ricketts said. This time, Thom checked Dyleane with a look of his own. "See, she had some of that red vino in her gut from just before she died, that blouse of hers was unbuttoned nearly down to her navel, her bra was undone, and her jeans were unsnapped, weren't they."

"Were they?" Thom said.

"Christ almighty, boy, I just said they was. And ain't no kind of struggle gonna cause all that."

"There was a struggle?" Dyleane said.

"Did I say there was? Fact is, there weren't no signs of any struggle at all. No defensive wounds, contusions, none of that. So, as I was about to explain, she was gettin' along mighty fine with this here fella 'fore he stuck her in the heart."

"Or girl," Thom said.

"Or guys," Dyleane said.

"Any one of whom could have forced her to disrobe at knifepoint," Thom said.

"Now just what are you two gettin' at? Y'all ain't withholdin' information from the police, are ya?"

"Well, Deputy Hagen, since you ask," Dyleane ventured, "we have heard that Brett Simms claimed to have been at a kegger out south of town that night. What if, say, that were all a ruse?" Nothing from the cop. "A made-up story?"

"Of course it's made up. Ever'one knows that. You goin' somewhere with all this?"

"That was Brett's alibi, the kegger," Dyleane said. "But it never happened. He lied. Why isn't he a suspect?"

"You, little lady, may know a thing or two about chilidogs, but what you understand about the criminal mind and police work couldn't but half fill a piss cup what's already half empty."

"Say *what*?" Thom said.

"He's got plenty of alibies involvin,' well, involvin' things all y'all ain't got no need to be worryin' yourselves about, don't he?"

"No—half filling a half-empty piss cup," Thom said.

"Thomas, shush," Dyleane said. "Now, Deputy, maybe it was just gossip and all, but didn't Brett and his girlfriend disappear before the end of the party they were attending?"

"May well have. Hell, I wouldn't mind a turn or two with that little firecracker of his, if you know what I mean." He directed this last comment at Thom before deciding Thom wouldn't know what he meant. With but a glance Dyleane's way, he seemed to conclude that she wouldn't know either.

"How about Mrs. Hogan?" Thom said.

"What about Mrs. Hogan?" Ricketts said, failing to conceal a certain longing. "I heard you two been pokin' around some. Now I believe it. Look, y'all best keep your noses out of po-lice business, know what I mean? You can't help none, but you sure as hell can waste a man's time. Right here's exhibit number A for that."

"So that's it?" Dyleane demanded. "The star quarterback gets a pass? His girlfriend too?"

"His best friend? His girlfriend's mom?" Thom added. "My dad?"

"You both crazy, ain't ya? And your dad—you're pullin' my leg now, ain't you? Let's just agree that he couldn't a been *up* to that task."

"What the fuck that's supposed to mean? You didn't see what he did to my mom."

"First off, I personally ain't never even seen him round these parts. Second off, that big boy what cleans this here pool, he sure coulda done it without even breakin' a sweat. So why bother? Look, next time all y'all gotta waste someone's time make it someone else's, hear?" He'd managed to clean the paper plate of all things edible and so waddled off with only the Big Gulp and a few chili stains dotting his uniform shirt.

Lost in thought, Thom and Dyleane watched Ricketts bend to avoid a limb extending from the live oak and disappear down the back pathway. Thom voiced his thoughts first: "The cops have obviously ruled out Brett. They must know something we don't."

"Are you actually suggesting that cracka knows something we don't?" Dyleane said.

"Fair point. But weren't the two of you all buddy buddy, I mean the way you were getting on? All 'sir' this and 'sir' that."

"Honestly. Are you that incapable of understanding why it just makes sense to stay on a person's good side?"

There was that, Thom silently conceded. And yeah, he did understand that bullshitting a guy to take advantage of him might make sense. This, it had become increasingly clear, was exactly how Dyleane was treating him. She obviously cared about Savannah May. Maybe there was more between her and Troy than he'd realized. Or her and L.T. Or someone else. What did Thom really know about her and all her time at home, at school, or wherever else she might be when she wasn't at the snack shack? After all, Dyleane convinced Thom that *he* had to figure out who did it—as long as it turned out to be Brett. And all that crap about repressed anger? Yeah—right.

Regardless of Dyleane's harebrained explanations, it remained true that busting the murderer might still help Thom regain his glorious aloneness. Solving the crime, in fact, appeared to be his only hope. Maybe by keeping her involved he was using Dyleane as much as she was using him. Much in the same way he had been playing Brett for information, right? Or had Brett been playing him?

Thom was grateful that Dyleane didn't make a big deal of him ordering a chilidog instead of the usual burger. He needed a change. Boy, did he ever need a change.

The stubborn rain showers left Thom ample time to ponder Dyleane's prior query: Just how *did* Thom know Corey wasn't yanking his chain yet again with news of the old man's sighting? Of course, that assumed Corey had yanked Thom's chain the first time around, whether about *seeing* the old man or then saying he had *not* seen the old man, which assumed that even if Corey had lied at first, one way or the other, it somehow robbed him of credibility going forward.

With these unanswered questions swirling about Thom's head, who could've blamed him if he'd just kept walking when Corey approached to announce, "I saw him again."

"Huh?"

"Oh, so now you're interested?"

"Look, Corey, are you serious about all this or just having me on?"

"'Having you on.' I like that. So like maybe I was at first, but this here is the straight shit."

And so Thom's faith, if any had existed, was justified—sort of. "Where? When?"

"This morning at the Dollar Store."

"What was he doing there?"

"What's anyone doing at the damn Dollar Store 'cept buying cheap shit or stealing it—and that mother weren't buying, I'll tell ya that. At first I just kind of watched, see? He's got on a long dirty t-shirt and baggy shorts, and I mean filthy. Out of nowhere, slick as shit, he stuffs a pair of blue socks in those shorts, around back. Then he lifts a three-pack of whitie-tighties, the kind all y'all wear, in the front of his shorts. Last thing, he takes this orange shirt off the hanger, button-up collar, real nice like. He looks around, sees me, winks, and, just as pretty as you please, he rolls it up and slides it into a front pocket and pulls that dirty old shirt down so you can't see none of the bulges. Smooth as goddamn silk, see? And anyway he's all hidden down between those tall racks and all."

"He didn't get caught?"

"Now *you* having *me* on, right? I go *pay* for my socks, 'cause that's why I'm there for. I'm almost out the sliding doors when he comes right up next to me like we're homies or something. We go out the door side by side. All of a sudden, some damn alarm goes off. And lights all start flashing and spinning like on top of a cop car. And now everyone knows someone's walking out the store with shit they ain't paid for. I stop since I'm the black guy and I do not want to get shot in case one of them cashiers is packing, hear? But him? Your old man? That little shit just walks off through the parking lot, down to the highway, like he's strolling through a park after Sunday service. He was even whistling something god-awful. Don't y'all got real music up there in Maine?"

"Canada."

"Whatever."

"Corey told them it was your dad, right? At the store?" Dyleane said while cooking Monday afternoon supper.

"The store employees? Hell no," Thom said. "Corey says he admires a true professional. And besides, if he rats out someone else, the cops get called, and he wants nothing to do with the cops. So he just played dumb and showed them the receipt for his socks."

"Smart boy," Dyleane said. "My mom and I had plenty of need for protection, but we still never called the police. They may protect and serve some folk, but those folk don't often look like me or Corey." Thom waited for more, but Dyleane switched gears. "So you still don't know if that's really your dad or not. I've done some reading, Thomas Loudon. And Florida just so happens to be very popular with little people."

"Of course it is. The risk of being blown away in a hurricane is nothing compared to getting buried by a snow plow."

"It *did* mention the weather."

"And jobs too, don't forget jobs."

"Wait. Our economy still sucks worse than anywhere else."

"Where else are legislators trying to lift a ban on dwarf tossing because it represents an unconstitutional infringement on freedom. Whose freedom? The dwarf's, of course. Getting hurt and humiliated has gotta pay pretty well, eh?"

"Oh, Lord. That didn't pass, did it?"

"Look, Dyleane, I'll bet whatever you were reading didn't also talk about little asswipe people who steal clothes and then frame black kids for it."

"Can't say it did."

"That's why it's my dad."

Thom, however, knew that Dyleane was right about Florida and its attraction to little people, bless its little heart—and it wasn't just the weather. For some five hundred years, Florida had been home to lost explorers, pirates, exiles, delusional retirees, persons escaping religious persecution, others intent upon perpetuating religious persecution, dreamers, drug runners, circus freaks, and whack-job swamp rats seeking to "live off the grid" (so long as bars and bait 'n gun shops lay within a fifteen-minute ride around the swamps on an ATV). Weirdness was endemic. In Florida, Thom wasn't just a freak; he was a freak among plenty of other freaks. Thom was a migga freak; his dad was a murder freak, but they were freaks all the same. In Florida, freakdom grand central, they at least had company, albeit company entirely composed of freaks. Thom and Dyleane embraced and pecked awkwardly upon parting.

Thom spent his insomnia time that night thinking about meeting his thieving, murdering freak of an old man face to face. The RCMP knew his dad was the murderer—it had to. Probably a double murderer—at least. Yet what were the chances that Ricketts would even look for him? Thom knew that answer: nil. Dude couldn't find an ant at a picnic. *Click*

Might Mr. Waldron know of other jobs? After all, Thom really was sixteen now, and he'd sure learned plenty about running a golf course. Maybe he could hire on in the lawn and garden department of one of those big box hardware stores? They seemed willing to employ freaks, at least as greeters. *Click*

But having no visa or green card ruled out most legitimate employment options. Even so, as Trooper Laboda suggested, Thom probably enjoyed a leg up on brown immigrants without documentation, at least among idiots like Ricketts. *Click*

There was always Canada. And snowplows. And suffocating normalcy that served only to spotlight the freaks. Where the RCMP wanted him for questioning about a murder. Perhaps Corey's reticence about becoming involved with the law wasn't so silly after all. *Click*

Chapter 15

Mrs. Ihms waved at Thom as she emerged from the storage garage wheeling her own clubs. She and her husband along with the Colburns and Martis comprised a regular Tuesday-through-Friday sixsome. Groups that large were typically discouraged because they would slow down everyone playing behind them. But these pleasant, easy-going white-, blue-, and no-hairs, despite an air of chronic distraction, were machines out on the course. None wasted a spare second looking for a ball or wondering how to make a shot she or he hadn't previously faced. This was because each round was practically a scripted carbon copy of the previous one—the bad shots as well as the good shots, the ribbing as well as the compliments, the simmering grievances and silent jealousy. Thom waved back. They were ready to roll, waiting only for Mrs. Colburn to return from emptying her urostomy bag.

"We saw the darnedest thing at the 7-Eleven on the way over just now," Frank Colburn said.

Mr. Ihms bit. "What'd you see at the 7-Eleven, Frank?"

"Well, there was this lady manager. And she was having it out with this little fellow, a midget of all the goddamn things. Couldn't have been taller than three, four foot. She'd caught him sleeping on the night shift. They was a cussin' each other up one side and down the other."

Thom felt the now familiar nausea rising from his gut.

"They can't get more than three customers on that night shift," Mrs. Marti said.

"I reckon they get a few more than that for gas and coffee, what with all those folk driving through town on the highway," Mr. Marti said.

"Then why wouldn't they just drive another block and a half over to the Gate—that's what I'd like to know," Mrs. Marti said. "Gas there's always a tenth of a penny cheaper."

"Coffee's fresher too," Mrs. Ihms added.

"They was damn near to blows," Mr. Colburn continued. "Her saying it was only his second night. Him saying what she could do with the job—that little guy was swearing up a blue streak, he was."

"What's taking your Jeanie so long, Frank?" Mrs. Marti said.

"They just gave her a new adhesive to stop the leaking and—"

"What color was his shirt?" Thom said.

"Huh?" Mr. Colburn said.

"Under that smock they wear, Frank," Mrs. Ihms said. "The boy wants to know about the color."

"Let's see. I guess it was nice enough. It buttoned up and all that."

"The color, Frank," Mrs. Ihms said. "Not the collar. What was the color?"

"I thought he wanted to know about the collar. Well, let's see.

Orange it was. A real nice, bright orange."

Thom sought refuge between the clubhouse and garage. He passed Mrs. Colburn on the way. She did indeed smell fresher than usual. The sun, however, was barely up and the day was young.

The chairs were gone, suggesting that the Nineteenth Hole had been busy enough the night before that someone fetched them inside. Thom settled on the rough concrete amidst the cigarette butts and crossed his legs, first gazing at the sky between buildings, then at the ground.

"Hey. Whatchu just sitting on your ass for? You the sleepy dwarf now?" Corey said. "You get up now and find me a job. Gotta get me thirty-six holes a day between now and Saturday."

"Okay. Yeah. Sure."

"You look like shit, you know that?" Corey said. "You been looking like shit pretty much every day lately. Like looking like shit must be normal for you. Now how about that job? We gotta deal you know."

"The orange shirt," Thom said to the ground. "You weren't lying."

"Course I weren't lying. Would I lie to you—least ways when I say I'm not? And I said I weren't lying, not about that midget. And now you mention it, I saw him last night."

"At the 7-Eleven."

"How'd you know?"

Thom shrugged. "Orange shirt."

Corey said, "Yeah, well, that place was hopping. Ain't no one go down to that ghetto Gate station no more. And there he was, standing on a box in front of the register, taking his own sweet time ringing people up, giving out change, getting cigarettes. Hell, *he* was smoking one, right there in the damn store."

"It's him."

"Damn straight. And he weren't checking IDs nor nothing. So I got me a case of Miller and a carton of cigs. When I finally get up to the register, I says, 'You were pretty slick back there at the Dollar Store.' He says, 'Yeah I was.' I say, 'You're Thom Loudon's old man, ain't you?' And his face all kind of lights up, so's I tell him how you're out here all the time. And he don't even charge me for the cigs. That's some old man you got right there. Now then, what about that job? *Hey.* Where you going?"

Thom paused at storage garage entryway. "Anyone in there?" he called. No reply. He entered warily. He grabbed a cheap nylon backpack from the lost and found. He stuffed it with a couple of changes of clothes, a toothbrush and comb. He dug his life savings out from under the bedside crate. Three hundred thirty-six dollars, $336.00 more than he'd arrived with, all of $338.25 once combined with what he was carrying.

He looked at his clubs, each possessing its own strengths, its own moods. The hybrid four, a stoic worker, complaining not a whit when Thom asked it to shape a shot well outside its typical range. The seven-iron, always seeking the limelight. "Look at me," it would cry even before Thom pulled it free of the bag, promising greatness and usually delivering. In other hands, the clubs might have comprised a reality TV cast complete with the obligatory narcissist, perpetual victim and slick liar. In Thom's fast fingers and calm palms they were a team with not a weak link in the bunch.

The tens and twenties stuffed into a deep front pocket could not stem the same lonely helplessness he felt three short years and countless long days ago on the cold night he fled the Pointe, a loneliness brittle and vulnerable. He lifted the putter from the bag. The custom-fit club on which, two years before, he'd blown what then constituted his entire life savings. From its leather reverse-taper thick grip down to the blade head and a flat-lie angle of nearly ninety degrees, Thom wielded it on the course as might a swashbuckler his rapier. Even now, the putter might serve as a walking stick, a weapon, or, if pawned, a night or two at a motel— a cheap motel because no person other than Thom Loudon would ever appreciate its full value.

He started towards the snack shack via the back pathway, trying out his new staff, and wondering what to tell Dyleane. He got as far as the live oak. There he spied a paint tray and roller and then Dyleane and L.T. idling in plastic deckchairs. He retreated before they saw him. And he'd thought that leaving behind his golf clubs was hard.

Thom tapped on the window near Dill's corner table. "I'm going," he said to the image on the other side of the glass.

"Huh," Dill said.

"I'm going," Thom said more loudly, exaggerating his words to facilitate lip reading.

"Where?"

Thom pointed at his backpack. "Friends. Just a few days. Don't worry."

Thom didn't need sound to know Dill was launching into another "what in the goddamn name of—" tirade. That was Thom's cue to split.

"You stop right there," a voice commanded. Thom stopped. "Now turn around." He turned. Jade stood atop the irreparably scarred steps, hands on hips, wearing a look that might have pulverized granite. She drew down on Thom like God: "Now just where do you think you're running off to now?"

"I'm not exactly—friends. A couple of old buddies."

"And just where might these old buddies live?"

"Gainesville. Or Jacksonville. I'm not sure yet."

"Well, you best decide soon, honey, 'cause they lie in opposite directions."

"Just for a couple days."

Jade descended the steps and approached until she could be heard in a quiet voice. "You know there ain't no place safer than where you're at right now."

Thom shook his head but could only manage, "Just a few days is all."

"You got people here what depend on you."

"Dill has Gram."

"Dill, shit. Gram, double shit." Jade nodded toward the front pathway. "How about that girl up there?"

"Dyleane?" Thom's throat constricted. "She'll be okay," he whispered. He turned away, started walking.

"You gotta place right here," Jade called. "You hear what I'm saying? Folks who care about you—right here."

Thom raised a hand, kept walking.

A quarter mile past the gates and along the dirt road, prepared at anytime to jump into the roadside brush upon sight of an approaching vehicle, he turned into a development of ranchettes opposite the BRGC. None were larger than a few acres, some with horses, others a modest field of corn or vegetables. The sun was high and uncomfortably warm by the time Thom wound his way through this slice of exurbia on streets named Pony Express and Sundance and finally Red Barn, which intersected the main highway a little nearer Palatka than the straight gravel road.

He stood on the shoulder, thumb out, a good two hours before a woman stopped her pickup and announced she was only going as far as Palatka. While he waited, Thom had recalled his trek to Sawgrass. The truck drivers had been good about using their radios to line up another ride at the next truck stop before dropping him off. He'd only had to hitchhike from the side of the road twice. Both times, however, he spent hours waiting. One time in particular, a driver apparently even more lost than Thom let him out on a narrow two-lane blacktop in the middle of nowhere. Thom kept his thumb out until darkness fell. Finally surrendering to fatigue and frustration, he curled up against a tree, hoping for protection from the cold. A farmhouse sat across the highway. It was surrounded by cars and pickups, a few still in running condition. He debated whether to knock on its front door. The lights inside disappeared one at a time even as Thom deliberated and trembled from the chill. The debate ended with the first hint of dawn. Back at the blacktop, by then feeling unsteady from hypothermia on top of hunger and lack of sleep, a jacked-up northbound Camaro passed, turned around. Guys in high school jackets occupied the front and back seats. The car slowed as it approached. Thom stepped to the shoulder's edge, beyond which lay a muddy ditch. He picked up a baseball-sized rock. "I'll bash your windshield," he called out. A plastic cigarette lighter came flying at him from a window as the hotrod spun out in a cloud of dust, throwing up loose gravel from the shoulder. Thom held the rock cocked behind an ear until the car turned a screeching one-eighty and raced past him, this time for good.

Then, as now, Thom was running—away from a corpse and away from his father the murderer—towards what he did not know. Then, as now, he felt consumed by a gnawing loneliness, the fear of passersby, and anxiety from all he could not know. Then, as now, he hoped that life elsewhere would be better than what he was leaving behind, perhaps even safer, but this he could not know either—and experience suggested otherwise. Once again, Thom didn't know jack.

Thom told the woman wearing a flannel shirt and jeans that Palatka would be just fine. From there he could catch US 17 north and over to Sawgrass or continue up to Jacksonville if so inclined. From Jacksonville, I-95 traversed Georgia, South Carolina, and North Carolina. It reached all the way not merely to Maine but to Canada itself. Canada would mean that the last three years, his love affair with golf, his whatever it was with Dyleane, were over. That, given their irrelevance to anything sure to follow, they had never even existed.

Thom rested against the passenger door, thankful that the driver did not expect conversation. They listened to twangy old songs about drinking and tragic love affairs. She dropped Thom off on Highway 19 just before it intersected US 17, at a Kmart that anchored one end of a block-long strip mall. Each highway offered an escape route to, well, somewhere. A massive pile of flattened cardboard boxes arose around one corner.

A Chrysler minivan pulled up and interrupted Thom's silent deliberations about what the hell to do next. It listed to port, the tires were bald, and rust pocked the anything-but-factory sky-blue paintjob. The driver, a shirtless, bald twenty-something going on forty-something, leaned out and asked what Thom was up to. Another shirtless man with a black stocking cap rode shotgun. Thom could've counted their ribs, if not their tattoos so numerous that each one seemed to bleed into the next. He wondered who in his right mind would wear a stocking cap during Florida's midday heat. He noted the driver's bad teeth and bulging eyes rimmed in red.

The picture before him would counsel any rational person to reply, "It's none of your damn business." Then again, how many drivers were likely to slow for a sweaty little person carrying a golf club, let alone express interest in his plans? "Looking for a ride north toward Jacksonville," Thom said.

"Well, ain't that a coincidence right there? Ain't it, Scooter? That's just where we was going after we earn ourselves a little spending cash. Ain't that right, Scooter?" The half-naked man with a cap nodded. "You want in?"

"Just how do you intend to earn this money?" Thom said.

The driver graciously spit tobacco juice where the splatter didn't soil Thom. "Yard work." Scooter nodded again. "You'd be perfect for helping trim the short bushes." The van's occupants laughed briefly—it could have been worse.

Yard work was Thom's forte. He might have pondered the absence of a trailer packed with mowers, leaf blowers and rakes, the same flatbed trailer that nearly every other vehicle in Florida seemed to tow. He instead considered another two hours or more standing at the side of the road consumed by a sea of exhaust fumes on a desert of sweltering concrete, thumb extended, watching as drivers looked the other way to avoid eye contact and accelerated as they passed. "Let's go," Thom said.

With Thom occupying the second of three rows of seats, they crossed the expansive and mostly deserted parking lot to a quick shop. The driver parked next to the gas pumps. Each man pulled a long-sleeved t-shirt from a pocket in his oversized, sagging, baggie shorts. The driver donned his own stocking cap as if it were cold outside. Each rolled up the window on his side of the truck. The driver explained, "We're going in to buy some, uh, some work gloves. Ain't that right, Scooter? But here's the deal, see? This van ain't registered, and I can't afford another ticket right now. So here's whatcha do, hear? If you sees some cops pulling up hereabouts, you reach over and honk this horn loud like. *Real* loud. Understand?"

"How is that going to save you a registration ticket?"

"You let me worry about that," the driver said. "We're doing you a favor here."

"And how am I supposed to honk the horn louder than normal?"

"Just do what you're told, you punk ass somabitch," Scooter said through clenched, yellow teeth. Agitated didn't quite describe his jagged anxiety. They left the motor running.

"Yeah, of course, sure," Thom called. "I'll honk extra loud." He would bail as soon as these guys were in the store. Except that, on the way in, they rolled down the stocking caps so that only their eyes and mouths were visible through neat little holes. Then, as the driver reached the entrance, he pulled a pistol from those damn baggy shorts. The driver and Scooter exploded inside and screamed so loudly that Thom could hear every word from the van with the motor running and windows up. *Get down—I'll plug your sorry ass—Ain't afraid to kill—* He also heard the hysterical cries of the young woman behind the counter. As quickly as he could, Thom locked the sliding door on the passenger side, then each front door, and laid on the horn. He honked as loud as possible—*real* loud.

The robbers didn't seem to hear. Thom kept honking, pressing even harder as if to elicit more sound. When the robbers finally noticed Thom humping on the horn as though he were performing CPR they became the frightened ones. Scooter ran out first. The driver hesitated but soon followed, even as he kept the pistol trained on the clerk until he was clear of the glass doors. With his immediate mission accomplished, Thom jumped around each row of seats to cower in the very back of the van. The men screamed and pounded on the locked doors. The armed driver struck the closed driver-side window with fists, elbows and the butt of the pistol grip. It held. He fired a shot through the window, which only caused a small hole before exiting through the passenger-side window where Scooter was pounding. It was then that Thom realized he hadn't locked the rear hatchback. He was discouraged from sitting up to finish the job by more shots, ones that pinged against the back just above his head.

Thom was going to die. They were going to get him from either the front or the back. His corpse would be found lying in a pool of blood flowing from the bullet that pierced his heart, blood exceeding what his polo shirt could absorb. Gram would take his job. L.T. would take Dyleane. A few acquaintances might dance a few steps to the mourning song before resuming their routines the same afternoon. Father C. might request a moment of silence during Nineteenth Hole coupling rites. Most wouldn't notice; fewer would care. Thom wasn't afraid of the pain. But Mary, God and Jesus, he hated the thought of watching the blood flow out, the pool growing larger in inverse proportion to the life force inside. He did not want his last breath to gurgle through the blood in his throat. He did not want to hear strangers laugh. He did not want to feel no hope, the purest, most insurmountably elemental no hope imaginable, exactly as his dying mother had felt while her own heart slowed to a complete stop. He did not want the last face he saw to be that of his old man.

"Please, God, let me die before that happens. It's only a little favor."

Bullets sufficiently shattered the driver window's glass to allow the driver to knock out the rest. He fumbled for the inside lock, jumped in, unlocked the passenger door for Scooter, who pressed a bloody hand to the side of his head, crying. Thom peeked over the seats. The driver glared through the rearview mirror, gun still in hand. "You're a fucking dead fuck as soon as we get out of here!"

Hey—at least then Thom would have a good reason for not golfing. He started laughing. And crying. Uncontrollably. He laughed and cried so hard he soiled his shorts.

"Shut up!" Scooter screamed, jumping in. The driver threw it in gear. "Shut up goddamn it!"

That's when Thom heard the sirens, and that's when the van swerved, ran into the concrete base of a light standard and lurched to a stop, which pitched Thom into the back of the rear seats, and that's when Scooter and the driver took off on foot. The van, for some reason stuck in reverse, rolled backwards. As if the windshield were a theater screen, a movie of the world moving from right to left played until the steering wheel turned of its own volition, causing the film to rewind and play the world from left to right. Tom might have contemplated jumping over the banks of seats to assume control, despite never having driven anything other than carts and a green tractor in which he stood on the floorboards so he could reach the pedals, but he remained consumed by the effluence of emotion and captivated by the movie playing on the windshield. That's when the van backed into a parked car. This launched Thom against the rear hatchback, which sprung open and ejected him onto the hood of that parked car, which belonged to a county sheriff. He rolled off, his forehead making initial contact with the concrete. His brain vibrated back and forth within its boney enclosure with repeated *boings* not unlike when the Sisyphean Coyote, foiled again by the Roadrunner, crashes headfirst into the side of a mountain. Thom stood unsteadily and turned, still ferociously laughing and crying, only to discover a gun pointed right at the bridge of his crooked, broken nose. From that perspective, the barrel might as well have belonged to a cannon.

"Out of the van—out of the van—now! Hands where we can see them. And shut the hell up already."

The world slowed. It grew smaller and more distant. Thom became detached. He watched the scene unfold as a third party. The little person covered by the cannon continued his caterwauling —he would not or could not just shut the hell up, despite orders to do so.

"Show us your hands. Get out or we're going to shoot."

But he was out; he was standing. And his hands were right there, waving about like those of a trapeze walker desperately attempting to regain his balance. So the poor freak escaped a cranked-up armed robber and his cranked-up buddy just to be shot dead by some crazy-ass cop?

Then a familiar voice: "Hold on, Jackson; I know this boy. He ain't dangerous, most times anyway, just loony as hell." Third-party Thom appreciated Ricketts's unlikely reference to the Canadian dollar coin.

The cop named Jackson asked if he could at least "tase his midget ass."

"Lemmie call an ambulance," Ricketts responded. "If those

dickheads aren't here in three minutes, light him up."

"Seriously?" Jackson said with a grin.

"With the Taser, idiot—the Taser."

Understanding that the man with the gun might be even dumber than Ricketts unnerved third-party Thom and even his otherwise incoherent counterpart on the ground. The shot administered a couple of minutes following the paramedics' arrival put them both to sleep.

"Wow," levitating third-party Thom said.

"Not sure why they're trying so damn hard. No one cared when I was alive," an undefined, translucent figure suspended at third-party Thom's side said, gesturing at the bald and mustachioed hulk in the hospital bed closest to the windows.

"I'm, uh, him, Thom Loudon—with an *h*," third-party Thom said, gesturing at the short body in the hospital bed closest the door, the unconscious patient who at that moment was being ignored.

"I'm him, Mick Kazcynski, the man with a three-to-one consonant-to-vowel ratio," the translucent figure said with half a grin. The Mick on the bed was surrounded by a half dozen young adults in variously colored hospital scrubs. Amidst the observations, orders and requests issuing with urgent yet practiced calm, beeps and a single incessant one-note alarm, they were alternately pounding, shocking, palpating and injecting Mick with businesslike intensity.

"You don't look so good," Thom said. "What happened?"

"Routine shoulder surgery first thing tomorrow morning."

"That's not routine, eh?"

"I checked out early. Against medical advice, you might say."

"Can you feel all that, those needles and paddles?"

"Not much anymore. But they really sucked at first."

"What happened?"

"A handful of pills I found on some dark website, guaranteed to stop your heart. And I'll be damned but they worked just as advertised."

"Why?"

"It seemed like a good place. It was easy to convince a surgeon that my perfectly good shoulder needed surgery. There aren't any neighbors or kids around to find me like if I'd a done it in my apartment. And you do it outside somewhere, who knows who's going to run across your dead carcass, right? I'm not going to stick some poor schmuck with that."

Thom laughed.

"You know what I'm talking about then?" Mick said.

"Oh yeah," Thom said, sounding very much like some poor schmuck. "I know. But why, like, why why?"

"Most likely something to do with my second tour in Iraq. Seeing guys—their parts getting blown off—grenades, IEDs—legs, arms, faces. Guys you live with, right? The ones you shared dreams with before they become nightmares, before everything just goes numb. Mostly that last op—my second-to-last day on active. Standing next to a buddy who gets it right through his nose. I didn't see it coming. I hate imagining what he saw last. Or thought."

No hope was Thom's guess, not one single goddamn bit of hope.

"Then there's more shooting in the building next door, yelling, dark smoke, people running every which way. Chaos, right? I run inside, right into this big room. There's a kitchen, couches, beds, TV, just like back home. And guys, my guys, six of them, laying this way and that, mowed down, every one of them, just as bloody as you please.

"Then it's just quiet all of a sudden. The bad guys had already jacked out with their AK-47s. 'Come get me, you bastards!' I'm screaming because I sure as fuck don't want to be the only one there, all alone, still breathing. 'I'm right here, mofos—bring it.' I'm getting ready either to cry or radio in when a bomb goes off. Alls I remember is the start of a flash. So maybe it's my lucky day after all, right? My time too? But no—no such luck."

Loudly enough to be heard over the choreographed mayhem below, a stubby woman with messy black hair announced, "I'm calling it." She looked at her watch. "Nineteen-oh-seven."

Another woman, this one holding a clipboard just beyond the most frenetic activity, said, "Got it. Nineteen-oh-seven."

The figures below, who just a moment before were dancing the dance of trying to bring a person back to life, stopped, hands at their sides, music silent. They permitted themselves a look at the dead Mick, but only a brief look. Then they began the cleaning up dance. A tall, gangly man approached his bedside.

"Hey, I know that guy," Thom said.

Against the tide of exiting doctors and nurses, Father

Crittenden shuffled forward. Repeating words and gestures that appeared all *too* routine, the priest danced *his* dance with the lifeless flesh-covered bag.

"Bet that helps one whole helluva lot," Thom muttered, watching Father C.'s ministrations.

"Know what?" Mick said. "It kind of does. I ain't felt nothing for years now—nothing good anyways. Some docs blamed the concussion from the bomb that didn't kill me; others called it psychological trauma. Depression NOS: that was a favorite."

"NOS—what's that mean?"

"That they don't have an effing clue, right? They gave me lots of worthless pills and shit. But that, what your friend did? That felt okay. And I ain't even religious, right? Just sort of Unitarian."

The two, hovering aloft like forgotten birthday balloons, watched the priest conclude his solitary dance and then the nurses and techs who resumed theirs, not stopping until that side of the room had been cleaned up and sanitized and a replacement bed bearing a bare mattress rolled in.

"They're pretty good for a podunk joint like this," Mick said. "I've seen more than my share of hospitals, and they're pretty good. It feels good to watch people who know what they're doing. Hell, it feels good just to feel good about something."

"Now what?" Thom said.

"Fuck if I know. Ain't never been dead before, right? Dead emotionally, sure, but not this kind."

"Dead dead."

"Yeah, that: dead dead."

"Hey, maybe if you run into people, you know, wherever, maybe a lady—a lady who's a little person like me, maybe some blood on her chest—"

"Thom," Mick said.

"Or this other girl, tall, like you, with blood on her—"

"Dude, Thom. Your table's ready."

Levitating third-party Thom looked down at Thom in the bed. That one was stirring.

"Okay, but—"

"I got it, Thommy. Will do. Thanks for hanging out. It's much appreciated. And good luck—I mean that. Good luck."

Thom, now just the only Thom, awoke in a hospital room. Father Crittenden sat on the naked mattress—one covered with faded green vinyl impervious to bodily fluids, rather than fabric quilting. "Greetings, my good man. So happy that you, at least, have chosen to join the living. You slept right through the excitement."

Thom's first words got stuck between tongue and lips seemingly caulked with adhesive. Father C. pushed a button that raised the head of Thom's bed. He poured ice water into a cup set on Thom's adjustable table. A man in scrubs entered the room, nodded towards Thom and the priest with no discernible emotion, inspected the room, and left.

"So, which do you wish to hear about first: How you got here, what you have just slept through, or the tray of food intended for you that I had removed before it permanently damaged *my* appetite?" As Thom continued to cleanse his mouth of muck with cold water, the cleric continued, "As for the former, following your receipt at the scene of what must have been a strong sedative, even Deputies Ricketts and Jackson were able to deduce that you were not conspiring to commit armed robbery. This was confirmed by witnesses inside the store and also by the real crooks, whom they found upon following a trail of blood that started very near a bit of ear lying on the ground."

"Ear?" Thom managed.

"At the passenger side of where the van was initially parked. The police surmise that the driver, while attempting to shoot out his own window, inadvertently managed to excise a portion of the other man's ear. Your kidnappers were discovered seeking cover behind a pile of cardboard adjacent to a nearby Kmart. They, shall we say, lacked imagination. As for what you slept through, your former roommate decided to end his association with this interminable and tortuous human existence. Not a day over forty and his heart just stopped. He was here for was some routine surgery or another."

"His shoulder maybe?" Thom said, with no clue as to why this seemed more likely than not.

"Perhaps. All I know is that the staff tried everything humanly possible to keep him here with us. Whether they act from sense of duty or from petty jealousy, I know not. But, alas, all to no avail."

Thom said, "Is it common for a sixteen-year-old to end up around as many dead bodies as I have?"

"I shouldn't think so," the priest said. The vinyl mattress crinkled when he shifted his weight.

"You were here in time to do the whole last rites thing?"

"On the tray of food?"

Thom shook his head.

"Oh, you mean your roommate. In fact, I was. Although I have no idea if it is ever appreciated by the departing soul, or if, merely by virtue of familiar ritual, it comforts only those left behind—namely, me."

"It helped," Thom said. Father C. raised an eyebrow and felt to ensure proper placement of his hairpiece. "I mean, I bet it helped. I think it did. Okay—I'm not even sure why I'm saying that."

"If you say so, Thomas. Or not. In any event, that excitement was just a bonus. In actuality, I was called for you."

"Was *I* dying?"

"Oh no, dear boy, no. That would have spoiled the whole purpose of my visit. Which, for better or worse, you've also managed to accomplish simply by avoiding arrest."

"Wait. Which kind? Cardiac or—"

"Police arrest. It's all part of a somewhat illicit enterprise in which I participate. When a member of my flock is arrested, or, just as likely, a distant cousin thereof, the boys at the jail give me a call to see whether I'm interested in throwing bail. I sign over a note for ten grand or a hundred grand, whatever some inattentive magistrate orders. When my ward appears as scheduled for each court proceeding and the matter is concluded, I get everything back. Minus, of course, incidental expenses assessed for each hearing, trial, etc."

"Isn't that how it's supposed to work?"

"To a point. At the conclusion of my charge's ordeal, however, the official books, for example, may well reflect that a full-blown seven-day jury trial occurred when, in fact, the unfortunate miscreant pleaded guilty straightaway. And those same books also reflect the extensive court costs subtracted from the initial bond to cover the county's expenses."

"But then you get a whole lot less back."

"So one might expect. Amazingly enough, I usually end up receiving considerably more than I put down for bail. In short, it's a Ponzi scheme. Certain jail staff pocket a fair share of the surreptitious additional costs, and as long as they keep adding conspirators, those of us who got in on the ground floor keep receiving a generous premium on our initial charitable and selfless investments. I'm not sure what happens when *every* church, mosque, bail bondsman, and synagogue in the county is finally in on the deal and there's no one left to add. But I'm sure my good co-conspirators are fully prepared for any such eventuality. This, after all, is Florida. It's not like anyone has to reinvent the wheel. Meanwhile, without having to harangue my parishioners too awfully for their habitual tardiness on annual pledges, I am able to pay the church's bills on time, enjoy the occasional pilgrimage to the Holy Land via Broadway or Vegas, and, I dare say, everyone is better off."

"Why in God's name are you telling me all this?"

"A fair question, my good man, and one that deserves a fair answer. But first, allow me to inform the head nurse that, unlike your former roommate, you appear ready to exit these premises under your own power. The doctor said that as soon as you are conscious, he would trust me to get you safely home and to monitor you for signs of a veiled brain injury. Your clothes and golf club are right here—minus a certain soiled underthing that I am confident no one will miss." Father C. handed Thom a bundle along with a certain putter sporting a leather reverse-taper thick grip and a blade head with a flat-lie angle of nearly ninety degrees.

A grandmotherly aide wearing pink wheeled Thom out the main entrance to where Father C. stood smoking beside a dark blue Caddy SUV. Thom climbed up and in. The interior still hinted of new-car smell not yet wholly corrupted by endless clouds of tobacco smoke. Thom started when the priest announced in his booming voice, "Transparency, my son, transparency. The key to a civil, compassionate and ordered society is transparency."

Everyone announcing what they were thinking and doing struck Thom as a sure guarantee for confusion, anxiety and conflict. Father C.'s appeal for transparency made no sense and Thom said so. In his experience, ninety percent of what people said accomplished nothing to make life better.

On the way back to the Breeders' Roost Golf Club and for half an hour in the parking lot before Thom retired to the storage garage and Father C. to the Nineteenth Hole of iniquity, the priest explained the inestimable benefits of transparency. Starting with the almighty: "In all likelihood, a belief in the existence of a single god in heaven originated among parents drowning in anguish over the senseless death of an innocent and beloved child. The characteristics humans first ascribed to God, such as mercy, fair play and compassion, offered an affirmative ideal for their behavior as well. It only made sense that we should emulate the qualities of an all powerful and merciful being, particularly if doing so guaranteed admission to the eternal paradise."

"Oh, right, because we all know how well people treat each other."

"Precisely. And where do we turn when the carrot proves insufficient? Introduce the stick, of course, this time in the form of hell. Knowing that ignoring God's dictates invites eternal damnation added a sense of justice. And fear! This, by the way, was not lost upon those interested in imposing civil order. The founding fathers were not particularly religious, popular propaganda notwithstanding. And look what still ends up in the very first amendment: Freedom of Religion."

"Got it."

"A good fire-and-brimstone preacher has always done more to promote the security of conformity than one hundred soldiers or policemen—which, of course, is why the government relieves churches of many obligations, taxes for example."

"Money well spent."

"Exactly. However," Father C. continued, "there remain those pesky nonconformists who deny the existence of God altogether, along with the hordes of wait, see, and hope-for-the-best agnostics. Moreover, the people who doubt His concern over minor transgressions such as speeding in school zones or adulterous trysts are swelling into a veritable mutiny."

"Or bail-bond Ponzi schemes, eh?" Thom said.

"Correct again. These types believe that God, regardless of His general disposition, isn't about to involve Himself in day-to-day minutia when He's got a whole universe to worry about."

"What's all this have to do with transparency?" Thom's forehead and the brain behind it throbbed with every heartbeat. "And make it short and simple, okay?"

"But, dear boy, that's precisely where transparency comes in. If we have no secrets, if we can get away with nothing, if a harsh light illuminates dishonesty in *this* life and exposes the perpetrator to severe consequences in the here and now, what better means of motivating *good* behavior could possibly exist? I personally count global positioning devices and internet surveillance conducted by corporations and governments alike as allies in the battle against furtive and injurious behavior. I should warn you, Thomas, that I for one have never guaranteed the confidence of the confessional."

"Have you ever told anyone that you'll blab their secrets if the spirit moves you?"

"Well, no, not in so many words. Do you think I should?" Thom shrugged. The priest continued, "In any event, I firmly believe that this constructive behavior modification occurring in the name of transparency enjoys the full blessing of our Lord Jesus and His Father in glory forever." Father C. smiled. Then he winked.

"Such transparency doesn't seem to have put much of a crimp in your Ponzi scheme."

"As you yourself must acknowledge, I do not hide my involvement, and I maintain that the greater good is thereby served. For example, I have used the mere threat of transparency as it relates to certain after-hours activities at the Breeders' Roost to convince Jimmy Simms to keep Troy on at the pool as a 'condition of release.'" One mystery solved—albeit a minor one. "Moreover, Thomas, you must realize that any great idea, as is the case with artichokes and onions alike, has multiple layers. Each resolved query serves only to expose another layer of potential confusion, as well as opportunity." Opportunity? "Let us examine these deeper layers some other time, shall we? For now I must tend to other members of my flock. I'm also out of cigarettes. If that bump on your forehead causes you to lose consciousness, I'll be in the Nineteenth Hole."

Wondering just how bad the tray of hospital food could have been, Thom consumed a nut roll and Sprite from the machines. A few ibuprofens later, the pain in his head diminished to the point that sleep became plausible. Tucked in with the fan on high, he chose to ponder neither which members of the priest's flock might be in greatest need of intimate attention, nor the nature of comfort he would offer. Father C.'s theory of transparency, however, struck a chord that still resonated when Thom awoke, per usual, a few hours later. If a husband knew his extramarital affair could not be concealed from his wife, kids or neighbors, let alone the other woman's—or man's—spouse and kids, surely it would stop the would-be cheater dead in his tracks, eh? But what about those who simply would not care if they were found out? And those too lazy or complicit to condemn others for doing wrong? *Click*

What if deceitful behavior was just so ingrained—perhaps

genetic, somehow essential for survival—that people would misbehave no matter what, punitive consequences be damned? Might the certainty of being discovered in lies that were inevitable, lies unavoidable, normalize the behavior? Simply immunize the liars from potential ramifications? Would the inevitability of misbehavior eventually remove the stigma altogether? *Click*

And what about the sociopaths? L.T. immediately leapt to mind. They never do wrong, no matter how abhorrent their behavior and tortured their reasoning. And anyone who suggests the contrary is not merely incorrect, he or she is evil. Just ask them. *Click*

Then, a whole 'nother layer: What of Dyleane? Achieving transparency with her would require Thom to reveal his wants and desires, his guilt, jealousy and insecurities. An effort along these lines would demand the baring of his soul, which, upon further reflection, Thom thought might best be left buried under a pile of rotting leaves in a gutter during an autumn sleet storm in the Pointe. Or at least clothed in an Alabama sweatshirt. Even Thom was scared about what might lurk there. *Click*

Thom's head hurt again, but not bad enough to summon the priest. He welcomed sleep's return before having to peel back any further layers.

Chapter 16

Thom donned the Alabama sweatshirt upon rising—the closest thing he had to an invisibility cloak, a shield against transparency. He'd rinsed the garment in the pool since using it to wipe throw-up from his face. The chlorine left it a lighter shade of gray and, thankfully, smelling fresh as chemical bleach. He looked down at the putter next to his bed. Was it a weapon, a tool for justice—an image Thom relished—or a security blanket—an image he did not? He seized the club by the head and stowed it none too gently in the bag with its fellow clubs, displaying as much devil-may-care as he could muster. It mattered not that no one was watching.

He made sure the handful of golf carts the seniors were likely to demand were gassed up. In Thom's absence, of course, each had been left wherever the last golfer to drive it had seen fit, and none had been topped off with fuel. Thanks for pitching in, Dill, Gram. No actual harm done, however. Each week the seniors turned back their schedules another few minutes to account for the later rising sun. Thom toweled off the dew that had collected on the seat cushions, would-be hoar frost in colder climes, and ran the carts to an overhead gas drum. He returned them to their proper spots and climbed the wooden steps to the clubhouse to open up the pro shop. He took stock of his face reflected in a window: the swollen nose, black eye, abraded and bruised forehead—he looked like he'd gone fifteen with Ali.

Then he looked up and read the poor-quality 8½ x 11 photocopy taped to the door:

PT Position Available Immediately
Hospitality Experience [Clothed] Preferred
Apply: Jade, 19th Hole, Breeders' Roost GC
Salary DOE

"Damn," Thom said. He read it again. "*Damn.*"

"Double-damn damn. That sounds damn serious," Corey said with obvious delight.

"Don't sneak up on a person like that!" Thom said.

"I weren't sneaking up on no one. You just one jumpy mother. I am happy to see your pale, little ass back here so you can get me my jobs. I needs a down payment by this weekend."

"On what?"

"Some fancy new wheels. Nigga, they be ballin."

Thom looked at Corey. He raised an eyebrow and said, "Migga."

"Say what?"

Thom nodded towards the photocopy. "Your own mom won't hire you?"

"No way, uh-uh. I don't want no step-and-fetch-it job like that."

"She won't, will she."

"If you laugh, I'll kick your ass." Thom took Corey at his word. "'Sides, she already hired someone. She made me take some of them papers downtown and spread 'em around. You know who she ended up hiring?"

Thom knew, of course he knew, but that did nothing to stem the shock every bit as jolting as if he'd plugged his pecker into a live socket. But why? He knew that too. "Fate," he mumbled grimacing skyward. The sooner it happened, the better. At least they would meet on Thom's home turf where he was surrounded by friends. Well, two, anyway, counting Dyleane and Jade. He reminded himself: *Each shot is a new opportunity; focus where you want the ball to go, not on the hazards blocking the way.* But what kind of friend was Jade to be pulling this crap. Okay, maybe one friend. Thom grabbed his putter from inside. Weapon or security blanket— what's the difference?

He stood aside while the seniors arrived and readied themselves and kept an eye trained on the parking lot. He twirled the putter as though it were a baton, a trick he'd seen countless others perform effortlessly. He stopped after dropping the club a third time.

Thom tracked the approach of a country sheriff's SUV. Per usual, it parked in the handicapped stall nearest the clubhouse. While Thom could picture his old man being hauled away in such a vehicle, harder to imagine was him being chauffeured to a new job in one. Ricketts, it turned out, was alone.

"Just the boy I need to see," Ricketts said to Thom.

Thom would typically have seized this opportunity for a completely nonsensical reply, but today superfluous communication lay beyond his focus.

Thom picked Scooter and the armed driver from a half dozen other mug shots of men who didn't look a thing like either Scooter or the driver. He provided a statement, which primarily consisted of nodding as Ricketts read through what he'd already typed back at the station. Thom signed and dated the last page. "Thanks," Thom said.

"What for?" Ricketts said, as though offended by Thom's gratitude.

"I seem to recall you stopping your partner from shooting me."

"Do you have any idea the extra paperwork that's gotta be filled out when you shoot someone? Nah, didn't think so. And it's twice as worse if you actually kill 'em."

"Will I have to testify?"

"They'll be plenty of hearings and what not. Plenty. But I don't suspect so, since they already pled guilty." Ricketts turned towards the SUV and stopped. He slapped his back pockets, then his shirt pockets, before finding what he was looking for in a front pants pocket. "Here." Ricketts tossed Thom a golf ball.

Thom dropped the putter and caught the ball in both hands. Here it was, complete with the *MN*. "You don't need it any more?"

"We ain't been needin' it for a while now. The state boys done tested and photographed it every which-a-way possible. Turns out it's a goddamn golf ball, ain't it? Laboda told me to give it back, but I ain't had no cause to drive all the way out here."

"You were just out here—"

"That was a . . . a . . ." He squinted at his shoes as if looking for a clue. Despite the unlikelihood of finding one there, he looked up with a triumphant smile. "Yep, a 10-33—riot in progress."

Holding the ball like treasure, Thom retired to a chair between buildings. He rubbed it, smelled it, shook it in both hands like a pair of dice, smelled it some more. He just barely resisted caressing it in such a way that might rub off the initials. (The ink, thankfully, had thus far proven indelible.) So occupied was Thom that he missed the arrival of a white four-door Honda Civic until it slowed to pull around the clubhouse into the employee lot adjacent to the back pathway. It returned to sight just beyond the dumpster. The fancy wheels and wide rear tires failed to dispel the impression that this beater could barely climb what constituted a hill in Florida. L.T. drove. His old man showing up with L.T. made sense like stink on crap. Dyleane, who emerged from the passenger side, did not. Shit—was the damn golf ball the closest thing to a friend Thom still possessed? So much for home-field advantage.

Dyleane closed the door and called, "Thanks a million, L.T. I don't know what I'd do without you." L.T. raised a hand and said something. Dyleane laughed. The car turned around—there was plenty of room to turn around in the employee lot except on special days when it was used to accommodate overflow from the members' lot. It disappeared behind the clubhouse again and reemerged with a smiling L.T. at the wheel.

Thom slid the ball into a pocket and picked up the putter. The seniors were self-sufficient. He approached the snack shop after what should have been sufficient time for Dyleane to turn on the grill and fryer, and to start on sandwich prep. He pulled himself up to the tips of his toes on the outside window counter. Dyleane sat on the chair inside. Whatever she saw on the ceiling apparently demanded her full attention. Thom tapped on the door and then a little harder. He heard the deadbolt slide and click. The door opened just enough for Dyleane to peer out. She threw it open the rest of the way, half squatted, and hugged Thom so hard she trapped his arms at his sides.

"Thank God you're back. Are you okay?"

Thom assured her that he was fine as best he could into Dyleane's shoulder—and explained that the new bump on his forehead and headaches weren't any worse than the previous broken nose, loose tooth, or muscle contusions. "Does everyone know?" he asked.

"Jade heard, so everyone—you know."

"And how about you?" Thom had not intended the words to sound accusatory, but Dyleane, conscious of her somewhat auspicious arrival, caught the inference.

"Do not use that tone with me, Thomas Loudon. I was doing just fine until I heard you had run away—without even a word. Not one single *word*."

She'd made her point; what else could she say to make Thom feel worse?

"Then you commit armed robbery. Then you're in the hospital. I was doing a little better when it turned out you were going to be okay."

Thom felt worse.

"At least I was until I heard the shattering glass at three this morning and grabbed the ax we keep just inside the door to go see what happened."

Thom prepared to feel worse still.

"Someone had heaved a brick through my car window, which proceeded to smash the speedometer and a bunch of stuff on the dash! And then I remembered that *you*, Thomas Loudon, had left without saying a *word* and might not ever be coming back. Oh yeah, I was peachy—just downright peachy." She was a leaky peachy just then, as tears formed rivulets down her rosy cheeks.

"I'm sorry." He wasn't sorry that, hopefully, Dyleane had run out of recriminations to which Thom had no plausible response.

"Sorry? I'll say you're sorry. Not even saying goodbye—what were you thinking?"

"That, well—I guess I wasn't." So much for transparency. Thom tried to sound as gracious as possible when he added, "So, uh, L.T. like tried to help or something? I saw you two, in his car, this morning . . ."

"Yes, if you really want to know"—Thom wasn't sure he really wanted to know—"L.T. did help. Honest, Thom, I didn't know who else to call. He came over early, swept out some of the glass, and I followed in his car when he drove mine to his uncle's body shop. It's that one on the highway just west of town. L.T. said they could fix it for the cost of the parts if he did most of the work. And then there was the note."

"Huh? What note?"

"In the car." Thom asked what it said. At first Dyleane hesitated; then, "It said to stay the hell away from L.T. But I'd already called him and everything."

"That's crazy. Who the hell would write that, you know, besides me and all?"

"You didn't, right?"

"Of course not. That's even crazier."

"I know."

"But maybe you should pay attention to it. Leave L.T. the hell alone."

"Thom, I can't work, go to school, anything without a car."

L.T. was a psychopath. Yet here he was helping Dyleane in her time of need, while Thom had blown town and, upon his return, still couldn't do diddly. Except maybe, "You want to use a golf cart until your car's fixed?" People in Florida used golf carts all over town, not merely driving to the golf course to play golf, but also to buy groceries, pickup dry cleaning, drop kids off at school. "They're not exactly street legal. But if you steer clear of the main highway, no one's going to notice. And I can gas it up for free." Dill was the last person to notice a cart missing with a couple of gallons of gasoline.

"Thank you, Thomas. I appreciate the offer. But L.T. said he could run me around as long as it doesn't interfere with football."

"What a swell guy."

"By the way, I was right."

"About L.T. not being psycho? Like hell."

"Yes, about L.T. But more about Savannah May." Thom followed Dyleane's eyes as she surveyed her workspace. She hadn't performed any sandwich prep after all. She prised two frozen patties from a stack in the freezer and tossed them on the grill where they clattered like hockey pucks on ice.

"So how does this game work, Dy. Do I get a certain number of guesses?"

"Savannah May—I think I know how others besides Troy found out about her little secret. You know her yellow V-Dub?" Of course—while Thom hadn't known to whom it belonged before the murder and all the talk that followed, there was no denying that the bug had stood out among all the dark-colored SUVs and chrome-plated pickups. "And her vanity plate?" About that he knew nothing. "It was one of those 'Share the Road' ones, the bicycle plates, and her number was STR36."

"Stir thirty-six. Star tree sex. Hey, I could use a little help here."

"You're getting colder. What are the first letters in the words 'share the road?'"

"Okay, fine. STR: 'share the road.' What about thirty-six?"

"It must have had something to do with that law about cars giving bikers three feet when they pass. So three feet, thirty-six inches."

"Never heard of it."

"Maybe that was her point. I personally would want at least five or six, but none of that even matters."

"Then why the hell are we talking about it?"

"Because of the BJP Weekly."

This conversation was going downhill in much the same manner as had Thom's talk with Jamison, only this time Jack Daniels had nothing to do with it. Dyleane may have noted Thom's angst.

"It's the alternative weekly around here. Named after Benjamin J. Putnam, the illustrious Indian killer and slave murderer after whom this idyllic county is named."

"So the paper's name is, what, irony?"

"Very good, Thom. Anyway, I've seen a STR36 posting on the BJP's online personals board. You know, before the murder, but not since."

"Posting."

"Posting—online—personals—looking to talk or hookup—in the She-She/He-He section."

"They have one of those things around *here*?"

"Yes, Thom. Because we also have *those* kind of people around *here*."

"Don't suppose they've got a Wee-Wee section, do they?"

Dyleane surrendered a giggle before continuing. "Now then, what was that about LT?"

"That he's a psychopath?"

"No. LT, the football position."

They were back to the usual meal—except for the occasional BBQ chips instead of fries. "Left tackle. Why?"

"And why is it a left tackle is so important?"

"I know you know. Why are you asking me?"

"Come on."

"Fine. He protects the quarterback's blindside when he's back to pass."

"Exactly," Dyleane proclaimed. "It's got to be him." She disclosed her discovery of a person posting as "Blindside Protector" on the *He-He* section of the BJP website. "He's a total cruiser," she said.

This, Thom knew, was complete nonsense. Nobody hated gay people as much as L.T. hated gay people. It couldn't be him.

"Is it that hard to understand?" Dyleane said. "Oh heck—never mind—of course it is. Let's start with you."

"*Me?*"

"In your eyes, you are different."

"You're hurting my head."

"Listen. You're really angry about being different, aren't you? You have completely bought into other people's biases that they are normal, that you are different, and different is bad. Being normal, taller, is good. So you don't like yourself. After all, you're bad. You're basically mad at yourself for being different in a bad way."

"Okay, sure, I'm pissed about being different. Who wouldn't be? Would you want to go through life as a freak?"

"L.T. is gay," Dyleane continued. "At the very least, he's scared out of his mind that he is."

"No way."

"Please just listen for one minute. L.T. has been raised thinking that gay is terrible, it's a sin, it's gross, it's worse than being a geek or a nose picker. All his friends mock anyone the least bit suspect. The word 'gay' is the universal putdown. So now he's afraid he's terrible, sinful, gross. That others will find out and he will become an outcast, just the way he casts out others on the off chance that they're gay. And who does he blame? Himself—especially that part of himself that might end up ruining his life, the gay part. The part he would cut out with a knife if he could. And he hates others who might be gay because if he thinks of them kindly, they become real, gayness becomes real, his gayness becomes real. So he hides among all the other ignorant haters for comfort. And he hates more than anyone else just to make sure there's no confusion—in others and especially himself—about where he stands on the issue."

"So why's he cruising the He-Hes if he's still in denial, Doctor Almost-Had-Three-Psychology-Classes?"

"You never heard about Hank Tooley, did you?"

"Well, actually I did. From Jamison."

"L.T. affirms his heterosexuality by hurting others he labels as gay—whether or not it's true—by pretending they aren't even people because of the way they were born. In the personals and comment threads, he can get a taste of the forbidden fruit all while telling himself he's only there to check out how gross all the other posters are."

"I don't know."

"You ever notice how when preachers or politicians get caught doing something, it's almost always the something they preached against the loudest? What we hate the very most in others is what we're scared of inside ourselves."

"So you're saying this is how Brett knows about Savannah May," Thom said. "Because L.T. discovered it from reading the personals on PB&J. And why L.T. was creeped out when Savannah grabbed his ass at that party."

"And how Savannah may have known about L.T.?"

"Which is why L.T. could be the murderer. Goddamn it, how can't you see that? Or my dad. L.T. or my dad."

"Or Brett."

"Or Cheri or her mom, eh? You know, Dy, we're supposed to be narrowing suspects instead of expanding the list."

"That's twice you called me Dy."

"Well, yeah, that's like your name, right?" Had Thom stepped in it again?

"It's what my dad, my real dad, used to call me. My mom too, back when things were okay. I like it."

With large Sprite in hand and the putter tucked under an arm, Thom made for the strategic observation point between buildings via the back pathway. Another Wednesday, another doctor-lawyer day, and another day of no golf for Thom.

And there he was.

Right on the other side of the opening, just beyond the chairs. Orange shirt—nice collar—blue socks, joking with the caddies for whom Wednesdays offered the best chance of work outside of weekends.

Thom retreated around the corner to collect himself. His knees and hands trembled. He could still breathe, albeit with some difficulty. Could he at least be civil? Go shake his hand and say hi —before calling Trooper Laboda? Or should he just call and wait for the lawman's arrival? Then again, what if Laboda merely promised to send out Ricketts? Ricketts, who would take his own sweet time in responding—if he responded at all. Still, Thomas knew, he had to make the call.

Thom stepped around the corner and reached for the wallet in which he kept Laboda's card. Then he set down the coke and gripped the golf club in both hands. He continued walking. He did not tiptoe, but it is fair to say he made as little noise as possible as he approached the figure from behind, gaining speed with every step. He raised the putter in full backswing position, ready to strike. The caddies saw Thom first. His dad turned in response to the astonishment on their faces. The old man also betrayed shock, then terror—yes, beautiful, sublime terror—spreading across that weaselly face, crooked yellow teeth, a five-day stubble, squinty eyes oddly big and round, arms raised preparing to fend off the inevitable blow. That delicious look of no hope on the man's miserable mug. Thom could already hear the sound of the metal head against his father's skull, see the gaping, bloody crevice extending through fractured bone all the way to gray matter.

Thom initiated a vicious swing aimed at a boney protrusion between the old man's ear and forehead when, "*What the—*" Something or someone cleanly snatched the club from his grasp. The force of a swing so abruptly aborted turned him around. There stood Corey holding the club, twirling it like a baton between nimble fingers. "Damn, boss, you can't just kill him. How you gonna help me with that down payment if you in jail for murder?"

Before Thom could respond, he felt a punch to his kidney, his feet kicked so hard they went right out from under him, his elbow, shoulder and head striking the concrete. He reflexively jumped to his feet, knowing that staying down likely meant death by stomping.

"There's your murderer," the old man said. He began circling Thom slowly, slightly crouched, hands ready. "You saw it: he was going to murder me with my back turned—his own father. Bet he never told any of you how he murdered my poor wife. Stabbed his very own mother right through the heart, he did. It don't make no sense that we raised a boy so full of lies and cold-blooded treachery, but there he stands."

He jabbed—Thom bobbed away. Father and son circled as lions readying to battle for control of the pride: The father, talking; the son, in the moment, ignoring the obstacles, savoring the opportunity. Father jabbed again—son brushed it aside.

"Didn't tell you how he killed that girl down here, did he? Found him right there next to her, they did, her blood all over his shirt. Another poor, innocent thing stabbed right through the heart, eh, just like his dear mother. A saint she was, a living, breathing saint." He launched a roundhouse; Thom blocked it with a forearm and landed a jab in the bastard's face.

"There ya go," Corey called. "Can't win shit dancing all day."

Thom landed another jab, a punch in the belly, then an uppercut to the chin. His old man had been drinking and sleeping rough the past three years. Thom had been raising thousands of awkward thirty- and forty-pound golf bags high above his head, getting them down, and carrying them around. He had dragged one-hundred-foot lengths of hose attached to industrial-sized sprinkler heads through long grass and around trees. He'd eaten two squares a day and played enough golf to hone his focus when need be.

And Thom fed off the smell of fear. Something inside Thom released, finally letting loose years of damned up pressure. His fury turned fervent. He followed his father to the ground without missing a punch. He hit his old man again and again. His knuckles and knees were bloody by the time Corey dragged him off the unconscious figure. Corey insisted, perhaps not for the first time but the first that Thom heard, "You gonna kill that mother if he ain't dead already."

Thom found himself sitting on a familiar bed upstairs in number seven. He wiped his scrapes with a bar towel provided by Jade just before the ambulance arrived and departed, its blaring siren silent for only so long as it took to make sure the old man was still breathing and throw him in back. Jade conveyed Trooper Laboda's initial instructions to stay out of sight when Ricketts showed up, and that Laboda's investigation had focused upon a stranger, a tall stranger, who attacked the little man somewhere in the trees before the fight played out next to the storage garage. The caddies, all of whom had seen something else entirely, naturally dispersed when Ricketts arrived in the sheriff department's cruiser. When Thom spoke to Laboda, on Jade's phone, still sitting on the bed in number seven, Laboda disclosed that Ricketts had readily filled in the cracks of Laboda's so-called investigation with theories involving perverted sex and/or drugs. He also said that as soon as Thom's old man was fit to travel, which wouldn't be until discharge from the ICU and maybe a week of basic rehabilitative care, he'd be deported back to Canada where he was wanted as a material witness and person of interest in the murder of Thom's mother, along with suspicion of auto theft, fraud, burglary, and various other felonies committed during his three years on the lam. Finally, that Thom could trust Corey with his life if it ever came down to it.

"You're making stuff up to help me," Thom said. "Stuff that could get you in trouble. How come?"

"Part of protecting and serving, I guess. Look, Thom, I got a sense of what's going on from asking around. I know enough to understand why what happened today happened—why hauling you in for aggravated assault or attempted murder just wouldn't be right. You got some friends up there to the Breeders' Roost, you know that? And, Thom, you sitting down?"

"Yeah," Thom said as he rose to pace the creaky floorboards of the upstairs bedroom.

"Your father has an airtight alibi for the night of Savannah May Paulson's murder." Thom stopped. Laboda explained that requests for information about a dwarf wanted for questioning had produced a clear surveillance video showing the old man's face, along with fingerprints, from the robbery of a gas station in a village fifteen miles south of Charleston. He'd made off with all of forty-seven dollars in small bills and change. "It was midnight, right around the time of Savanna May's murder."

Thom's head swam.

"You okay?" Laboda said.

Thom handed the phone to Jade.

Dyleane delivered Thom's lunch to his sanctuary on the clubhouse's second floor. The two spoke briefly before Dyleane returned to the snack shop because it was doctor-lawyer day. Jade returned to the bar because it was doctor-lawyer day. As Thom returned to the storage garage via the Wife Escape, Dill lit into his ass because it was doctor-lawyer day and because Dill had forgotten (if, in fact, he had ever known) how to get all the foursomes off the first tee in order and on time. All Dill knew about the fight was the abbreviated version of the fabricated story that Corey had cooked up with Laboda.

Outside of a few sideways glances from the other caddies and a fist bump from Corey upon Corey's return from a second eighteen-hole gig (one where Corey handled two bags in return for nearly double the pay and tip), nothing more was said or done about the fight between father and son at the BRGC. The only evidence that a fight had even occurred, outside of a Canadian dwarf who spent forty-eight hours in intensive care and a few more scrapes and bruises on Thom's increasingly blemished exterior, were the splotches of the old man's blood on the cracked concrete. That evening, Jade handed Corey a bottle of chlorine bleach and made him clean up the stains before leaving. Florida: where people and their stories disappear as absolutely as gator prey dragged beneath the murky water.

So the old man didn't murder Savannah May. That at least reduced the list of potential suspects by one. On the other hand, it only reduced the potential suspects by one—without so much as casting a ray of new light on just who the hell did murder the girl everyone so admired.

Thom had just checked in the clubs and carts of the last doctor-lawyer foursome. If he hurried, he would have barely enough time to gas up the carts, park them in a neat line, and dash up to the snack shack before Dyleane turned off the grill. That's when Cheri and a girlfriend approached on the main pathway leading from the pool. To Thom's surprise, they not only stopped to request Cheri's and Mrs. Hogan's putters along with a few range balls with which to stage a putting contest, but also behaved somewhat civilly. Thom heard their giggles from the practice green as they wagered a six-pack of Corona—although nothing was said about how these eighteen year olds would arrange such a purchase. Cheri returned alone with both putters just as Thom was about to make his getaway between the buildings and up the back path.

"Who won?" he said.

Cheri still wore her pink bikini top decorated with what looked like black tadpoles and silky white gym shorts. "Me, of course." Thom struggled to focus his gaze on the putters she was tendering. Cheri said thanks; Thom managed you're welcome. Then, speaking at the same time, both said, "Can I ask a quick question?" They laughed and simultaneously responded, "Sure," and laughed some more.

Thom said, "Ladies first."

"Am I like you?"

"Well, for starters, we're built quite a bit differently." They giggled. But Thom knew what she was asking. She couldn't be much more than a hair over five foot. She was worried she was a dwarf. She needed someone to reassure her that she wasn't. Thom presumed that would rank up there with the worst of imaginable nightmares. Yet Cheri's face betrayed little more than genuine curiosity. She crossed her arms and Thom forced his eyes to gaze elsewhere. "And I don't do that," Thom added. They both looked at her anxiously tapping foot.

"That?" She laughed. "My dad says I got that from my mom."

"Fay?"

"God, no. Fay's been my"—air quotes—"'mom' for, like, a year and a half now. My real mom. Which was like three 'moms' ago."

"I'm sorry."

"You're sorry? How come? I'm not sure anyone ever said that before."

The mention of her *real* mom had made Thom sorry, if not for her then at least for himself. The day's emotional roller coaster had taken a toll.

Perhaps she noticed. "It's okay. I barely knew her. As much as Dad loves saying, 'The bitch just up and ran off,' more often than not he complains about how much he had to pay a lawyer to make sure he got custody, and then how bad he feels for his divorced pals stiffed with paying child support. 'What a racket,' he says. So basically he fought for custody to get out of paying support. That and how my mom was such a bitch and how much I take after her."

"That sucks, him saying crap like that." She appeared to agree. "So, no. The official definition for dwarfism is 147 centimeters or under. That's about four-ten for you Yanks. You've got a good couple of inches to spare."

"It's just that everyone calls me a midget—no offense or anything."

"For future reference, you are allowed to sock anyone who calls you that. Midget *is* an offensive term. People used to use it to describe certain kinds of dwarfs way back when. But now when people use it, they're doing it to hurt someone."

She said she was sorry. Thom said it was cool—she didn't know.

"Okay," she said all schoolgirly. "You next."

"First, you have to promise not to tell Brett."

"Sure," she said. "There's lots of things I don't tell him." She looked up to the sky and put her lips together, feigning innocence. Thom bit.

"Like what? This is important—I don't want to end up with another one of these." He pointed at his misshapen nose.

"Oh, I dunno. Like this?" She held Thom's head and kissed him. Really kissed him. Her tongue insisted that his come out to play, and both tongues fairly frolicked. She tasted of spearmint from the gum she chewed and skillfully kept out of the way. Thom touched her hips and just a little higher to feel bare skin. A moment later she backed away, just like that. Reflexively, Thom wiped away the excess moisture on his lips with the back of his hand.

"Oh God, was it that bad?" she asked, knowing damn good and well it wasn't.

Just then, a car door slammed shut. Thom turned to see Dyleane getting into L.T.'s beat up Civic just beyond the dumpster with a clear line of sight to where Thom and Cheri stood. L.T. turned the car around and slowly drove through the members' lot on the way to the gates. Was he looking at them through the tinted windows? Had Dyleane seen? Was she watching via mirrors or otherwise as they drove away? Thom's woody went flaccid more abruptly than a hurricane dissipates the calm.

"Uh-oh," Cheri said. "I hope you're not in trouble with, you know, her." She had passed from conspiratorial schoolgirl back to sincere.

"Her—me—I—but you—L.T.—Brett—" The kiss and then Dyleane's possible detection had discombobulated Thom.

"*Que sera, sera.* And hey, I think Dyleane is nice. I only pushed her on a dare. It was stupid. I've felt stupid ever since. I've been meaning to tell her, but . . . "

What the hell had they been talking about? About Cheri, right? About not telling Brett. And Cheri wasn't going to tell Brett— although L.T.'s sudden drive-by didn't exactly inspire confidence that their conversation would remain confidential. Thom nonetheless blundered forth. "So, uh, you didn't like help murder Savannah May, did you?"

"God, no. Why would you even say such a thing?"

"Well, I mean, you guys were kind of fighting and stuff right before that, right?"

"I got pissed major at Brett. He shoulda known better than to be flirtin' round with her. But we made up later that night. If you haven't noticed, I have a certain way."

"I noticed, I noticed. Did you guys, like, make up for very long? Maybe until midnight or, say, three?

"Well, ain't you the nosey one?"

"Look, I'm just trying to figure out—"

"I know. I get it. Folks around here are so quick to jump to conclusions about any damn thing and too ignorant to admit when they're wrong. They just as soon assume the worst no matter what. It's lots easier that way."

Thom said he knew. Cheri said she sure as hell did too.

"So who was it?" Thom said.

"Everyone says it was Troy, right?"

"Do you have any real reason to think it's him? I mean, did you see something, hear something?"

"Well, either him or you. And you definitely strike me as more a lover than a fighter."

"Whatever," Thom said, thinking about Dyleane. "Your mom —?"

"My stepmom," Cheri insisted. "What, did Fay murder Savannah?"

"I don't—I mean—you know how people gossip so much around here."

"Sure do."

"Well, could she have, I dunno, maybe gotten a little jealous too? Like maybe if she saw Savannah and Brett?"

"People say that, do they? Fay's jealous, all right. Jealous about me—about *me* and Brett. Can't no one have something she can't have. Brett swears there ain't never been anything between them. Stupid bitch is even jealous about me and Dad."

"You mean—"

"Oh Lord, no. Nothing sicko. She thinks he spends too much time"—more air quotes—"'doting' on me. Yeah, right. The guy who says how much I remind him of my bitch of a mom is *doting* on me? When Fay isn't getting all the attention she wants, she's gotta take it out on someone, and it's usually me."

"So you don't know where she was that night?"

"Like I said, me and Brett was making up and till pretty late if you have to know. I didn't check the time."

They stood silently. Thom thought about Savannah May, Cheri, Brett, Mrs. Hogan—Dyleane.

"Hey, this has been real and everything, but I've got to run," Cheri said. "Someone's gotta help our star quarterback get Ds and Cs so the teachers don't mind so much giving him Cs and Bs. Even FSU's got admission standards, so they say."

"You won't say anything about what we were talking about?"

"Not unless you say something about what you did to me."

"*I* did to *you?* But—oh, yeah, I get it. Message delivered."

She smiled kind of sad. "A girl's gotta protect herself."

"I'm sorry about how stupid your dad is, and whatever about your mom, Cheri. You're nice, a nice person."

"I'm sorry about the whole midget thing. Because you're nice too."

"Tell you what. You can be part of a secret club if you want. But, wait, how do I know you can keep a secret?"

Cheri laughed. "Nice try. You'll just have to trust me this time. And I do like secret clubs."

Thom believed her. She was dying to belong, wherever and however she could. "It's the Migga Club. So far you and I are the only members."

"Migga?"

"Long story. We can talk about it some other time. But I'll have to be extra very sure you'll keep it a secret."

"Keep trying." She gave Thom one of those handshake cheek pecks. Thom liked it all the same, as soon as he made sure no one was watching.

Later that night, after a candy bar and coke for dinner, Thom tossed a soggy Kleenex in the general direction of a trash can and slid the magazine back under the mattress, thankful at such times, if not others, for his windowless and locked-door solitude. He pondered the last few days—fights, guns, a hospital, whiskey, kisses. The excitement and the guilt. How he still couldn't play golf and no longer needed to live in fear of his father, yet how he still wanted the putter close by when he turned out the bedside lamp. How none of it added up. He was sore, exhausted, and overwhelmed by the artichokes and onions, to which they might as well add a few pounds of boiled gulf shrimp and hard-boiled eggs, all in desperate need of peeling.

Chapter 17

Not a mere knock but outright pounding on the metal door of the storage garage jolted Thom awake. He rolled over to check the clock radio—6:13. He glanced at the antiquated time clock on his way to the door—6:14. It wasn't like he'd slept in or anything. More pounding as he fumbled with the brass padlock. "Hold your horses."

"Hold your own damn horses."

"Brett?"

Another two resounding thumps just as the lock released and Thom freed it from the latch. Thom's first glance of the soft light of dawn beyond the door was narrowed by Brett, hands on hips, wearing baggy gym shorts, a sleeveless tee and black swooshy sandals. "I'm already running late for morning workout, so I talk, you listen."

"Of course. Honesty and transparency—that's the ticket." Thom couldn't say whether he was being serious or just ad-libbing in a surreal drama in which he was the only character without a script. Who was the star? When was intermission—had he missed it?

"I know about you and Cheri," Brett said.

"Huh? What about me and Cheri?" Thom said, not particularly looking forward to the answer.

"I said I knew. So just shut your mouth and listen."

"From who?" But Thom already knew it was either L.T. or Cheri. Or Dyleane? Knowing which at this point didn't make much difference. Besides, Brett's hands were balled into fists. "So, like, what's up?"

"What's up is that I'm damn sick and tired of you and all your questions. Just butt the hell out of the damn murder and out of our goddamn lives."

"You're not pissed about the kiss?" Why did Thom keep asking questions that could only get him in more trouble? Because he didn't have the script, that's why—he needed the damn script.

"Kiss? You and Cheri? See—that's why I changed my mind about those guys pounding you. You're a smartass, a smartass midget. I used to like that about you. *Used* to."

Thom at least thought better of saying, "I'm not kidding—we seriously sucked face." He also managed to resist yelling, "I'm not a damn midget." Although what finally did emerge likely wasn't any more helpful: "It couldn't have been Troy."

"Well, that's just too damn bad then, ain't it? Because you and your nigger bitch are the only ones who think that way."

Thom pushed Brett. "Her name is Dyleane." Thom's push forced Brett back all of a half step. Brett said, "Cut it out, Loudon. Look, I'm telling you just this once and you better hope I never have to tell you again: I had nothing to do with any of that shit with Savannah May. She was hot. That's why I asked her out."

"But she said no. Nobody tells you no."

"Close but no cigar. The deal is that I never take no for an answer—unless I choose to. That's the difference."

"So you did—"

"Stop. Just stop right there. Unlike your doofus buddy Troy, I had options. There was always Cheri. I wanted to know if she was a screamer like her stepmom."

"So you—"

"Screw whatever *I* did or didn't. What don't *you* get about *none of your fucking business*? And make sure your black whore understands that too, because she wouldn't want to learn it from me in person. That's a promise."

"Because you never take no for an answer."

"Not if I don't want to. You're finally catching on. I also know she's been hitting up L.T. with a million questions."

"I know, I know: He hates questions as much as you do."

"Got that right. But maybe he wants that bitch. For her own good—hell, for all of our good—she'd just better stay the hell away from him. My L.T. don't *never* take no for an answer."

"That's what the note said, the one they found in Dyleane's car."

Brett's expression turned to pain, and he looked skyward, as though trying to resist an urge. It didn't work. He pushed and Thom careened back into the white-painted cinderblock and crumpled to the ground. "That's what I mean, goddamn it. Neither one of you knows shit about what you're messing with. And trust me, you sure as hell don't want to find out. So quit nosing around —just *stop*—and keep your bitch away from my L.T., 'cause you got no idea how sorry y'all gonna be if you don't." Brett raised his arms, palms skyward, as if to say, "What's not to understand?" He turned and swaggered to his SUV, still the only car in the members' lot.

"She's not a bitch," Thom called from his seat on the ground. No response. "I'm not a midget," he added with more volume. Brett shook his head and kept walking.

Thom stood. His knees felt stable, breathing wasn't labored. Aside from a new lump, this time on the back of his head from his collision with the cinderblock wall, he felt oddly at ease. Never mind the lower body bruises evolving from blues to yellows, loose tooth, swollen nose, shiner, diminishing forehead knot, the raw knuckles and knees. The seniors began arriving soon after Brett's departure, and Thom stood aside to let them do their thing. He helped where he could as the normal assortment of couples, foursomes, and the occasional sixsome trickled in and then out.

It was as if he had a plan and, if not a way out, perhaps finally a script. Even as he watched Dyleane arrive in the jacked up white Civic, even as she and L.T. fist-bumped followed by some practiced routine of finger spreading and hand waggling. Even as Dyleane took the path around back of the clubhouse without so much of a glance in Thom's direction. Even as L.T. laughed and drove off. Even as Thom knew they must be communicating frequently enough to coordinate transportation between work, school, football workouts, and—was there an and? Even if there was, for the first time in weeks, Thom felt more like the club, not the ball.

Thom tapped the window opposite Dill's table in the Nineteenth Hole to signal his breakfast break. Because Dill took his sweet time draining whatever was in his coffee cup, Thom got stuck helping a foursome of women more intent upon catching up with their busy lives than making clear who needed new balls or a set of demo clubs, which bags went in which cart, or which of the members were paying for the guests, whomever they were. When glassy-eyed Dill finally did emerge, he again confronted Thom about the time he had been missing.

"You can count the number of days I've taken off the last three years on one hand—without using your thumb," Thom said.

"Don't give me that. You've been scarcer 'round here lately than a sober man on a dance floor. That just ain't gonna wash no more, sonny. I'm a gonna be making some serious changes around here any day now, you hear?"

"Like what?"

"That ain't for you to worry about."

"Dill, I'm assuming any such serious changes involve me. Are you planning to let me know before I'm supposed to change or afterwards?"

Dill's cheeks, tracked by spider veins, were turning purple. Such coloration constituted clear warning to back off before contributing to a Dill Pickle explosion, an eruption likely to include screams, thrown objects, cursing the likes of which was rarely heard even on the golf course during couples' day. Thom did back off, but only after asking what Dill could possibly know about dancing sober.

Thom peeked inside the snack shop's order window by pulling himself up on the sill and standing on tippy toes. A tray containing a cold burger and fries clattered down on his fingers. The ice in his Sprite had either melted or there hadn't been any to begin with. The extra garnish, a single dill pickle slice, could hardly be called extra.

"Dyleane, let me in. We need to talk."

Dyleane spoke in a voice oozing forced nonchalance. "We do? Whatever about? Is something wrong with your meal?"

"About me and Cheri, you and L.T., about Brett's little sunrise visit to the garage this morning." The script called for ruthless honesty. This once, Thom felt up to the role. "About you and me, Dyleane. You and me."

Still exuding frigid drifts of *I could give a shit*, Dyleane said, "What day is this again—Thursday?" She glanced at the prep station. "I suppose I can spare a moment." She unlocked the door, leaving it for Thom to open and enter. She took the chair, leaving Thom to stand. "Explain." He only briefly felt like a disruptive student summoned to the principal's office.

Thom started with an abbreviated version of Father C.'s ode to transparency, then the surprise, pleasure, and guilt of his encounter with Cheri. He shared all the details of the confrontation with Brett, particularly emphasizing the warnings about her and L.T.

"So *you're* jealous?" Dyleane said. "That's rich."

"I didn't say that." Oh, transparency. "Maybe I am—and jealous jealous to boot. But mostly it was just damn creepy how he kept saying '*my* L.T.'"

Dyleane sat and Thom stood barely a foot apart. He looked at her, she at him. "And…" Dyleane said.

"And?" Thom said.

"You and me, remember?"

Thom took Dyleane's hand, pulled her close, and *he* kissed *her*. It took a while—it felt a very long while—before his effort was rewarded with anything resembling warmth or passion. Dyleane finally scooched to the edge of the chair, freed her hand to draw Thom close—very close.

"Jesus H. Christopher Columbus," a voice exclaimed through the order window. "Jeanie—come here quick. This you gotta see."

Thom jumped and turned to see old man Colburn at the order window, his wife Jeanie just behind him, both craning their necks for a clearer view and each grinning wider than the automatic door on a three-wide garage. Thom turned only his head out of fear what a profile of his torso might reveal. "Oh, hi there, Mr. Colburn, Mrs. Colburn."

"Don't stop on our account, Thom," Mr. Colburn said. "This beats the hell out of anything I've seen since Jeanie here caught me on pay-for-view and installed those goddamn parent controls."

"I was just leaving," Thom said.

"We can always swing by later, can't we Jeanie?"

Despite the unexpected audience, Thom couldn't wipe the smile from his mug. He slid almost backwards to the window and grabbed the breakfast tray from the ledge. He was halfway through the door before turning back to Dyleane. "Transparency," he mouthed.

Inexplicably, if there was hope in Dyleane's expression, it was subtle at best.

So it was that Thom approached the snack shop that late afternoon feeling both excitement and trepidation. No sooner had he passed the live oak and rounded the corner than the order window slammed shut and the door swung open. Thom's still-warm, well-garnished dinner and sufficiently-iced Sprite sat on the prep table, and Dyleane in the chair. Dyleane's face dispelled Thom's initial thought that the improved cuisine promised more of what they'd shared that morning before the old codgers interrupted.

"Look, if you're worried about the Colburns, don't. They haven't talked to Dill in years. They aren't going to say anything."

"Well, that's at least one thing off my mind. But there's still another."

Thom waited. What could possibly have smothered Dyleane in such gloom?

"Transparency, right?" she said.

"Just tell me what the hell's going on already."

"So, L.T. kind of asked me out for tomorrow night, and I kind of said yes."

Thom had to smile. "Kind of kind of?" Dyleane nodded. "After the game?"

"They don't play until Saturday afternoon this week. I guess it's something they do once each year to make it seem like a big college game or something. The starters' names are announced when they come onto the field and all that stuff like it's a big deal or something. He asked me after I saw you and Cheri."

"Where are you going?"

"Take a deep breath. We're supposed to go to Cheri's. Her stepmom is still throwing one of those Friday night parties, *plus* a BBQ for whole families after the game Saturday.

"Well, *that's* probably the most horrible idea I've kind of ever heard. You can't do that."

"I knew you weren't going to like it. Please believe me—he doesn't mean anything like you do. Nothing."

"Thanks, Dyleane. But it's not that. Well, maybe a little. It's still just a crazy idea. All that 'my L.T.' crap."

"Thom, that's what the note in my car said: Stay away from my L.T."

"Dyleane!"

"I know, I know. It's really weird, isn't it?" Dyleane dropped her head into her hands.

"That's definitely not coming from L.T.'s jealous girlfriend."

"You think his jealous boyfriend?"

"Maybe. Anyway, you've got to tell him no."

"I can't," she said looking up.

"Sure you can. Say that *we're* doing something that night," Thom said boldly. "Or make up some other excuse," he said less so. "But you have to say no. End of story."

"Of course I could say no. But I—I don't want to."

"You what? I thought you said—"

"I did—and I do. Okay, transparency, right?"

Thom rolled his eyes. "I'm not so sure anymore about all this transparency stuff."

"There's a reason I was on the BJP's personals."

"There's a reason you were on the personals," Thom said, testing out the words he'd just heard. "Okay."

"I like girls."

"Girls? Well, whooptie-doo. Me too. Help me out here. What about me, Dyleane? Us? L.T. and now girls?"

"It's really a lot less confusing that it seems."

"Waiting."

"I like boys *and* girls. Maybe it's more that I like boys *or* girls. I really love having one very special person in my life. And that's you, Thom with an h. Just for the record, I wanted that, you and me, way before you finally figured it out. But before that, I might have been happy with a girlfriend or a boyfriend. As long as the person is special and earns my trust and—promise me you won't get scared, okay?—and as long as I love that person, really feel love. Hey, I think I just said I love you."

Thom heard this as well. It threw him off track, but only momentarily. "There's something wrong with him. Maybe he and Brett—you know the whole 'my L.T.' thing—maybe Brett gets jealous when L.T.'s with a girl. I don't know what it is. It's just scary. And I—" Thom shifted his stance and extended his arms as might a sailor on an open deck preparing for rough seas. "—I think I love you. I mean, I sure as hell never felt like this about anyone else. Not even close."

"What about Moe Whatever-his-name-is?"

"Damn it, Dyleane."

"I think I can help him, I really do. He's killing himself. I went through that too, back in Marietta. I know what it's like being a freak. I know I can help him."

"You're not a freak."

"Now who's talking?" She took Thom's hand. "I'm different from everyone else. I'm something others make fun of, don't even *want* to understand. But what I figured out, what you and L.T. are still working on, is that it's their problem, not mine. I'd be a fool to let them decide how I see myself. I'm a damn good person, and that's a fact ain't no one gonna change. If someone can't accept that about me, then they're the freak, not me. Is any of that getting through that thick skull of yours, Thomas Loudon?"

Thom heard the words, perhaps even some of their meaning. Yet all Thom really understood just then was not only was he being challenged about long-held perceptions but he was also being badly outflanked.

"What it comes down to is that I'm done letting other people say who I am. I'm done judging myself by *their* stupid standards. I can be who I want according to my terms, not theirs."

"Yeah, yeah, yeah."

"I know I can help L.T. start figuring all that stuff out. Lord only knows, maybe even you someday. Maybe I can get away early. I'll try really hard."

Dyleane reached for Thom. Thom hesitated but a second before acceding. What began as an emotional embrace gradually became less soulful and more electric.

"Oh shit," Dyleane said.

Thom had just been working up to exploring some unknown territory. "What? Did I—you know."

"Oh yeah, I think I know 'you know' perfectly well, Mr. *H*. And you didn't notice me throwing up any roadblocks now, did you? It's just that L.T. is probably waiting. I gotta run."

It peeved Thom that once they were outside and had shared a quick mouthful, Dyleane did run, and he couldn't keep up. The image of Dyleane and him making out in front of L.T. provided no small measure of pleasure. Perhaps that's why Dyleane ran ahead. But if she was being truthful about her feelings for Thom, why should she care what L.T. thought? Why should Thom care? Oh crap, Thom Loudon, give it a rest already. He switched focus to where he and Dyleane had just ventured together and where they might still go tomorrow night if she could get away early as she'd promised to try.

The night sounds had dialed back only slightly with the cooler temperatures, shorter days, and lighter air at dusk. Then there was Dyleane's scent, one so pure, so invigorating. Even sullied by the remnants of grease and onion that, sooner or later, permeated everything in and around the snack shack, Dyleane put Thom right on edge and left him wanting more, needing more. Besides, Thom loved greasy food and extra onion.

For a brief moment, Thom regretted the early sunset that foreclosed a few quick holes of golf. Just then, immersed in the perfume of early evening, garnished with the recent memory of Dyleane's, he felt nothing of the all too familiar panic that had attended any thought of golfing over the three weeks since his unfortunate foray into the depths of that steep-sided number two bunker.

Chapter 18

More members than usual on a sunny Friday morning, including a few mixed foursomes, were starting their weekend off early with a round of golf. When Thom finally broke away to grab breakfast, Dyleane opened the door just as he passed under the live oak and rounded the corner. Dyleane cooked; Thom ate. Their conversation journeyed from the weather—increasing clouds with storms likely later on—to Thom's misgivings about Dyleane meeting L.T. that night, no matter her laudable intentions and assurances, to the wordless tension of unfulfilled desire.

Thom said, "I called Laboda about Brett basically repeating what was in the note."

Dyleane said, "I know. When I called Ricketts, he said you were still interfering in the investigation by calling Laboda. And, of course, that I was still interfering in the investigation by calling him."

They agreed that Ricketts's mere existence generally constituted interference.

They chanced a passionate kiss in a corner that would deprive anyone at the window of a clear sightline absent half climbing in.

The way Dyleane said, "Not now" as Thom slipped a hand under her shirt seemed to suggest that not now did not mean not ever.

Shortly after six, with the window firmly shut and locked until the next morning, Dyleane's enthusiastic participation in exploration confirmed Thom's optimism—until she again uttered those horrible words, "Oh shit." This time, Dyleane sprinted off with an even more emphatic promise to return to the BRGC as early as she could gracefully manage despite her plans with L.T.

Thom felt admiration, anticipation, frustration, awe, love, and lust all wrapped together like a sweet candy-coated sour gumball. His mouth even watered.

Slowly, almost nonchalantly, Thom strolled toward the elevated tenth tee box ostensibly to gain a better view of the sky in hopes of gaining a clearer read on the weather. No wind. The low clouds were ripe, juicy. He stopped at the edge of the tee box as the beating in his chest became uncomfortable, but before it became painful.

Back inside the storage garage, Thom retrieved the putter from beside the mattress and returned it to the bag. With a smile, he straightened the sheets and covers, the ones he'd changed just the day before from the linens stacked high in the bar's forsaken kitchen, linens typically reserved for the beds on the second floor. Given that his bed, over the last three years, had rarely been "made," it then appeared to Thom almost worthy of, say, a visitor. Thom, however, understood that others might not see it that way. He still slept on an old stuffed mattress no one else wanted, in the back corner of a storage garage on a concrete floor. Yet, in the vernacular of the Pointe, when something was as good as it was destined to be, little was left to say but, "Whataya gonna do?"

He retrieved the recently stowed putter from the bag, grabbed a couple of range balls, and strolled out to the rusty blue cart with three small wheels and a tiller attached to the one in front. The air remained still, almost expectant. He pulled the cord that connected the electric vehicle to a 220-volt outlet. Thom set the balls among random tees left in a small plastic tray beside the tiller and rested the putter against the cushioned passenger seat. The cart hadn't been driven since Thom's disastrous attempt to play the back nine one day after finding Savannah May Paulson's body. He walked back inside the garage and emerged a moment later with a towel. With the benefit of a light drizzle whose primary effect was to hasten the dusk, Thom wiped the dirt from the padded seats and fixtures within. The towel had accumulated enough grime from the interior that it merely spread the grit like finger paint when Thom attempted to wipe down the blue-metal exterior.

Thom rested in the cart, enjoying the solitude afforded by the threatening weather. He turned on the power with a round knob located between the seats, observed that the cart still held a charge, and drove it while standing the short distance to the practice green. There, he sat some more. He wasn't waiting, merely sitting, sitting where, just then, it seemed right to sit. He held the Moe Norman ball in one hand and the putter's worn leather grip in the other. He experienced—no, relished—a shortness of breath and lightheadedness that stemmed from something other than terror.

The light drizzle became a steady drizzle that created halos around the tall fluorescent lights in the parking lots. This pleased Thom. Just then, practically everything pleased Thom. After fifteen minutes of sitting and feeling, by then happily drenched, Thom drove up to the pool along the unlit back pathway as if this was his routine every evening. He showered in the hottest water he could tolerate. Holding the ball signed by his hero and clad only in a clean towel borrowed from the locker-room stack maintained for the members' convenience, he wheeled back to the garage. He plugged the blue cart back in with an affectionate pat. Carrying the club, he reentered the storage garage and extinguished the banks of overhead fluorescent lights, which left his bedside lamp as the only source of illumination. He toweled off the putter and returned it to the bag, donned a clean shirt and shorts, and slipped the Moe Norman ball into a front pocket. While not nearly as demanding as Brett's pounding that morning had been, Thom still jumped a half-foot when an assertive knock on the metal door broke his reverie. Another knock and the unlocked door pushed open. Might it be . . .

"Hey, quarter-pint, you in there?" Corey said.

"Over here," Thom said from an aisle of stored and stacked clubs. "What the hell do you need? And what's with the vest and long pants?"

"Don't you worry your really little head about them," Corey said.

"You're working for your mom in the Nineteenth Hole, aren't you?" Against his better judgment, Thom laughed. A little. He couldn't help himself. With the door open, he could hear the calm, steady rain creating puddles for succeeding drops to splash in.

"Well, since you can't find work for a bee in a hive and damn near killed the first man she hired, someone gotta do the job. Look, itsy person, I brought you out a visitor. Figured I better come in first—save both of you the shock of seeing whatever it is you do in here all by your lonesome with your itsy parts."

"What the fuck are you talking about?" Thom wondered if Corey *might* know what Thom did in there all by his lonesome with his parts—which were not itsy by any reasonable measure, thank you very much—once the door was shut and locked for the day. And it *was* embarrassing.

Cheri poked her head in behind Corey. "Hey."

"Hey," Thom said, more than a little surprised.

"Here he is, girl, and thank God he's at least presentable, you know, as presentable as he gets. I'd tell him not to do nothing I wouldn't do, but then he ain't never even gonna do what Ima *not* gonna do. Know what I mean?"

Cheri nodded as if she did and smiled uncertainly, suggesting she didn't.

"Hey, Corey," Thom said, "Nice apron."

"Ima kick your ass one of these days just for the sheer joy of it. Maybe tonight."

As the sound of Corey's dress shoes scratching against wet pavement receded, Cheri said, "He was kidding, right?"

"About what?"

"Kicking your ass tonight?"

Thom sighed with relief. "We're friends. He was kidding. I

think."

Cheri stepped in. "This is where you live—your house?"

"I guess you could say that."

She closed the door. "Give me a tour?"

"Sure. Okay." The aisles were cloaked in shadow. "On your left, ladies and gents, you will notice clubs for members D through H with I, J, K, and some of L on your right. And away back there in the corner you will see . . . "

Thom hesitated, placed hands on hips, and suspended his role as guide. What would another person see if, say, that other person was looking at this—his house—for the first time? Stuffed twin mattress on the floor; sheets purloined from a whorehouse; a crate on one side—his bedside table—on which sat a gooseneck reading lamp, tissues, keys, sunglasses and the digital clock with a radio that only played static; harsh shadows cast by the lamp. In the narrow space between the mattress and wall on the other side, a stack of books that Dyleane had checked out from the high school library; the wet clothes from earlier strewn next to the books; and his precious few changes of clean clothes, not exactly folded and neatly arranged, next to them.

This was his living room, study, bedroom and den. This was where he ate, read, slept, couldn't sleep, cried, hid, slapped the snake. No dresser, closet, adjoining bath, TV, or mirrors. (No magazines sticking out from under the mattress, thank goodness.) No one to make the bed nor even to yell at him for not making his bed. Certainly no one to tuck him in, to say goodnight, to chastise him for reading too late. Ah hell, Thommy Boy, get over it. This wasn't home and wasn't ever gonna be. It wasn't even a house, let alone his house. It was where he took shelter, the spot he used while everyone used him.

Thunder rumbled immodestly in the distance.

"That's sweet, anyway." Thom said.

"Huh?"

"A good hard rain and I won't have to irrigate anytime soon. Autumn means more golfers and less humidity. The greens dry out like nobody's business."

"I hate lightning."

"Yeah?"

"When I was like six or seven, there was this huge storm. I thought I heard barking, so I looked out my bedroom window upstairs. Sure enough, there was Peggy—she was this dumb little pug we'd raised from a puppy. Dad says we got her a few weeks after I was born. He called her Piggy, which was not entirely unfair. She drooled and had the worst gas. But she was still my, you know, like my best friend. How pathetic is that?"

"Not pathetic at all," Thom said, clueless as to where this was leading.

"She was just sitting there, down by the lake. The water gets so green between the whitecaps during storms like that. God knows what she was waiting for. What any of us is ever waiting for. Then there's this lightning bolt. It like ricochets off a tree and hits Peggy. I swear to God, she's there one second, and when I open my eyes after the hugest thunder ever, she's gone. Absolutely nowhere in sight. I run down to dad's room, probably screaming my fool head off, and pound on the door. He's with one of his wives or girlfriends, I forget which, and tells me to go back to bed; he'll check on the damn mutt later. She musta just got scared off a little ways, he says, she'll come back. But she never did come back. When I looked the next day? Sure enough, you could see where the lightning hit a branch and on the ground. But she never did."

"It sucks to lose someone you love, just like all of a sudden."

Cheri didn't answer. She'd turned her face away from Thom. Thom touched a shoulder. She looked back, her eyes wet. She reached out and Thom held her. Coughs and hiccups became sobs, sobs gradually gave way to sniffles, and then a self-conscious, half-choked giggle. Thom was not proud of his sudden state of arousal that was wholly inconsistent with the role of caring friend. They drew apart. Thom pulled a couple of tissues from the box on the crate.

Cheri blew her nose like a trumpet. They laughed. The time clock ticked. "What's that?" she said.

"This damn old clock on the front bench. It keeps me awake at night."

"You can't sleep either?"

"I've always kind of had insomnia. But it seems like it just keeps getting worse."

"Like since Savannah May?"

"No. Well, maybe."

"You can't golf either."

"It's this damn shoulder." He moved one back and forth, faked a wince, and wondered again if it was the one he'd earlier claimed was injured.

"Come on, Thom. That's not it. I heard you're good. Like, really good." Cheri sat on the foot of the mattress. She wore a sleeveless sky-blue blouse, white shorts, and rainbow flip-flops. She patted a spot next to her. "Tell me what's going on?"

"Well," Thom said. He settled just around the corner from Cheri. He told about his mother, her murder, how it reminded him of finding Savannah May, how he'd been getting panic attacks at the mere thought of golfing. Cheri reclined back on her elbows while Thom hugged his knees. About hope and no hope, about how maybe he might actually have been feeling more hope of late.

"You really do know about losing someone you love."

Thom smiled. "I'm not really sure what I know anymore."

"I'm all over that no hope shit," Cheri said.

"You?" Feigning indifference, Thom continued, "Prettiest girl in that school, head cheerleader." This was flirting, wasn't it?

"Thanks, but not even. There are so many beautiful girls there. Tall, slender, graceful. Like Dyleane. You really like her, don't you?"

So much for flirting—which, in and of itself, was not necessarily an exercise in transparency. "I guess you could say that. Actually, yeah, I really do. But you're going to FSU, right? A plan and a way out—that sounds like hope to me."

"Just a way out of Putnam County is more like it. But I'm still me on the inside. Tallahassee ain't gonna change that. Jealous, needy, doing whatever I have to so people like me—I hate being that way. You're not like that."

"Some things you can't change, some you can. As for what you can't, maybe it just doesn't make a ton of sense worrying about them." Did Thom believe this? Had Dyleane's message sunk in to where it at least qualified as aspirational? Or was he simply regurgitating Dyleane's talking points?

"Sometimes I have fun making sure I fit in, like when I pushed Dyleane. You know, at the time I did it. Then I hate it even more for enjoying doing something that's wrong. Brett calls me a high maintenance cunt. My dad and Fay are always saying that same kind of stuff."

"To you? Seriously? Screw those asswipes."

Cheri giggled. She rolled onto her side and touched Thom. She rubbed his back. Thom's shock gave way to hyperawareness of her hand caressing the muscles of his shoulders, massaging his neck. Fingernails down one side of his spine and up the other—he arched like a cat against her touch, quivered with goose bumps.

"You're nice, Thom. Really nice. How nice ought to be. Come here."

"God, it's stuffy. Sounds like the rain is really picking up out there."

"I could tell you liked our first kiss. You know what gave you away, don't you? I liked that too."

The door was unlocked. Dyleane might enter at any moment.

"You did like it, didn't you?" Cheri persisted. "You like me?" Her dangly silver earrings shimmered as she tilted her head.

"Oh Lord, Cheri, if you only knew."

"Come here then."

Hey God. What's up with all this happening all at once? Nothing but rocks and coal in my stocking forever, and now this? You're either trying to make up for all that other crap you've dished my way or this is one of those damn tests you love so much. Okay, I choose we split the baby—me, I'm the baby. Dyleane gets part; Cheri gets part. What could it hurt, eh?

Thom considered how to turn and lie next to Cheri without looking like a klutz. Just as he made to lower onto an elbow, she sat back up.

Oh, so first you giveth and now you taketh away? Cheap trick, old man—well played, but cheap.

"It is her, isn't it? Dyleane. You don't like me either."

"Cheri, I'm telling you—you have no idea. I wasn't kidding when I said you were the prettiest. I dreamed about you the other night—not kidding. And it was, like, a pretty nice dream. And *you* are nice—the kind of nice people ought to be. I wasn't sure what to think at first, I admit that. I didn't like the part about pushing Dyleane. But now I am sure. It's when you just talk I can tell."

Cheri's pout was rather fetching as well.

Thom continued, "But, well, yeah, I do like Dyleane. A lot. She's been helping me figure out a ton of stuff like the no hope crap I've been fighting since forever, dealing with all those things I can't change about myself. As much as I want to—and seriously, you have no idea how much I want to—I guess I can't. I gotta stay loyal."

"Loyal? What about her and L.T.?" The pout turned defiant. "They were at my house, off in the trees alone talking like forever.

And do you think that's all they were doing? Talking?"

Thom thought. "Yeah. I guess I do." He became more confident when Cheri did not contradict him, despite the time he'd offered in which to do so. "Yes, they were just talking. And why are you here, anyway? Shouldn't you be at your own party?"

"Fay's party you mean. I told Brett this wouldn't work, not in a million years."

"You what? Told Brett?" Who the hell had changed scripts again?

"I told him you were different, that you liked Dyleane. But he made me. If I don't do what he says, he'll tell everyone about him and Fay."

"What?"

"I'd just die. And if I didn't, my dad would kill me. He'd blame it on me, I know he would."

A thunder clap, closer, louder. Thom touched the bulge that was the Moe Norman ball. He chose focus over panic—at least for the time being. He stood, helped Cheri up, and held her shoulders firmly, not roughly. The look in her eyes—if any hope dwelled there, it didn't show. "Cheri, it's okay. Everything's okay. Just tell me what the hell you're talking about."

"Don't hurt me."

"No one is going to hurt you." Thom would have slapped her silly if he'd thought it would help. "Just tell me what's going on."

"Brett and L.T. were so pissed about you calling the cops. Then L.T. and Dyleane were talking like forever tonight at my house. He got really, really weird like he does sometimes. Brett said L.T.'s going to bring her here. They want you to stay out of the way. He promised not to hurt you or me if I could keep you busy for a couple of hours. He made me. Honest, he made me."

Panic drew even with focus and was threatening to take the lead.

"She'll be okay. Brett promised she'd be okay."

"Brett's a lying sack of shit."

"But he promised."

Thom raced to the door deciding whether to grab Corey first for backup or just take the blue cart and find Dyleane. He threw open the door, raced out, and took a blow to his head just above the ear. The very earth vibrated as he went down, or perhaps it was simply brain bouncing against boney skull, just as it had two days earlier in Palatka. Rain, steady. Big storm, gathering. Lightning and thunder, growing more intense. Brett and Cheri—she, reaching for him; he, pushing her away. Thom struggled to gather his legs and senses, not necessarily in that order.

"Fucking cunt couldn't even make it with a midget. You make me sick."

Gears, grinding in Thom's head, just beginning to mesh. "Not a cunt—she's not a midget—"

"You promised you wouldn't hurt him," Cheri cried.

From a puddle, looking up. "Where's Dyleane?"

Brett struck Cheri with the back of his hand. Her howl rang out like that of a wounded animal and resonated with betrayal more than pain. The rain pounded; lightning flashed. Thom lunged at Brett's knees, thunder, Brett stumbled but a half step, shook his leg free from the mere inconvenience of Thom's desperate grasp and kicked Thom in the gut and then in the ribs for good measure. Gasping for air had become a regular occurrence for Thom of late. He'd learned that struggling for breath accomplished no more good than simply awaiting its return—so far, at least, it had always returned.

"Go home and stay inside until I call," Brett said to Cheri. "*That's* why we took two cars. I knew you'd screw up and I'd have to finish things my own self."

"You promised," Cheri screamed.

Brett slapped her. The smack of palm against wet skin and Cheri's shriek rivaled a simultaneous thunderclap.

The paralysis of Thom's diaphragm eased. He looked for Cheri just as Brett tucked him under an arm like a roll of carpet, a short roll, and set off for the parking lot. Thom took a shot at Brett's nuts. Without breaking stride, Brett responded with a shot to Thom's nose.

Thom came to just as Brett steered the black SUV through the BRGC gates. He desperately looked back for any sign of Dyleane, Cheri, or the white Civic. Brett chuckled, "Nothing back there for you, Thommy Boy."

Brett piloted the SUV down the gravel road, windshield wipers slapping ineffectually at the deluge, slowed and turned left onto Highway 20, towards Palatka. Thom's upper lip tickled as fresh blood flowed from his nose, around his chin, and down the front of his shirt. How soon until all of Thom's clothes sported bloodstains? Brett had fastened the restraint straps with Thom's arms trapped inside. They were just seatbelts; Thom could easily free himself.

"Don't even think about it," Brett said.

The SUV gained speed over the rain-slicked pavement. Despite the frantic thwack-thwack of the wiper blades, visibility hovered near zero. Brett drove with one hand, the other resting on the shifter extending from the center console. Thom 'thought about it' only briefly—he wasn't about to jump from a speeding truck or wrest control of the steering wheel from Brett. More importantly, any hope that he might still rescue Dyleane only dimmed each time he was knocked senseless.

"She's right, you know, old cunt-face back there. I did promise. And if she'd only done her part, I might even have kept it. But you shouldn't never have squealed to the cops. That's just the kind of shit that could cost me and L.T. our full rides and, who knows, maybe even a shot at playing Sundays."

"So are you two, like, gay? Together?"

Brett laughed. The SUV braked hard as it neared a dimly lit parking lot on the right. A tall, unlit pole sign announced:

SIMMS

Building & Supply

Since 1969

Brett turned in, shut off the headlights, and pulled around the store's far side. He parked where a fenced lumberyard extended from the rear of the structure.

"Nope, you guys shouldn't never have called the cops. Big

mistake right there. And that bitch of yours shouldn't never have mentioned Blindside Protector around L.T. Seriously extra big mistake there." He hit the power button, the engine died, the wipers froze mid-swipe. The pounding rain and rolling thunder punctuated by sharp claps drowned out any competing nighttime sounds. "Let's do this, Thommy Boy. Unclip yourself." Thom freed an arm and unclicked the belts. Brett opened his door and grabbed Thom's unkempt hair roughly enough to make Thom wonder whether the strands might rip out in clumps and take a chunk of bloody scalp with them. Brett dragged Thom across the console, out the door, and through the sheets of rain at a jog, stopping only upon reaching the canopied entryway. The scent of wet lumber filled the air between raindrops. Guard dogs barked viciously from the lumberyard. Brett pulled a ring of keys from the pocket of his light jacket and unlocked the deadbolt and a handle lock. "All this shit goes digital when I'm in charge." A car on the highway slowed as it reached the parking lot.

They stepped inside, Brett still dragging Thom by the hair. "See, when someone brings up stuff like that around L.T., something goes off inside him. Totally off. True story: During a game one time I told him how this defensive guy was calling him gay, and L.T. nearly killed the dude. He hadn't really said nothing, but I told L.T. he did. No penalties, nothing like that. L.T. didn't lose his head. He just crushed that guy every time we snapped the ball, and he crushed each replacement they brought in for him. That was poor little Savannah May's mistake too." They made their way towards the back of the store. "And unlike your black bitch,

Savannah hadn't never even called the cops. That's only gonna make it worse for her. One or two drinks off L.T.'s bota after he doctors it just so and it's pretty much lights out till he gets her alone. He wants her awake at the end. And then, boy oh boy, is he ever gonna have *his* way."

Thom swung at Brett's balls again, missed again. Brett only hit Thom's nose hard enough to cause excruciating pain and turn the stream of blood into a river.

They reached the back of the store where a set of double doors opened into the lumberyard. Brett pounded twice on the glass. Two pit bulls instantly hurled themselves against the barrier without ceasing their ferocious barking.

"It took some talking, but I finally convinced L.T. there were better ways of getting rid of y'all than just leaving bodies lying around afterwards."

"Too many people have seen you and L.T. and Dyleane too. You're never going to get away with this—Bretto."

Brett launched Thom headfirst into the door. As unlikely as it seemed, this elicited an even greater fury from the dogs.

"I'll make sure Cheri don't talk—whatever that takes—and then leave the rest up to our county's very own Barney Fife."

"Corey saw Cheri and me."

"That's one boy smart enough to keep his stupid mouth shut. 'Cause if he don't, no one's gonna believe him *and* bad shit's gonna happen to his momma. 'Sides, I seen what these dogs did to a doe we shot out of season once. We keep 'em hungry. There ain't gonna be much left of you two out-of-towners once they get done with you. Everyone'll figure you two freaks up and eloped to California or somewhere else where your kind of shit's normal. You're gonna make one tasty appetizer before the dark meat."

Brett inserted a key in one of the doors and pulled a small black box from his pocket. Thom caught a reflection in the glass of movement in the front of the store, ever so slight. Brett pushed a small red button on the box that emitted an ear-piercing screech. "Just a little something the pups been taught means back off or something bad's gonna happen. You know"—Brett grinned—"just before something extra good happens if they obey. They been trained just right."

Brett pulled Thom to his feet. Thom saw the dogs' eyes aglow, teeth bared, anticipatory drool. Brett pushed the button again. The dogs remained frozen. "I hate long bu-byes," he shouted over the screech. "Don't you?"

Thom glanced over his shoulder as Brett reached past him to unlock the door. Cheri dropped to all fours just behind Brett. It was the oldest schoolyard trick in the book, one by which Thom had been humiliated a dozen times at his school. How many times had Cheri been the perpetrator at hers?

Thom pushed Brett with everything he had. Brett's expression was more bemusement than outright surprise as his arms flew out in a struggle to maintain his balance before tumbling backwards over Cheri. His head struck the edge of a paint can neatly stacked with others into a pyramid display.

Lying on his back, a smile spread across Brett's face at the realization of what had just occurred. "You fucking cunt," he said, seeming to relish each word. He raised himself almost to a sitting position when Cheri stepped between his splayed legs and kicked him in the nuts harder than Thom thought possible. Brett let loose a single cry and curled up on his side.

But Brett Simms, the greatest athlete in Interlachen High School history, knew how to deal with pain, to overcome adversity. Every great player understands that such feelings can't be allowed to distract. Mind not merely over matter but over weakness. The elite warrior could—would—overcome. Misfortune meant opportunity. Brett got to his hands and knees. A palpable rage radiated from his every pore. He progressed to a kneeling position just as Cheri raised a gallon paint can with both hands and brought it down on the back of his head with all her might. Brett collapsed face down on the hard tile floor. No sooner did he raise his head an inch than Cheri crashed down another gallon can. It struck with such force, driving Brett's face back into the tile floor, that the lid popped off.

Thom and Cheri waited. Outside in the sustained downpour, the dogs hurled themselves against the glass doors in a fury that, whether taught or genetically driven, transcended horrific. No movement from Brett other than white paint oozing down the sides of his head and creating pink where it mixed with blood pooling on the floor.

"What'd he do with that black noise thing?" Cheri said as if she were alone. "Those dogs deserve a special treat. A special meal."

"Cheri—you can't do that. You've already bashed his brains in."

She appeared surprised by the presence of another. "Who says I can't?"

"L.T.'s going to kill Dyleane. He's going to murder her." Cheri perused the scattered paint cans for the black box. "He's going to murder her just like he did with Savannah May. We don't have time."

"You're *too* nice for your own good," Cheri said.

"Please, Cheri. For Dyleane. For me. Please."

She stepped behind the motionless prone figure, between its legs, and landed another brutal kick.

"Now?"

"Wait. This one's for Peggy." Another kick. Still no response—not so much as a twitch or noticeable inhalation. "Okay. Let's go."

Cheri ran ahead through the front doors and to her two-door silver BMW roadster. She strapped in and revved the engine. Despite the raging storm, she was lowering the convertible top as Thom reached the car. She spun out towards the highway, spraying gravel in every direction even as Thom struggled to pull his door shut. Water cascaded down harder than in a carwash. She pulled onto the highway without pausing. The faster she drove, the less rain fell into the passenger compartment. Thom beheld the digital speedometer—105 mph, then down to ninety as they practically hydroplaned around a gentle bend.

"Turn on the wipers," Thom yelled.

"Right," Cheri said, reaching for a switch that extended from the steering column. Thom secured his belts, quit watching the speedometer, didn't tell Cheri to slow down—she wouldn't have and he didn't want her to. Minutes later, Cheri executed a perfect power slide from the highway's slick concrete onto the saturated sand and gravel road. The Bimmer fishtailed slightly in the crushed rock and puddles as she jammed the gas pedal to the floor. She executed another surprisingly deft high-speed turn off the gravel road through the BRGC gates. The white Civic was parked opposite the first tee near the bench Thom had once shared with Jamison and Jack Daniels. Cheri glanced at Thom. He pointed forward. "Where?" she demanded.

"Up to the clubhouse."

Cheri slammed the brakes seconds later. Had it not been for the curb marking the edge of the fire lane, they'd likely have careened through a picture window onto Dill's corner table. Cheri looked at Thom. Thom had no idea what was about to happen. He wanted her help, likely needed her help. "No," he said.

"No what?"

"Go inside. Tell Jade." He pulled a card from his wallet. "Here. Call the number on back first, before 9-1-1."

Thom was grateful Cheri didn't argue—he'd have given in despite the danger that might lay ahead. He jumped from her car and ran to the blue cart. A bright blue flash as he pulled away signaled that he'd forgotten to disconnect it from the 220-volt outlet. It still ran. He aimed up the eighteenth fairway, tapped his left foot, reminiscent of Cheri and her real mom, to urge the obsolete vehicle forward, then cut through some trees and reached the number two fairway just beyond the elevated tee box. He pointed the cart straight for the green.

"Let them be here, let them be here—where else could they be? —dear God, you son of a bitch, let them be here."

The gale had relented slightly; rain fell steadily in drops the size of bird eggs. Thom crested the small rise and saw movement in the steep-sided bunker. It sure as hell wasn't a gator. Thom redirected the cart towards the sand trap's nearest edge with a push of the tiller just as the small front wheel entered a puddle of standing water. The wheel caught in the boggy grass and the cart tilted onto two wheels. Thom jumped clear as soon as he realized it was going over. He rolled once on the spongy turf and regained his feet. After one step toward the figures, he returned to the upended cart to yank free the fairway iron that served as a lightning rod. With the club in hand, he ran full speed toward the trap of sand.

Still some thirty yards off, a sustained flash of lightning illuminated Dyleane, naked, and L.T., grinning. His hands and the yellow cord from the wine bag encircled her neck. He was simultaneously choking and slamming her head against the rain-compacted sand. Each impact of Dyleane's skull made a thud and splashed a little water.

Thom's initial shout was drowned out by an explosion of thunder. After the last rumble, he screamed so loudly his voice cracked: *"Stop it—stop."* The words echoed.

L.T. looked up, released Dyleane. Her limp body tipped sideways, her head coming to rest just above the small lake formed in the crater's bottom. L.T. rose, casually pulled his shorts up over his boxers, zipped and snapped them. "You're supposed to be dead," he called.

Thom stood silently. Since L.T. had released Dyleane—now what?

"Where's Brett," L.T. demanded.

"Somewhere," was all Thom could muster. He gazed at what was visible of Dyleane over the bunker's edge—her bare back, shoulders, head turned sideways, yellow cord around the brown skin of her neck. It might have been a necklace, a choker. "Somewhere."

"Well, ain't this my lucky day? 'Cause I gonna love killing you too. But first your thin little bones gonna go all snap, snap like chicken wings." L.T. calmly scaled the steep slope of firm sand. "You gay little faggot. You and your bitch done caused plenty enough trouble 'round here." A metal rake with blunt tines lay at the trap's edge. L.T. picked it up and grinned more savagely.

Thirty yards.

Thom raised the golf club, his hands around what remained of the grip, hoping to appear menacing. L.T. laughed. "You better make your first shot count, 'cause I'm gonna comb more than just your hair with this here rake before you get a second."

Twenty-five.

"Dyleane," Thom called. L.T.'s cackle constituted the only response.

Twenty.

My first shot. That was all Thom had: one and only one shot. He grabbed the ball initialed *MN* from his pocket, dropped it. The downpour made for heavy turf, yet if he struck the ball too thinly, it might sky off the short wet grass.

L.T. howled with laughter the moment he understood Thom's intentions.

Thom struck a stance then glanced up to confirm distance and direction. L.T. broke into a run, bent slightly, arms out, prepared to launch himself at Thom.

Fifteen yards.

Thom swung. L.T. was still grinning when he stumbled to his knees, stunned by the impact of the ball against his forehead.

Thom ran as fast as he could and jumped down the steep, sandy slope into four inches of water.

"Dyleane, it's me. Can you hear me?" Thom had never seen her naked, had never even seen his mother naked, had never imagined Dyleane looking like this. He reached for her clothes but didn't know what to do with them. He wrung water out of the blouse, held it out. He shook out more water as if it mattered while the rain continued to fall. "Dyleane, here."

Thom knelt in the water, reached for her. He touched her bare, cool skin, leaned closer. "Dyleane."

Thom loosened the yellow cord just as a massive force launched him through the air and against the sandy bank nearest the green. L.T. grasped Thom's throat, choked him, and pounded his head against hard-packed sand. No longer smiling, L.T. tossed Thom around like a ragdoll, then held Thom's face in the water. So Thom wasn't meant to die in that van after all, nor at his father's hands. He wasn't fated to become a meal for vicious guard dogs. What had he been thinking? He was going to die right here, at night, in the same damn number two bunker alongside Savannah May. And his mother. And Dyleane?

A figure appeared above L.T.'s head. *Mick, three-to-one consonant guy, is that you?*

Only this apparition was more angular, dark. It flew like a screaming missile and exploded against L.T. who tumbled hard onto Thom, elbow first. Thom's ribs cracked (like chicken wings). L.T. rolled and swung wildly at Corey who swung back. L.T. made a break for it, but Corey tackled him before he could scramble over the bunker's edge. They stood and threw punches; neither retreated at the impact of the other's fists. Corey tackled L.T. again. Thom crawled up the embankment free of the standing water, away from the writhing bodies locked in combat, to reach Dyleane. He put an arm around her, pulled the yellow cord over her head, tossed it aside, drew her close, tried to breathe for both of them.

A siren sounded above the vicious slugs, punches, and grunts, even over the constant roll of thunder. Thom gasped for air as might a fish trapped on land. The siren grew louder and then fell silent as the turning lights mounted on top of the sheriff's department cruiser cast shifting shadows.

The crackly, amplified voice of Deputy Howland Ricketts rolled over the glistening grass and against the trees: "Stop that fightin', you hear me? Stop that fightin' there." Corey and L.T. remained locked in mortal struggle. Corey landed two lightning fast jabs to L.T.'s jaw. A flash and a *boom* exploded from the deputy's car window. A smoking pistol pointed skyward. "Goddamn it, I'm serious now—quit your fightin.'"

Corey and L.T. warily disengaged and rose from the standing

water. L.T. aimed a final kick at Corey, which glanced off Corey's thigh. "You know Ima get your punk ass for that," Corey murmured for L.T.'s benefit.

"Thank God you made it, and just in time too," L.T. said between pants, hands resting on knees. "These here maniacs been making to kill me just like they done to that girl over there."

Thom's head began to spin. His attempts to breathe were like walking on glassy-smooth ice—he went through the motions, tried with all his might to inhale but made no progress. "Ambulance," he gasped.

Ricketts reached the bunker's edge. He drew down on Corey with the pistol and helped L.T. from the bunker with his free hand.

"Life flight," Thom whispered.

"He's turning blue," Corey said.

"You shut your trap, boy, and keep your hands where I can see 'em," Ricketts said.

"No, Dyleane . . . Goddamn it, God, life flight." But no one heard Thom's whispered plea, at least not those on the ground.

"I was gonna meet her out here," L.T. said, with an offhanded gesture towards Dyleane, "like me and her talked about earlier." Thom caught the wink in L.T.'s voice. "I parked my car and heard a commotion—the girl screaming, that big ole boy right there all a moaning. It was sick and I just knew there was trouble. I ran out here and then them two boys started going off on *me*. Then the midget hit me with a goddamn golf ball,"—L.T. rubbed his forehead—"and this here nigger drug me down there into the water, all a scratching and choking like a girl, trying to drown me."

"You gone and done it now, boy," Ricketts said to Corey.

"I ain't done shit. But I just might if you don't get these two some help. That boy there is turning even bluer. And the girl ain't moving neither."

"Didn't you hear me say shut up?" Ricketts said, waving his pistol at Corey. "You just lay down on your front with your hands behind your back."

Corey, hands still raised, looked at the standing water before him, then at Ricketts as if the deputy was a fool.

"Hey, sir," L.T. said, "I've got to go find Brett, Brett Simms. He's supposed to call earlier and I ain't heard nothing."

"That can wait, son. We're gonna need statements and all that. Then you free to go."

"Dyleane," Thom mouthed.

"Brett Simms, you know, Jimmy Simms's boy. I'm afraid these two mighta got to him before they started in on me and that girl."

"Ah hell." Ricketts appeared frustrated, confused. "Okay, sure. But you call in with anything as soon as you find out, hear? That statement's important. You the only eye witness we got."

"You got it. Yessiree. Just as soon as I find anything out."

Thom heard L.T.'s footsteps as he jogged away, maybe felt them—any distinction was illusory. He tried blinking away the clouds swirling before his eyes, within his eyes. Brett was right all along. They were going to get away with it. Their plans may have gone completely awry, but they were still getting away with it. Thom felt raindrops on his face but could no longer see. Another siren. Another tinny, amplified voice, this time Laboda's. "Hold it right there. That's a good boy. Now put those hands above your head. No sudden moves."

Then the chop-chop-chop of a helicopter, growing louder, closer. A blast of wind. Jostling, sharp pokes. *Hey, asswipes, that hurts.* Nothing.

Chapter 19

Thom looked down at himself lying in another hospital bed, this time the only bed in a small room where large windows served as a wall. Beyond the windows, in a dimly lit room surrounded by other windowed suites, sat a half dozen persons wearing purple hospital scrubs and looking at computer screens. An IV ran into each of Thom's arms. A green plastic mask connected to a bubbling jar on the wall by a green plastic tube covered his mouth and nose. Another tube, this one thick enough for rust-flecked fluid to pool in a low spot, emerged from a patchwork of bloody tape and gauze below his left armpit and plugged into some sort of suction contraption protruding from the wall alongside the bubbling jar.

"Didn't expect to see you so soon," an ethereal Mick Kazcynski said.

"Oh hey. Thought I saw you a little earlier, but it turned out to be someone else," the Thom looking down said. Just as before, Father Crittenden leaned against a wall, arms folded, one leg crossed over the other, his hairpiece slipping ever so slightly.

"They're saying you'll be okay, in case you were curious. Something about cracked ribs and a collapsed lung."

"Thanks," Thom said, although he felt neither relieved nor particularly thankful.

"Your friend—Dyleane, right?"

"Yeah, Dyleane. Where is she? Can we just sort of go to wherever she is?"

"No, not you, not yet anyway."

"Why—where—how's she doing?"

"Not so good. That body was a real mess. Your priest friend got here just as they gave up on her, you know, like he did me. He did that whole last rites thing he does."

That body? Thom felt suddenly submerged into a tub of water where hot and cold didn't mix, his head swimming and unable to stay afloat. Dyleane—*that body?*

"He sure looks like he could use a cigarette, don't he?" Mick said with a nod towards Father C. "We talked, your friend and me, just for a second. She's going to be okay."

"You mean she's not dead?"

"Nah, man. Not that. She's okay, like me."

The Thom in the bed moved, yanked his hands against sturdy straps that lashed his wrists to the raised bed rails. "That's your cue," Mick said. Father C. ambled stiffly to the bedside.

"Suppose so," third-person Thom said.

"Got a feeling I'll be seeing you later," Mick said.

"What if I don't want to go back?"

"You'd be wrong. Don't ask how I know. This side's a little different that way. Things just are."

"Less guesswork?"

"Yeah, maybe. Could be that we just accept the uncertainty without all the angst."

"I don't want to go back."

"Hey, I saw your mother. She wasn't hard to pick out—she looked just like you, her face I mean. She said you gotta have hope. That's it—you gotta have hope. That's like a song from some old movie, right?"

"Calm down, Thom. *Thom.* Calm down." Thom peered into the priest's weary face and watery eyes, his collar askew, toupee close to committing lemming suicide off his brow. Father C.'s breath reeked of acrid smoke and coffee. "They're going to tie down the rest of you if you don't just lie still."

"Me?" Thom said.

"Yes, you. Do you know who *I* am, where you are?"

Thom stopped struggling, took a breath. "You're you and I'm here, right?"

"That nicely sums things up. I had to make sure—Lord knows you've been through a lot."

"Whatever."

"Here then are the headlines. You're going to be okay. But your friend—"

"Dyleane?"

"Correct, Dyleane. I'm afraid she—"

"She's—she's dead, isn't she."

"You know?"

"I'm—I guess. But you got here in time for all the crosses and prayers, right?"

"And to console her distraught mother. Although distraught doesn't even begin to cover it. The poor woman was torn into heaving, teary bits—and she looked to me for consolation. *Me.* As if I could resurrect her daughter, lessen the loss, fill the terrible void. I'm not sure how much more of this I can take. I'm really not sure."

"There's always Vegas, eh?"

"Perhaps." The priest nudged his carpet back into place and dabbed his eyes with a hanky. "Although I am not sure which of us is most in need of an escape right now."

"I already tried that, remember? It didn't work out so well. Go have a smoke. No offense but I don't need you."

"For that, this once, I am grateful." Father C. turned towards the door.

"Wait," Thom said. The priest stiffened, turned. "They've got L.T. and Brett in jail, right? Not Corey?"

"You sure you want to talk about this, now? Maybe you should rest."

"Just the headlines."

Father C. pulled over a motel-quality vinyl recliner and settled in. "Yes and no, my son. Corey is not in jail. The young Hogan girl told the state trooper everything that you and she had done even as said trooper was racing to the golf club. That included the part about Corey sprinting out onto the course when he heard what you were up to. Upon the trooper's arrival, it all checked out. So they arrested that L.T. fellow and released Corey—over Deputy Ricketts's vigorous protestations from what I understand."

"Brett?"

"Here's where it becomes rather strange. Perhaps this part should wait."

"Brett?"

"If you insist. The Hogan girl—"

"Cheri. It's Cheri."

"Cheri," the priest said as though the name didn't taste right. "As I was saying, she described helping you at the Simms store and inflicting several, shall we say, potentially debilitating injuries upon Master Simms, whom, I must add, is also dead."

"What? How?"

"Cheri is under arrest at the insistence of Jimmy Simms, among others, most notably including our good Deputy Ricketts. I'm afraid there was so little left of the Simms boy that determining a precise cause of death will prove very difficult, if not impossible."

Thom's eyes above the plastic mask evidently made clear his confusion.

"The dogs, dear boy, those guard dogs. They made quite a mess of the poor fellow."

"But we didn't let them in. Brett, he damn well meant to feed *me* to them. That was *his* plan! But *we* didn't let them in." Pain shot through Thom's left side upon the effort of trying to make himself clear. "We sure as heck could have but we didn't. Honest to God, we didn't."

"Honest to God—an ever fascinating entreaty. But I digress. It is clear that the dogs gained entrance by miraculously breaking through the double-pane glass in one of the rear doors. Perhaps they were driven crazy by the sight of a potential meal lying in a pool of fresh blood. But the question remains: Who caused his actual demise, the dogs or Cheri? And you, my good man, are the closest person to a disinterested witness they have, particularly as the young lady was advised by counsel to say no more as soon as the subject of culpability arose."

The round clock on the hospital wall read 2:15—a.m.—when Father C. finally escaped for a desperately needed smoke and then home. A young doctor and old nurse, each wearing scrubs, pulled, pushed and prodded particularly wherever Thom was most tender. The doctor announced that if all went well, they would "yank" the chest tube around noon that day. If Thom's "sats" remained above ninety-four percent as they dialed back the supplemental oxygen to room air, he would go "home" later in the afternoon.

"Home."

"You didn't hear it from me," the nurse said after the doctor left, "but if you had any insurance worth a damn you'd be in here for another two or three days. They don't understand how this trauma is worse on folks like you. Or they don't want to." Thom said he understood, although he wondered at there being other folks like him. He thanked the nurse for untying his restraints. She filed out still shaking her head just as Trooper Laboda filed in.

"That should be a revolving door," Thom said.

"You should see how crazy it gets up here during the daytime when all the regular folk are around too."

"You're not regular?"

"Not for me to say. Look, Ricketts is gonna take care of all the statements and paperwork stuff. I just need to know one thing. And I'll be honest with you. No matter what you say, either old man Hogan or Jimmy Simms is going to be pissed off all to hell. Most likely both. What a couple of sorry-ass pricks, those two."

"What shape was Brett in when we left?" Thom said. Laboda nodded. "Why should Simms care? His darling beloved son is still a dead murderer either way."

"A dead accomplice, technically speaking. I'll give you three guesses why he cares, and the first two don't count." Laboda shook his head, shrugged. "Jimmy Simms couldn't ever afford liability coverage on those dang dogs. They'd had them or others for years, and only folks what they caught breaking in got hurt, so no big deal as far as anyone was concerned. So if they killed Brett Simms, that's it, end of story as far as any hope for remuneration goes. But if Cheri Hogan killed the boy, along with his potential future earning capacity, Cheri and her old man are on the hook to Jimmy Simms big time. And the Hogans have plenty to go after."

Thom's neck was so sore that it was all he could do to shake his head. "Money—got it."

"Cheri Hogan confessed to dropping a couple cans of paint on the boy's skull and kicking him in the balls. That's when her daddy's lawyer told her to clam up. So."

"So."

"So for one thing, that tells me Brett Simms had to be unconscious at the time. Or maybe dead. Otherwise she doesn't get a second shot, let alone a third, fourth, whatever."

"He was perfectly lucid. As lucid as you and me."

Laboda squinted at Thom. "Perfectly lucid? Never mind that you damn near died just a while back and still got plenty of drugs on board, which, I don't mind saying, places *your* current state of lucidity squarely at issue."

"Not nearly enough if you ask me. Who do I ask about more drugs?"

"Are you telling me that young, strappin' fellow just laid there and let his girlfriend kick him in the nuts?"

A focused confidence of the sort that could give rise to a below-par round of golf on Sunday at a major seized Thom. Despite not having spent much time on the lying practice range, opportunity is still opportunity, and God only knew anymore where the limits of Thom's world started and stopped. "He might have been a little groggy from his head hitting those paint cans at first." Thom's recent vows of transparency be damned. "Then I held him down."

At Thom's first mention of half nelsons and arm locks, incredible as it all sounded, a dubious Laboda warned Thom that he could be incriminating himself in the commission of Brett Simms's murder and read him his rights.

"I don't care about any of that," Thom nobly replied. "I'm telling you the truth. He wanted to kill me. He was going to feed *me* to those damn monsters, then Dyleane. That's why we were there, eh? And he sure as hell wanted to kill Cheri after she showed up to help me. It was him or us. I'm leveling here. Until she dropped that second can, it was him or us."

"Self-defense."

"Until that last can, the only thing on his mind was feeding

Cheri and me to those dogs. And you know how easy it would've been for him to do."

It felt as though Thom's side had been pierced again, this time by a dull, jagged spear. He was growing short of breath. He pushed the call button on the bedrail.

Laboda shook his head. "You understand that to Jimmy Simms that makes you a murderer too, right? Ain't no one going to call you a hero for helping do all that to the best football player ever from this part of the state." This, in fact, had crossed Thom's mind about halfway through the yarn. "And while I wouldn't expect too many folks around here to believe a damn word of what you're saying, I do not doubt for one second that Cheri Hogan would have a jury of her peers, particularly those male peers what have eyes, eating right out of her outstretched hand before she even finished taking the oath."

Laboda confirmed that he was again holding the Moe Norman ball for evidence and that he would see that Thom got it back—perhaps more promptly this time than last.

"Tell me this, Thom. The way L.T. describes it, you must have hit some incredible golf shot to stun L.T. like that. They already did an MRI to check the damage, and sure enough, there's a hairline fracture practically square between his eyes. How'd you do that?"

"Short game."

Later that day, after he proved he could keep down his hospital dinner—no small feat under any circumstance—Thom gingerly climbed into Father Crittenden's Cadillac SUV, any hint of new-car smell banished forever by that of an airport smoking lounge. Its windows were blurred yellow on the inside, a bit like Thom felt after popping two pain pills the size of Florida palmetto bugs just minutes before being wheeled out by another elderly woman, this one wearing a yellow smock. On the outside, the early evening sky beyond the palms and pines teased hues of pink and gray. "Where to, Mr. Loudon?" Father C. said.

"The doc said home. Know where I can find one of those?"

"I'm afraid not. It apparently falls to me to inform you that your engagement at the Breeders' Roost Golf Club as assistant to the head pro has been terminated."

"No surprise there," Thom said. Even before the new deaths, Thom understood this was the change Dill had promised. Thom's veneer of resignation did little to dispel a rush of desperation. "Screw it. That wasn't ever home anyway."

"Jade and Corey's? More compassion resides in that woman's plentiful bosom than in all the saints combined." Thom shook his head. "The Hogans? With Cheri out of jail thanks to you, despite the incredulity of certain aspects of your story, I'm sure they'd be more than willing to begin paying down their debt of gratitude with room and board, at least over the short term."

"You don't get it, do you? There's no such place as home."

"The proper reference, I believe, is, 'There's no place like home.'"

"Maybe for some girl and a damn dog. Not me."

"I know the loneliness you must feel. But with time and, dare I suggest, a measure of faith—"

"No offense, Father, but you don't know shit. Not about this anyway."

Father C. tapped free a cigarette and lit it with the Caddy's lighter. "I'm listening," emerged in the initial cloud of smoke.

"Dyleane was the kindest, smartest, most generous—" With a raised hand, Thom stopped Father C. from filling the ensuing silence with platitudes as he struggled to regain his composure. "The most—ever. Well, you know, along with my mom, maybe Savannah May . . . " More silence as Thom shook his head to rid it of corpses, with Dyleane's stripped, brutalized and unmoving brown form the worst image of all—more cruel even than his mother bleeding to death on a bare wooden floor. "I'm done, Father—with people I mean. I tried, goddamn it. With my mom. With Dyleane. Like nothing before with Dyleane. And just where in goddamn hell did that get me?" Thom punctuated each word that followed with a fist pounding the padded dash: "Where the hell did it get *them*?"

Except for Thom's intermittent and choked sniffles, they drove the rest of the way in silence.

The priest pulled the parish Caddy through the club gates. One gate was actually drawn across the road, reducing the point of entry to a single lane—Thom had always regarded them as irrevocably open. They passed an empty police car parked near the first tee and drew up to the storage garage. The members' lot was empty. No golfers, no caddies, no one. Thom's clubs leaned against the cinderblock wall just outside the padlocked metal door. The lock was new. Not that any reason existed for Thom to go inside, as one half-full garbage bag containing the rest of Thom's worldly belongings lay alongside the clubs.

Lights were on inside the Nineteenth Hole. Dill would be at his corner table. Corey was quite likely inside helping his mother despite the lack of business. It was time for Thom to move on. He should acknowledge those who had helped him since he landed at the BRGC—because, indeed, some had. Thom should thank the priest. Thank Corey. Thank Jade, for that matter. Thank Cheri—perhaps convene at least one meeting of Migga Club. Thank Dill? Why not—"thank" and "you" are just words.

"After three years, this is the thanks *I* get," Thom mumbled.

"Where will you go?" Father C. said, throwing a butt out the window and tapping out a fresh cig.

"Haven't a clue, never mind how I'll get there or how I pay these hospital bills." Thom waved a half dozen sheets of printouts and carbon copies that had been resting in his lap. He lowered the passenger window, fully intending to launch into a gentle breeze the charges for the helicopter ride, medical treatment, anesthesia, supplies and other assorted expenses adding up to nearly forty thousand dollars, which, on a separate page, he had agreed per his signature to satisfy by the end of the month. Father C. overrode the window's descent from the driver's side. "Don't litter, dear boy. Besides, your failure to pay those could very well lead to your summary deportation."

Thom couldn't say whether getting kicked out of the US might be good or bad. Actually, he could. Deportation would be bad. Everything was bad—with one notable exception. While Thom couldn't say for sure that identifying the murderers who'd bloodied Thom and Moe's world with Savannah May's corpse had unlocked the door that permitted his return to the wondrous, solitary world of golf, he knew it had been unlocked. Rather than solving the young woman's murder, perhaps the door opened upon Thom's full release of anger, grief, and guilt. Nah, that wasn't it—he had never before felt so mad, broken hearted, and culpable. Nonetheless, the door was open. He could feel it, just as he could feel how a golf ball would break, how it might slow just before reaching the cup. A courageous voice whispered inside that it may have been Dyleane and her unqualified acceptance of Thom that provided the key. Her love that, however briefly, made him feel worthy of hope, worthy of a home, an acceptance that enabled Thom not merely to see love as more than cynical manipulation but also to envision loving in return. Thom, however, drove that voice away. He simply couldn't go there. Not then, perhaps not ever. Besides, what did it matter *why* the door had swung open? Quit peeling the damn artichoke and simply accept that it had.

"My boy, you recall my having previously extolled the value of information imparted by parishioners, particularly information imparted into the hands of a cleric committed to transparency? How such information might generate leverage, particularly leverage to influence behavior, particularly the behavior of the imparting parishioner?"

Frankly, now that Thom's future loomed before him like a giant black void broken only by one pinprick of light, he was done with Father C. and his particulars. "Are you about to make a point?"

"I know the following to be as true as anything in the Bible—hell, *truer* than most things written in that damnable book, for all the trouble it causes. There comes an hour late at night in haunts such as the Breeders' Roost, at least among those lonely souls left downstairs in the bar, when some are so forlorn that they become incapable of lying."

"Stupid drunk?"

"More or less."

"Yeah, I've seen that."

Fifteen minutes later, Thom exited the SUV thankful for the fresh air and soft veil of near darkness. He took his time shuffling up the scarred wooden steps one at a time. He was stiff and sore, aware like never before what it meant to be tired to the bone. Inside, the silent TV replayed the final round of the 1999 Ryder Cup at Brookline. That was where the US staged a remarkable come-from-behind victory against Europe on the event's final day, and in so doing, violated nearly every rule of etiquette known to golf. Tom Lehman running up and down fairways to egg-on an already boozy and disrespectful crowd; half the US team dancing all over the 17th green after Justin Leonard sank a long putt, even though Spain's José María Olazábal still had a shorter putt left to halve the hole. Although Thom knew the Americans were in the wrong, and also that the American team had since apologized ad nauseam for their disrespect, he acknowledged the unbridled passion so unique to Yanks, so courageous and childish at the same time.

Corey approached Thom. One of Corey's eyes was blackened, his cheek a montage of blues and browns that even his dark complexion could not conceal.

"Thanks," Thom said.

"Thanks don't even begin to cover it, mutha. I still ain't got no down payment on those wheels I need."

"I'll see what I can do."

"She-it."

They shook hands, not quite embracing but patting each other's backs three times in the manly manner then fashionable.

Jade came around the corner of the bar. Her eyes were swollen as if she'd just gone fifteen with Ali. Tears old and new marked her cheeks. She reached for Thom. The dread of suffocating within her breasts was offset by the security they provided—as well as the time it gave Thom once again to compose himself.

Once freed, without looking her in the eyes, Thom nodded towards the corner table. "Dill," he said.

"And that goddamn Gram cracka," Corey said.

"Watch your damn mouth, boy," Jade said, although a crack in her voice robbed it of its usual authority.

"Another round of whatever they're having—make it doubles," Thom said.

"Gram's just drinking crap beer," Corey said.

"Whatever," Thom said. "I'll take a shot of Jack. Put it on Dill's tab."

Jade raised an eyebrow and commenced to mixing drinks.

Thom walked over and claimed a chair. Dill said, "What in the swamps of hell are you doing here? Thanks to you, we might have to close down this entire operation once and for all."

"Shut up, Dilly. I'll bet this was your busiest morning since Savannah May."

Gram nodded affirmatively.

"Careful, boy, you don't know who you're dealing with here," Dill said.

"Look, Pickle, you ain't shit compared to what I've been dealing with the last few days. So *you* just shut the hell up."

Thom explained that he knew all about Dill's albatross at the 1965 Greater Jacksonville Open, the one that led to his best finish on the PGA Tour and served as his primary claim to regional fame and celebrity. It was a sham! Dill had been so embarrassingly drunk that Sunday morning on the old Selva Marina course that not even the tour marshals, let alone his playing partner (and heaven forbid, a gallery) were paying him any attention whatsoever. So that when Dill took his second shot on the eighteenth and completely whiffed at the ball, no one was there to see Gram pick it while replacing a divot as big around as a tractor tire. Only when Gram approached the green several minutes later, ostensibly to tend the flag, looked inside the hole, and by sleight of hand appeared to pull out Dill's ball did anyone finally take note. How could anyone not have noticed Dill hooping and hollering, doing a jig on the green's fringe, falling down, and hollering some more after Gram helped him back up? The winds preceding a smack-down nor'easter then rolled in, and Dill's falsified score held up to keep him third on the leaderboard.

"I thought you said you never told no one," Dill said to Gram.

"I thought you said you ain't never told no one neither," Gram said to Dill.

"How the hell did you find out, Loudon?" Dill demanded.

"God only knows," Thom said. "But here's what I'll be needing in exchange for keeping your cheating a secret."

"You can't blackmail me, boy," Dill said.

"Sure I can. If this gets out, your tour results are void along with your reputation, your teaching credentials, and your job. Hell, you'll end up no better off than Gram right here. And where he lives, no one runs a bar tab." This final prospect appeared to grab Dill's rapt attention.

Once during the following thirty-minute negotiation, Corey approached under the guise of wiping down a nearby tabletop. "Get the fuck away from here, sonny boy," Dill growled.

Thom left the table one time after that to grab a sheet of blank paper, pen, and a refreshed shot of Tennessee's finest. When Dill and Gram finally stomped off with Gram carrying Thom's medical bills—each old man having just chugged the remaining dregs of his drink—Thom sat alone and reviewed the document signed and dated by all three parties. In consideration for keeping secret Dill's skullduggery, the agreement required, in pertinent part, for Dill, personally or through the BRGC, to establish a $7,000 line of credit at Dewey's Used Car Sales in Palatka for Thom's exclusive benefit. Also covered were all expenses related to Thom's two prior hospitalizations, payable before the end of the month, as well as the prospective expense of surgery to straighten out Thom's disfigured and nonfunctional nose and the dental work required to address Thom's loose tooth. The agreement also stipulated that Dill had to give Corey the job of golf pro assistant with a generous hourly wage, as well as to secure fake documents showing one Thomas Loudon to be an eighteen-year-old American-born citizen and high school graduate. (Dill nodded at Thom's suggestion that Father Crittenden could be relied upon for just such a task as if everyone knew that.) Finally, per their agreement, Dill was to cover Thom's expenses for the first six months on one of the minor-league pro golf tours popular in South Florida.

Thom wobbled just a bit as he stood and walked back to where Jade and Corey had been intently watching while attempting not to be too obvious. Thom said, "No thanks," when Jade made to refresh his whiskey, adding, "I need somewhere to sleep. Just for tonight." He didn't feel up to dancing on any greens. His improbable come-from-behind victory could not touch the sorrow.

"Lord knows it's going to be quiet upstairs," Jade said.

Thom hesitated, shook his head. "Do you think I could . . . "

Jade nodded. She grabbed a key ring from under the register and then a particular key. One lengthy, suffocating hug from Jade and a three-pat man-shake with Corey later, Thom shouldered his clubs and lifted the the garbage bag. With the blue cart still captive beyond roll upon roll of yellow police tape, he walked up the path around back of the clubhouse. From the live oak, Thom could see the neatly spaced plastic loungers arranged earlier by the recently vindicated pool manager. Thom showered his beaten and bruised body one final time in the men's locker room until the steaming hot water ran tepid. He unlocked the snack shop door. Once inside, with the window closed and door again locked, he powered up the grill and deep fryer, just as he'd watched Dyleane do so many times to feed her family in preparation for the day ahead. Minutes later, he sat the steaming hot double cheeseburger, fries, extra garnish, salted nut roll, and large Sprite on the prep table. He shut off the grill and fryer and bricked the grill to a shiny gleam, just as Dyleane had always done after serving her family their end-of-day meal. He drew up the lone chair to face an empty coke syrup cylinder. Not long after, he turned off the lights and returned to the chair.

The next morning, Dill sent his new golf pro assistant up to run the snack shack as best he could until they hired Dyleane's replacement. There, next to a pile of books from the high school library, Corey discovered not one but two complete meals sitting untouched on the prep table.

. . . So the salesman and lawyer, they amble on down to the end of the bar, just as pretty as you please, to where a bunch of others are sitting. They're all joking and laughing, buying each other rounds. The midget climbs a stool and sits by himself.